THIN
RISING
VAPORS

SETH
ROGOFF

Sagging
Meniscus

Printed in the United States of America.

Set in Mrs Eaves XL and Remington Noiseless with LaTeX.

ISBN: 978-1-944697-70-9 (paperback)

ISBN: 978-1-944697-71-6 (ebook)

Library of Congress Control Number: 2018939411

Sagging Meniscus Press

www.saggingmeniscus.com

To my parents

THIN
RISING
VAPORS

Foreword

It has been over six years since I went to Abel's house in Casco. From that time, the time of his death, the house has belonged to me. Despite this, I haven't been back there on a single occasion. It's likely I'll never return. When I left the house on that morning in late November 2011, I took all of Abel's papers with me. I had intended to do a thorough study of them to discover something like a deeper truth about my friend's life. In the weeks and months that followed, I managed to produce an account of my seven days in Casco—to retrace my steps. I could go no further.

Since my initial surge of work during that winter, the massive stacks of Abel's papers, notebooks, and boxes have remained where I placed them—piled high on the floor of my office in Whitefield Hall, on bookshelves, and crammed in drawers. For sure, the stacks have now and then been knocked over. A breeze has blown some pages around. Coffee has spilled and stained them. Dust gathers everywhere. But they are here with me and form an archive I feel compelled to preserve but cannot bring myself to examine. At some point, who knows when, the time for such an investigation will come. The publication of these tracings is, I hope, the beginning of the process, a beginning that at the same time could very well be an endpoint. I don't know. I sense, though, that at this moment of disquiet and rising extremism, I cannot keep Abel Prager to myself any longer. His all-too-brief life suggests a type of radical resistance—a perfectly struck note of discord. Such a note of discord has become, for me, part of the general earth song, the likes of which, as you'll find later on, Henry David Thoreau would hear when the sound of the crickets in the field would fade toward silence.

Ezra Stern
Whitefield Hall
January 1, 2018

Day One

It was early morning and still dark when I arrived at Abel's house. I had driven for close to seven hours through the night to get there. Despite predictions that the first snowstorm of the year was to hit around midnight, I had left the city in a rush, taking nothing with me besides what I was wearing—a pair of old Levis, a white T-shirt, and a gray woolen button-down. Sophia, my wife, had tried to convince me to wait for morning to go. But that wouldn't do. It was clear to me that I had to leave immediately and get to his house as soon as I could. It felt like the one thing about the situation I knew for sure. Knew—I knew nothing for sure. A lawyer's letter had arrived at my office earlier in the day saying Abel was gone. That's all I knew.

The snow had held off during the drive, but as I turned onto the winding and narrow dirt driveway that led from Mayberry Hill Road to the house, sparse flakes started falling gently around me. I got out of the car and lifted my head to let some of the snow gather on my cheeks. The coolness felt good. I hesitated for a moment before unlocking the door and stepping inside. Only moments after I entered, the wind and snow picked up. The blizzard had been trailing right behind me.

There was a total darkness here that didn't exist in the city, and though I had grown up in a small town in Vermont, I had been in the city for more than two decades. In my quasi-blindness, I groped against the wall for a light switch, found one, and flicked it up. No light came. I took the phone from my pocket, activated the screen's light, and flashed it around the living room. There was something bordering on criminality in my actions, I considered, as I scanned the walls of the house of my dead friend. The screen of my phone went black. I was suspended once more in the darkness.

With only my phone for light, I moved through the living room and into the kitchen. I rummaged around in some cabinet drawers, finding a package of candles and a book of matches. I lit a few of them and placed them around the room. In the corner of the living room, there was a Franklin stove with two baskets beside it, one empty and one full of old scraps of paper. I grabbed the empty one. In back of the house, beside the door that led from the kitchen, I found firewood stacked against the wall. I gathered some logs and started a fire. Then I moved a candle to the center of the coffee table and sat down in an armchair as the flames inside the stove grew larger and brighter. Soon the stove was giving off good heat. This would have been a perfect moment to share with Abel, like we had in the past—countless campfires of earlier times combined into one towering mnemonic conflagration. But all that was gone now, suddenly lost to an irretrievable past.

How close to and at the same time distant from childhood I felt. Abel had been one of very few people in my life who straddled the line between then and now. With most others from those early years, I had lost touch. The relationship with Abel had been different. Abel had stuck with me and I with Abel, though it had been a long time since we last saw each other. It had been over six years since Abel left the city for this house. Six years. I couldn't believe it had been so long.

The room was getting warmer, and I went over and stretched out on the sofa, finally allowing my eyes to close. It was nearing four in the morning. There was nothing to do but sleep.

Day Two

I woke up with a start, confused by the unfamiliar surroundings. My phone was ringing and I reached over and held it in front of my face. Through the blurriness, I saw that it was Sophia.

"Hey," I said, "what time is it?"

"It's already after ten. Where've you been? I've been up for hours worrying about you. I haven't been able to get through until now."

I sat up on the sofa and looked around, trying to dispel the strangeness of the scene. "I'm at the house in Casco. By the time I got here it was too late to call."

"You should've at least sent a message. How was the drive?"

"The drive?" I repeated, as I tried to steady my vision by rubbing my eyes—for some reason it was taking longer than usual to come back to me. "The drive was fine," I said, "more of a blur than anything else." I looked out the window. It was still snowing. Gathered on top of my car was a pile of snow at least twelve inches high.

"It's the largest snowfall in three years," she said, "and the most snow in one day in November in a century. Can you believe it, before Thanksgiving? The kids are home from school and I've taken the day off from work. The city is peaceful; there's hardly a noise. I'd like to take the kids out, but we don't have boots yet for Sam. He's grown out of last year's pair. With how busy this fall's been, I hadn't noticed."

"It's been busy," I agreed. "I'm sorry, Sophia, but I don't feel like talking now. I've got a lot to do in the house. I haven't even looked around."

"It's a terrible thing to die alone like that. It's such a tragedy." After a pause, she added, "Just to let you know, we have plans with Ellen and Dave tomorrow evening. You left so quickly I didn't have time to tell you. Anyway, I'm sure they'd understand if we cancel. And Sam has his first basketball game Saturday afternoon. He really wants you there. Let me know if you think you won't make it back for it."

"I'll make it. I'll start back tomorrow morning. What time are the plans with Ellen and Dave?"

"Eight. We're meeting them at the restaurant. Sally is coming at 7:30 to babysit."

"I'll be there, and I'll call you later once I get a handle on things."

I hung up the phone, leaned back into the sofa, and thought about Ellen and Dave. Ellen was Sophia's friend from college. She taught English at the Woosley School, a private school for girls on the Upper West Side. Dave, her husband, was a psychologist whose practice was located only a few blocks from my office in Whitefield Hall.

I recalled a lunch I'd had with Dave just days after Abel had quit his job and left the city for Casco. Dave had various theories about why Abel had done it, but in the end summed it up with what seemed to me a rather facile chess metaphor, claiming that Abel was "resigning"—or perhaps he said, "tipping over his king"—instead of "playing out the game."

I sat up on the sofa and thought about Dave's notion. I'd met Abel when we were nine years old, during our first summer at camp. From the first day, I had been drawn to him—pulled in by the force of mutual affection, or maybe by a blind desire to be near a greatness of some indeterminable sort. Abel was no star athlete in a camp that glorified physical prowess. He was not a skilled outdoorsman. His sailing, archery, tennis, and swimming were either below average or outright lousy. Abel's talents were in other, less common, domains. He always played the lead role in our group's annual play, which would be performed in front of the entire camp sometime in August. He sang beautifully at the camper talent show. I'll never forget his delivery of Paul Simon's "The Sound of Silence," which he sang to Ethan

Weiss's piano accompaniment when we were fourteen. Nor could I forget that the following year, our last, Abel ended the camper talent show with Simon's "I am a Rock." I closed my eyes and imagined that young boy with his thin body and black, curly hair standing on stage in the camp's assembly hall, singing passionately while gazing into the dusty greens and browns of old camp memorabilia: *Don't talk of love, but I've heard the words before; it's sleeping in my memory.* Sleeping in memory—yes, this was it, this was the reference to the death of Abel's mother between that second and third summer at camp. My mother came into my bedroom one February day and sat down on the bed to tell me. The camp director had called with the news.

By the second week of that first summer we were already best friends. Abel had even invented a nickname for me, "Allstar," which called upon, he told me, the German translation of my last name, *Stern*, and at the same time evoked my dominance of the group's baseball games—I was far and away the best player. In addition, the name played on what he called my "fixation" with Major League Baseball's mid-summer All-Star Game, around which, I admit, orbited the whole pageantry of the sport. Allstar stuck, and I loved it because it came from Abel's mind, created just for me.

Was Dave right? Was Abel afraid of the endgame, afraid of ultimate defeat? For my whole life, I couldn't imagine that my talented friend could fail at anything. On the contrary, it seemed as if he had achieved far more than what I thought was possible. During our final year at camp, for example, Abel had written and performed his own one-act, one-character play. It was the story of a fifteen-year-old boy who had been caught doing something forbidden at school and was waiting in a drab antechamber for the assistant principal to call him in and administer his punishment. The play had a bewildering range, from outbursts against the reigning authorities to quiet, self-probing contemplations about life, morality and justice. The entire camp sat spellbound as Abel performed. There was silence when the lights went out and the curtains drew together following the play's final scene, a scene that still sticks with me two and a half decades later. The play was a triumph, a "huge success," I said to him later that night. Success continued at the university, where we roomed together for two years and where it seemed like Abel floated through his classes plucking high grades like low-hanging fruit, while I labored over every assignment. Then after college, the jobs leading massively important environmental projects, the books, the international fame. Success defined Abel, I thought, as I gazed at the fire in the Franklin stove. There was nothing in his life that evoked failure, that indicated defeat.

After the third summer at camp, we started to write letters. I wrote at least one letter each month to Abel, and Abel, in turn, responded with typewritten letters, which I'd read—savor—and then carefully deposit—in a sort of ritualistic act—in a special dark-green cardboard box in the bottom drawer of my dresser. To my utter shock, these letters were lost when my parents renovated my bedroom while preparing for the arrival of my sister's first child. I wondered if Abel had saved my letters—my utterly prosaic letters, or worse, letters in which I tried and, I'm sure, failed to imitate Abel's easy brilliance, his eloquence and elegance. I wondered whether my letters to Abel had meant as much to Abel as Abel's letters had to me.

These were questions I could think about after returning home. I had work to do. I needed to get a sense of what had gone on here with Abel's life, with Abel's incomprehensible death. It was time to get off the couch and look around.

"Abel. Abel Prager," I said aloud. I couldn't believe he was really gone—and in such a fashion. The letter from the lawyer claimed that it had been a suicide, that "Abel had purposefully eaten poisonous mushrooms by the name of *Galerina autumnalis*," a common brown-capped fungus, I subsequently discovered by looking online, which grew plentifully throughout the Northeast in wooded areas. I made a short Internet search and couldn't find a single reported case of suicide by mushroom poisoning, which, it seemed, led to a painful and quite gruesome death. But where did he die? And who found him? And most importantly, why did he do it, if this was indeed what he did? The lawyer's letter said nothing of this. How could this be reality? This "reality" had nothing in common with the reality I had assumed was real.

I made my way over to use the bathroom. Then, feeling suddenly quite hungry, I went to the kitchen and searched the refrigerator and cabinets, discovering that the house was empty of food. I looked out the window. The snow was easing but still coming down. I explored the entryway, finding a pair of rubber-and-leather boots and a thick jacket. I put them on and went out to inspect the car. My car, a small Honda, made some desperate noises but refused to turn on. The snow, meanwhile, was over a foot and a half deep, in some drifts over two or three feet. Even if the car had started it would not have been powerful enough to force its way back down the path to the road. Prospects of dislodgement seemed dim, as I calculated based on previous shoveling experience—I'd grown up in Vermont after all—that to clear the road by hand would take me a full day at minimum and potentially much longer, assuming that the snow didn't transform into one giant block of ice. The boots and jacket fit nicely. Abel and I were basically the same size. I had been sturdier than him in youth, but the long years of library and archive work had made me frailer, while rural life must have strengthened my friend.

I saw no choice other than to walk back up Mayberry Hill Road to the small store, which I'd passed the previous night on my way in. I went back inside, found a wool hat and a pair of gloves, and started on my way. It was slow going on the dirt path to the road and even slower on the road. Nonetheless, an hour after I set out, I arrived at the store, a ramshackle wooden construction with a hand-painted sign in black letters (CASCO GENERAL STORE), a porch, and two old-fashioned gas pumps in the parking lot. As I entered, I noticed that the man behind the counter, a stout figure with a graying beard and a red-and-black checked shirt, shot me an odd sidelong glance. I ignored it and made my way among the aisles. My hunger had grown immensely and I couldn't help but tear open a very large bag of potato chips and devour nearly half of them in a matter of seconds. I loaded the basket with everything that seemed suitable under the circumstances. This included a block of cheese, salami, two loaves of sliced bread, apples, bananas, milk, a small bottle of maple syrup, peanut butter, a package of ground coffee, and a bottle of whiskey. I threw in a box of candles and a few lighters at the end.

"Got everything?" the man asked as I placed the basket on the counter.

"That should do it."

"Excuse me for asking," the man said as he quickly punched the prices into the register, "but it's about your clothes. It seems to me like you've got on things belonging to a local resident, a man who recently died. In fact, for a second when you first walked in, I thought you were him."

I felt a peculiar combination of anxiety and relief. "You're right," I said, "these are Abel's things."

"Prager. That's what I thought."

"I'm a friend of Abel's. He actually left me the house and land. Abel and I spent summers together at a camp a couple of hours away from here."

"My condolences for your loss," the man said. "Here, I know it's nothing much, but take some of this moose jerky. Made it myself. I've got the damn stuff hanging from just about every inch of rafter in my barn, not to mention the boxes of it I've got out back in the shop. It's on the house." The man took a large fistful of jerky out of a tall glass jar, put it in a paper bag, and stuffed it in among my groceries. "It'll help keep you warm, nothing like moose meat for that. It's supposed to get very cold over the next few days."

"I've never eaten moose before."

"I think you'll enjoy it." As he said this, a shout came from the back of the store that a delivery truck was just pulling in and boxes needed to be moved. The man turned up the flap that allowed him to exit the space behind the counter. As he maneuvered his rotund form through the narrow gap, swiveling first this way, then that, he paused and added, "Abel loved the stuff. The moose, I mean. Probably ate more moose jerky than anyone in town."

I reflected for a moment on this information without knowing how to think of it, to organize it, to frame it within the broader context of Abel's life and death. Then I said, "Do you know anything about what happened to him?"

"Not much. I bet you know more than we do."

"But I don't know anything."

"Since you ask, there were some things about the situation that surprised me, like that the young lady, one of the Klein girls—can't remember if it was Leah or Juliet—found the body out back behind the house, in the woods. The Kleins aren't usually around at this time of year. They're summer folks. Then there were the packages Mr. Prager sent from the store a few days before he died. We've got a postal sub-station here. The damn thing is like a curse, especially in the summer. We've got to hire an extra kid in July and August just to deal with it. Abel sent three or four packages. Not sure why it stuck with me."

"I see," I said, trying to think of what to ask next. Questions eluded me. I felt muddled, out of place, both tired and agitated. In addition, I couldn't shake the man's reference to Abel as "the body." Abel had been much more than "body" for me; he was an intellectual, spiritual guide, a force emanating through words and ideas, a mystic sage, a guru. But he was body, too, profoundly so—a young boy in a camp uniform, a swimmer with rib cage jutting out as he took deep breaths in prelude to his dive, a pubescent teen in the communal shower, a thin, bearded man, almost unrecognizable, arriving back from a project in Kazakhstan. Now that body was gone forever, buried without ceremony (according to the lawyer's letter) next to his parents in the cemetery Beth-El.

"Pardon me," the man said, "but I need to get to those boxes. The driver's always damn impatient. If there isn't space, he's bound to just drop the new ones in the snow."

"Sure," I said and turned to go. Then I stopped. "One thing. Do you know someone who could plow out Abel's dirt path to the road? My car's stuck and I think I need a jumpstart."

"Call the Reynolds boys, Bill and Fred. Card's on the counter."

"Thanks," I said, picking up one of the red cards with blue lettering. "I'll be leaving in the morning, but I'll probably be back with my wife and children in the spring."

"There's no spring here. Winter slams right into summer in these parts."

Before leaving the store, I fished around in my pocket and retrieved my phone. It was already nearing noon and I'd done nothing in or around the house. I took the two heavy bags and went outside. The snow had stopped. The clouds had moved away, and a cold sun was gazing down at the winter landscape.

The walk home was even slower going. I had to take care with each step to keep the weight of the bags in perfect balance. By the time I trudged up the path and set the bags down on the kitchen table, I was exhausted. I fixed myself two salami-and-cheese sandwiches and consumed them while still dressed in Abel's jacket and hat. I finished the open bag of potato chips and reproached myself for not buying another. Sophia didn't allow potato chips at home, and I had a weakness for them, at times surreptitiously eating a couple of small bags in my office after lunch—minuscule rebellions, useless and pathetic decadences. I drew a few cups of water from the faucet and drank them quickly. I felt calmer and flicked on my phone to call the Reynolds boys. The phone wasn't getting reception. I added a few logs to the stove and closed it up.

I sat in the chair next to the stove and warmed my feet. For the first time, I let my eyes wander around the living room. The Franklin stove, the room's most prominent object, was on the half-wall separating the living room from the adjoining kitchen, on a raised platform of blue-gray rock. The wall behind the stove had the rock until about mid-way to the ceiling, at which point it gave way to old wooden wainscoting, once painted white but now a dull shade of yellow. Across from the stove was the outer wall that contained the door and two windows facing the driveway. The wall was painted a pale blue. It was clear from the quality of the color that this had been done long ago. The adjacent exterior wall also contained a window, beyond which pine branches, laden with snow, drooped to within inches of the house. Next to the window, there was a painting of a lake in winter.

"Abel," I whispered as I turned to the Franklin stove, "Where are you? Where are you in all this?" Maybe, I considered, the trip up here was a big mistake. "What good can it do?" I said aloud. I flicked at the phone and saw that it still had no signal. I grabbed a stick of moose jerky from the bag and ripped off a chunk. The meat was salty and spicy and had a pleasant tangy flavor. Abel, the guy at the store had said, was the biggest moose eater in town. What nonsense!

I decided to go upstairs. I climbed the narrow staircase and continued down a short hallway. There were two rooms on the second floor, one on each side of the house, and a bathroom at the end of the hall, facing the woods. Next to the bathroom was Abel's office. His bedroom was across the way facing the road. The office had an additional wood-burning stove.

I entered the office and sat down at the desk. Without thinking about it, I pulled open the top-right drawer and discovered that it was crammed with papers. I pushed it shut again. I repeated this with the top-left and again found it completely full. The others were the same. On top of the desk was Abel's antique Remington typewriter, still in perfect condition. For some reason, I was surprised to see it there. I had long thought of Abel's retreat—and I did, I realized, always think of it as a retreat—as an attempt to reject those thick layers of the past, and nothing conjured more thoughts of the past than the Remington.

The typewriter had belonged to his grandfather, Herschel Prager, who came to the United States from Vienna and taught Abel German when he was a boy. *Stern*, star, Allstar, I thought—it all connected to the Remington. Yes, I recalled, as I sat back in Abel's chair and gazed out the window, Herschel Prager came to New York in the late 1920s. In 1938, he got a job as a European correspondent for *Newsweek*, which took him first, briefly, to Berlin and then, as the situation deteriorated, to Paris, where he lived until the German invasion.

In Paris, Herschel met and married Vera, Abel's grandmother. Soon after they arrived in New York, Abel's father Abraham was born. From a young age, Abraham was driven, serious, and practical. He went to City College and then to work for a bank, where he excelled, moving, within five years, into senior management. By the time Abel started camp, his father was a vice president of New York Merchants Bank. By the final year of camp, he was president and, I assume, a rich man.

Along the way, Abraham married Lillian Blumenthal, Abel's mother. I knew her from those first two parents' days at camp before she died. She had wavy black hair, greenish-blue eyes, and a smile at once tender and forlorn. She had a special type of beauty, none of which Abel inherited. Abel was the image of his father, though shorter, smaller, somehow less substantial, less weighted to the earth.

I peered out the window into the woods as the scene started to fade in the afternoon light. The Remington—it was this Remington that Lillian Prager had used to type the letters Abel received every other day at camp. My mother would write letters full of the dullest matters. Lillian, on the other hand, wrote long and poetic letters to her only son. She typed them on rich, creamy paper that held the ink perfectly. They were not scrawled in some intolerable bubbly letters, the likes of which my mother used. Each vowel and consonant seemed to me struck with utter resolution. M. Y. D. E. A. R. E. S. T. A. B. E. L. They were hammered into place, chiseled into the page with a determined love. The Remington held many ghosts—Herschel Prager, Lillian Prager, Abel Prager—and now it belonged to me, left to me with everything else in Abel's will. Abel was dead. It was on this Remington that he had written to me. Those letters, those words, more than anything else, had shaped my life. For many years, those letters had guided me—they had been my touchstone, my inspiration.

I ran a finger along the top of the Remington. Its austere functionality seemed, at that moment, the height of elegance and dignity. It had one purpose only: to record the thoughts of any person who sat before it. What a far cry from my current machine. My computer seemed built for precisely the opposite reason—to think for me, to interrupt me, to connect me with all that was not myself. Yes, perhaps it had been built precisely to obliterate my selfhood entirely. I took a fresh piece of paper from the stack on my left and loaded it into the Remington. I typed, *Dear Abel.*

For some reason, alarmed at what I'd done, I rose to my feet. "What am I doing?" I asked myself and ran my hands through my hair. "Nothing good can come of this." And, I thought, what could I possibly have to say to him now that he was gone—now, after all those years of silence?

The lawyer's letter had requested that I come to the office on Park Avenue as soon as possible to discuss the totality of the inheritance. Only at this moment, leaning over the Remington, did it dawn on me that this inheritance might go well beyond the house and the land. The letter said that it was Abel's request that I be sent the keys to the house in the initial note. "You will find them in a small yellow envelope stapled to the back of the letter." "Abel Prager," it read, "requested that you be able to access the house without delay."

These were the words that unsettled me. I had concealed this piece of information from Sophia for some unclear purpose. "Access the house without delay." There was nothing in the house that seemed to warrant such haste.

These thoughts were confusing me. I had turned forty a few weeks before and had been working long hours to finish my second book—a book, I hoped, that would elevate me to full professor and the peak of my career. I was writing about the Karaite challenge to the rabbinical order in the waning years of the Cordoba Caliphate. It was the story of the greatest internecine struggle in the history of medieval Judaism— a story untold, largely forgotten. As I saw it, it was my last chance to break out of the ordinary ranks of the professorial herd and to join an entirely different group—the community of real scholars, Jewish scholars. If the book succeeded, it could reshape the entire field of medieval Spanish Jewish history. If it failed, I failed, and my career would be doomed to a slow stream of mediocrity for the next thirty years. Success, on the other hand, would bring a flowering of some elusive genius.

For much of my life, I would never have considered pursuing genius. To the contrary, I couldn't help but feel my mediocrity time and again, especially when I compared myself to Abel. I had succeeded at many things, it's true, but I'd done so by simply following a path cleared for me. It was a matter of walking straight without diversion— being steady and focused. Abel, on the other hand, blazed a trail that led from New York to the Congo, to Egypt, Ethiopia, Israel, Central Asia, and ultimately into the dark, thick woods of Casco.

I turned back to the desk. Six years, I thought, of isolation, of seclusion in the face of mounting disaster and crisis in the world. During these six years, during the wars in Iraq and Afghanistan, the financial meltdown, Abel had been here. Resigning—I thought again of what Dave had said—instead of playing out the game.

I needed to get a handle on this situation. It would be dark soon and my ability to sort through the papers would be restricted. I sat back down and opened up the top right-hand drawer. I drew out a large stack of papers; all had been typed on the Remington. I began to leaf through them, at first inattentively or even dreamily, until my eyes passed over the title, "First Canoe Ride on Pleasant Lake." Intrigued, I took the pages from the stack and moved over to the old rocking chair, in the corner by the stove. I didn't feel like making another fire and instead wrapped my body with the woolen blanket that Abel had draped over the back of the chair. Undoubtedly, Abel used to do the same. The thought pleased me, and I began to read.

First Canoe Ride on Pleasant Lake

I push my canoe into the lake and feel an intensity churning in my chest. I am Ahab, only without a whale to pursue, a fresh water Ahab. Or perhaps I am Ishmael, alone on board without Ahab, without captain or crew, without a grander pursuit either divine or demonical. My canoe is old and red. I bought it together with a wooden paddle from the Wilkinsons, who soon will be selling their little cottage, a cottage that has housed Wilkinsons (so they say) for two hundred years.

An Ahabian pulse beats inside me. I am driven by a blind rage after something. No, it is a rage after nothing; there are no whales in Pleasant Lake. Who is Ahab, then, without his whale, without the endless expanse of ocean in which to hunt? I have been thinking about his mad story during my sleepless nights. I came to Casco in search of sleep and discovered instead its impossibility. It tempts me. It comes within reach and then withdraws to lurk in the shadows.

As I set off on the lake, I think of Ishmael, penniless and alone, signing up to join the voyage. He has nothing left on shore, nothing binding him to the land. This is it – this is the feeling of launching a canoe. It is liberation from "shore" and everything shore implies. I make a few strong strokes with the paddle and glide over the water.

It was a damp, drizzly November in his soul. So be it. Depression drives Ishmael into that demonic tale. What drives me into this red canoe in such a state of weariness? I haven't slept in two days. The lake has a deep green color and is streaked with yellows and reds, reflections of the shoreline. It is early in the morning, just after daybreak, when I push off. The sky is pinkish. Blue emerges from the deeper blackness. This seems to me the perfect time of day, the birth moment of day. Only the death moment has a similar splendor. What separates the birth moment from the death moment is that the latter contains anguish. Daybreak, rather, spirals back to creation: "Let there be light." Day breaks over Pleasant Lake. I glide across its liquid reflection.

There emerges a complex spectrum of blues, purples, oranges, reds as the blackness slowly drains out. What kind of God is here on Pleasant Lake? It is certainly a sleepless God, the God of Insomnia, son of Nyx and Erebus, brother and enemy of Morpheus. I try to push these thoughts away so that I don't find myself actually believing in this transcendence, in this waking dreamscape. Such is the power of the lake amid an autumnal dawn. One forgets about sleep entirely - or perhaps more accurately, one forgets about being awake. I focus instead on my paddle as it dips into the lake and rises out of it, marking my rhythm.

The summer residents have all gone home. The locals remain to withstand the winter. I scan the lake in all directions and see no other vessels. For sure, around some bend and hidden in a fold of shoreline there is a fisherman with his rod, casting gently into this calm water. On shore, boys throw sticks for their dogs, which leap without hesitation into the cold water. I paddle.

The Wilkinson paddle is a fantastic object carved from a single piece of maple wood. On the butt of the handle is the stamp of the maker - Morehouse. Poland, ME. The graceful curve of a duck's head, branded into the wood, represents the Morehouse brand. I stroke the paddle into green-blue, then into green-black, then green-black-yellow, then green-black-red-orange, and so on. There are endless variegations, which depend on a multitude of factors: the shoreline placement of pines, maples, birches, and oaks, the movement of clouds overhead, the angle of the sun, the strength of the wind and its traces on the surface of the lake, the path of a duck or loon, the flight of a bird.

I have launched my canoe from the end of my forest path. Unlike my neighbors on either side, I have no dock or beach. What an absurd sight it was in July when the McKenneys had a dump truck drop a load of sand onto their portion of shore. Pleasant Lake requires no such cosmetic improvements. The McKenneys on one side and the Lasalles on the other have subjected their small bits of forest to the dentist and orthodontist. My forest, sandwiched in between, still has a touch of wildness in it. It is raw and rotting in parts. Trees are left to decay. The road is gradually being choked off. The real estate agent who sold me the house told me that I could pave it down to five hundred feet before the lake, just as the McKenneys had done. But no, my little patch of wilderness will have to fall to somebody else's axe.

In truth, I know nothing of the woods here, these woods that I own by deed. By contrast, I feel like I have established some basic intimacy with the lake. I have known other lakes before. I fell in love with a lake as a boy, and as I paddle I sense that this love repeats itself with Pleasant Lake.

On the other hand, it is impossible to say for sure where the lake stops and the land begins. During my first plunge into the lake in summer I encountered cool streams of water from some sub-surface current. These streams pulsed into the lake through underground arteries. Where was the lake's heart, that mysterious and invisible machine? Yes, it was not in the lake at all but far from it, perhaps miles away, deep beneath the woods somewhere. If the heart is the essence of a being, and the lake's heart is in fact bound by earth, what does this say about the lake itself? The entire lake, I think, is but an expression of something else, like that far-off mountain, like that unreachable, austere and craggy peak, so devoid of life.

I move across the lake in my red canoe. Thoughts of its pulsation have made me thirsty. I reach down and cup some water and bring it to my lips. This is as close as it comes to transcendence. This, I say quietly to myself, is as close as I will ever come to God.

To the east, the sun has risen above the treetops. There are clouds in the sky, but they have been thinning, and it seems as if the sky is destined for perfect clarity by noon. The sky and the lake will soon find their harmony.

I can feel the pressure changing and the temperature dropping. Fall is cozying up to winter. As I intensify my strokes, I start to feel warmth coming from my core. I am pleased to note how effortlessly I can paddle. The muscles in my arms, shoulders, and back easily contract and stretch out. I feel like I have finally shed some of that city brittleness, that city weakness. I am no longer that self. I have lost my whale.

At camp, we learned to steer a canoe through calm and rapid waters. As a child, I had lacked strength. No matter with whom I was paired, I would be made to sit at the front of the canoe. I came to suspect that I had been born to sit at the bow and that the whole world could be divided into those who sit bow and those who sit stern in a canoe. The bow-man points the way forward, calls out danger, spies flora and fauna on the shoreline to entertain the man in back. The bow-man is freed from heavy labor and can contemplate quietly or tell stories. The man in stern, of course, is the opposite. He is silent, stoic, powerful, and manly. What I would have given to be a stern man for a single day! To guide the vessel, to power it through the rapids of life!

For months, I have been eyeing a small beach with a white shed or boathouse situated on a point protruding into the lake. I have never seen a person on this little oasis. There is no doubt about it; this is the best spot on the lake. The sun strikes it nearly all day. The beach glows like white gold.

To make it there, I need to leave the shallows and venture out toward the middle of the lake. I am happy to do it. I will leave civilization behind me, at least for the ten or fifteen minutes it takes to make it to that little house. I cannot be Ishmael. I am not an adventurer at heart and my despair does not push me there. My difficult days pass with doors closed, curtains pushed together, and shades pulled down. It is a process of entombment. My jewels and statues are mostly books. My internal organs are preserved in jars of homemade jam that a kind neighbor brought for me in a state of mid-summer euphoria. There, in my wintry tomb, I die and am resurrected.

I close my eyes. In the imaginary reflection of the lake within my eyelids I see myself as a child, a child with a mother still very much alive, a mother waiting for her son in the city, paintbrush in hand, hair pulled back, neck craned forward to inspect a hue, a tint, a movement of paint toward or away from form. In any case, I am standing on a dock before breakfast. I have woken up earlier than the others. The previous night had been cold, and though it is the middle of July, the lake water, I'm sure, is even colder than the new day's air. I brace myself and then rip off my shirt. I run my hands along my ribs and take deep breaths. Two, three, four, and then my muscles tense and release as I dive into the water, knifing through the surface with perfect form.

My young body was made for diving - and how I loved to dive from that dock! It was not just any dock and any lake, but this dock, this lake. It was this morning, this and no other, when I knew for sure that my perfect diving form was a gift of youth, a temporary gift, and that I needed to indulge it to the full.

I have become timid. Now I am barely able to stick my toe in the water as a tester, and only in deep July or August do I feel confident enough to wade slowly in. I have gone from diver to creature of the shore, at best a wader in the shallows. Somehow I must align the rhythmic beating of the lake's heart with my heart and let its deep, hidden spring babble through my veins.

I think of nothing for a while as I paddle. The sky has turned blue. The shore is a mix of browns, greens, and yellows, with blurry streaks of red and orange blazing here or there. Birds fly overhead - including two hawks, which wheel in sweeping arches over my canoe. The canoe enters into a new zone of the lake. The current shifts and heads directly against me, slowing my progress. I don't mind. I have no reason to hurry. Nothing is waiting for me at El Dorado. Slowly but surely, the little white house creeps closer.

I pull my canoe onto the beach and sit in the sand. The sun is now producing slight warmth, perceptible through the cold autumn air. My cheeks have a pleasant flush. Suddenly, I feel as if my mind undergoes a rapid expansion, as if a vise-grip has let go its hold and I've been allowed to stretch to my full capacity. All at once the ordinary calm transforms into a boundless silence. A Promethean urge grips me - calling on me to pursue the "secret" of this lake, and through that the secret of - who knows? Who knows!

I lie back and close my eyes. The expansion stops. I realize that my mind is not an ocean after all, but a lake bound like Pleasant Lake by its shore. The thought is both upsetting and calming. Doubt seizes me as I realize how much more of the journey towards the infinite is left to go and how little I have gone so far. Some desire, or rather something beyond desire, is pushing me to that place, or in that direction. Whether it is a place or a direction I do not know. Perhaps I am Ahab after all. I wonder about his whale and mine.

The height of morning has arrived. It is an ordinary (meaning extraordinary) October day. I get up and make a

quick tour of the beach, including a circumambulation of
the little house. It has no windows. Its door is padlocked
shut. Even if the house contains the many promised trea-
sures, I am happy not to have them. I would rather have the
house maintain its secrets and store some of mine. I give it
stillness and silence, the great promises (illusions? delusions?) of the lake.

Mental gravity presses down on me. Thoughts of my father
come. It is time to push off, for thoughts of father will
lead to thoughts of her. My mother's image flashes before
me like a Fata Morgana. It is the moment of real danger,
and it means that I might not, in fact, make it back to the
end of my forest path. I will lose myself on this lake. My
demise on Pleasant Lake will not rank with the adventures
of Ahab and Ishmael. And they will say - because she called
him there, she called him back to her.

I return to the canoe for the trip back to my small sliver
of frontage. I decide to keep to the shore now, even though
it increases the length of the trip. As the sun strikes my
face, I stow my paddle and let the current carry me. I lean
back, with my arms resting against the gunwales, and try
to clear my mind of all but the most immediate impressions.

I float like this for a while, only now and then direct-
ing my boat away from shore. Eventually, the mental dam
breaks. The damming came at a price. She comes back to me
not as a Fata Morgana but as flesh and blood. I fight to
think of something else - and my mind turns to the last
project I undertook, an analysis of doomed plans to restore
the Aral Sea. Its naivete, ambition, and rational beauty
beguile and repulse me.

Better to take up the paddle again. Before long I find myself in port. For sure, I have brought no whale oil back for market. At least I have preserved my ship and crew, my crew of one. Deep in my heart, I sense that I am not Ahab or Ishmael but Queequeg, that master of the harpoon, that lover of the kill. Such fantasies can and must be indulged on a quiet autumn day on Pleasant Lake. I chase them, no matter where they lead.

Abel, Abel, Abel, I thought, or rather hummed or chanted. As I looked out the window at the snowy field, my mind turned to rivers: Moose River, the Kennebec, the Penobscot, and the Allagash. As campers, we had canoed them all. Each summer brought a new river, each summer the journeys grew longer. Three days on the Kennebec, five on the Penobscot, seven on the Allagash. During both the Penobscot and Allagash trips, Abel had sat at the bow of my canoe. These two trips belonged to my finest memories. They were the jewels of an otherwise rather ordinary childhood, or at least this is how I thought about them as I gazed out into the wintry scene behind Abel's house.

It was dusk. It's time for a glass of whiskey, I thought, and planned to prepare materials for the morning while I drank. The morning would have to be extremely productive if I were going to make it home for the evening with Ellen and Dave, not that it mattered. I went downstairs and threw a couple of logs into the stove. I went into the kitchen and poured a whiskey, twice my usual amount.

Perhaps there was something Ahabian in my friend, I considered as I took the first sip. I remembered when Abel read *Moby Dick* during that final summer at camp, that sweet, dolorous swansong to childhood. At fifteen, a world only made up of boys was not bound to last.

I picked up my phone and flicked it on. A message from Sophia popped up on the screen. "Where are you? What's going on there? Let me know, Ezra." Something about the message bothered me—or maybe I was bothered by the very existence of the message itself, infiltrating into this zone. I hesitated and then hit the button to call her back. It went to voicemail immediately.

"Soph, sorry I missed your call. I'm just getting your note now. I've been sorting through some papers but barely scratched the surface. I've basically only opened one drawer and now it's getting too dark to do any more. There's a ton of stuff up there—upstairs, that is. I'm not sure how I'll manage it. The car's still stuck and I haven't been able to reach the Reynolds boys. But I'll be back tomorrow. I'll see you tomorrow."

I sat down by the stove. Ten, then fifteen, then twenty minutes passed—or longer. The thinning light was making it more difficult to see. The light was hazy and comfortable, and I took a few deep breaths. I was starting to feel or imagine a little bit of Abel in the house. It had been nice to be among his words again.

The whiskey was gone and I poured another. The light drained slowly from the room. The candlelight grew more intense. There was no point calling the Reynolds boys now. It would have to wait till morning. Two opposing impulses worked on me. The first was to go back to Abel's office and continue to sort through his papers. The other was to close my eyes and feel the stove's heat on my cheeks and try to think as little as possible. I reached over to the bag of moose jerky and pulled out a stick. The spicy jerky combined with the whiskey brought a deep flush to my cheeks.

There was no question of heading back to the office. It was too dark and I felt too tired to work through those papers by candlelight. My thoughts turned to Sophia. I had met her while visiting my friend

Harvey Dunlop. Harvey had moved to Burlington after getting his law degree, to work for a local firm. After a week visiting my parents in south Vermont, I borrowed my father's car and drove up to see him. Harvey and I were eating dinner at a typical Vermont place, equal parts ethnic, hippy, and yuppie. The food was good. Sophia was our waitress. I tried to catch her attention now and then but in the end left without asking for her number. That night I lay in Harvey's guest bed and thought about her. She had dark brown hair with a certain orange tint, like the bark of a redwood. She had a narrow face, a slightly bent nose, and rich eyebrows. As I lay there, I vowed that I'd go back to the restaurant the next day and find her. Harvey and I had plans to meet for lunch. After that I would go.

The following afternoon I parked the car across the street from the restaurant. I got out and crossed but at the last moment didn't go in. It was foolish. I lived in New York. I was a professor of medieval Jewish history. Instead of going in, I walked down Main Street toward the lake and went into a coffee shop to grab a drink for the drive south. When I entered the place and glanced around, I saw that she was by the window drinking a cappuccino and reading a book. My heart started to pound. I decided to get the coffee first and then approach. The line seemed to take forever. In front of me, people seemed to be ordering the most complex drinks imaginable. When the coffee finally came up, I took it over to her table. She had one foot splayed out on the chair next to her and a cheap ballpoint pen in her mouth.

"Hello again," I said.

"Do I know you?"

"I was at the Emerald Garden last night with a friend of mine."

"Wait, yes, I remember. Spicy peanut chicken with rice noodles."

"Actually, that's what my friend had."

"What did you have?"

"Sesame tofu and vegetables, brown rice."

"I don't remember."

"I hope I'm not disturbing you."

"I've actually just reached the end of a chapter."

We talked for a while at the café. I learned that she had just finished her junior year at the university and was majoring in English. I told her I taught Jewish history. She said that she didn't know much about Judaism but had always been intrigued by it, especially by the sounds of Hebrew prayer being chanted. After we left the coffee shop and took a walk through the city, we drove out into the countryside, pulled over on the side of a rural road, and had sex in the back seat of my father's car.

I fell in love with her immediately, or at least that is what it felt like at the time. In retrospect, the sensation might be better described as an unquenchable and unshakable lust. It was May. My first year of teaching had ended only weeks before. I had planned to spend the summer in the city working on my book.

I couldn't leave her, not after this first encounter. I took a room at a motel in South Burlington for a week. She came over each day, either before or after her shift. Sometimes she came in the morning, sometimes not until after midnight. She was twenty-two years old. Her father was a furniture maker. Her mother was a librarian. I was drawn to her body with a ferocity I had never known I possessed. Previously, I had always thought myself in possession of a rather weak libido.

I left after the week. I needed to get back to the city and back to work. When I returned to my apartment in the city, I discovered, however, that it was impossible to work. Books found their way to my lap. I would stare out the window and think of her.

I called her and tried to convince her to come to the city. She agreed to come in two weeks, when she had a weekend off from the restaurant. The knowledge that I would soon see her calmed me, and for the next days I worked furiously, as if I could work away the time like whittling down a stick.

We hardly left the apartment while she was in the city. We went once to the Metropolitan Museum of Art and out to dinner. On her last day, we went downtown to meet Abel at a bar in the East Village. The next night, after Sophia had gone by bus back to Burlington, I met him again in the same bar.

"I thought," he said, "you were required to throw fish back if you catch them too young." I hesitated. It was not a typical statement Abel would make. It was too conformist, too sexist, and way too moralistic for Abel. "In any case," Abel continued, "I don't know many fishermen who would be able to part with such a catch."

"She's not that young," I said. "She's already twenty-two. There's nothing wrong with that. I would've thought that of all the people I know, you'd be the least concerned with things like age."

"Calm down, Ezra. I didn't mean it seriously, at least in the way you're taking it. Maybe I'm jealous. It could be that I'd like to have a young student of my own."

I sipped the whiskey and gazed into the Franklin stove. The conversation had annoyed me. It could be that it had offended me. I had never felt angry with Abel before then—disappointed, sure, but never angry, never mad.

Then there was her departing. When the Green Mountain Busliner pulled out of the station, I was thrust right back into that state of desperation. After a few days of intense self-pitying, I called her and announced that I would rent an apartment in Burlington for July and August. She seemed pleased by the news.

I found a small place not far from the lake. By mid-July, we were practically living together. I had brought boxes of books and materials from New York, but even though I spent my mornings and afternoons at the library, I accomplished virtually nothing.

When the summer ended, I packed up my things and returned home. The school year started. Life lurched back into its usual form.

Then something changed. Sophia started taking longer to return my calls. My emails often went unanswered. By the end of September, she seemed to be preparing to cut me off. Those were the darkest days, I thought, as I poured another whiskey. The lowest point came in mid-October when she finally broke it off. My world unraveled. My stability, my career, my future started to pull apart at the seams.

I got up from the chair. This was too much, I thought, too damn much. There was no need to get back into all that now. I was in Abel's house and Abel was gone. That was the point. What was the point of remembering that meaningless comment about fish and the fisherman? Why should I open this smallest of old wounds? I went to the kitchen and fixed a salami sandwich, eating it together with an apple. I finished my whiskey and followed it up by chugging three glasses of water. I blew out the candles and unbuttoned and stripped off my gray shirt. I got under Abel's woolen blanket and immediately fell asleep.

Day Three

In the deep recesses of my mind, I heard the faint sounds of Reveille playing over the electric bugle system, as it did every morning at camp, waking the campers up from dewy, misty slumber. I opened my eyes.

The fire in the Franklin stove had gone out in the night. Beyond the blanket, the air was cold, in the forties if not below. I lay there for a few moments and then sat up, wrapping the blanket tightly around my chest. I bent over the stove and stuffed in a few handfuls of old papers and a couple of logs. I struck a match and the fire immediately started to blaze. I quickly went to the bathroom and then returned to the sofa and the still-warm blanket.

I thought of that final year at camp. By then, the group was just eight of us. Besides Abel and me, the group consisted of Ethan Weiss, a freckled, awkward boy from Cleveland; Danny Kaplan and Paul Freeman, from the suburbs of Boston; Adam Grube and Walt Myerson, from Westchester; and Stevie Berman from Austin, Texas, or "Tex" as we called him. Apart from Abel, my best friend at camp, I was closest with Walt, Ethan, and Tex, though in truth all eight of us were very close. For whatever reason, though, I found real intimacy only with Abel.

During the first week of August, the eight of us had headed out with two counselors in a flotilla of five canoes to paddle the 92-mile length of the Allagash River. The Allagash was the longest trip during our years at camp, seven days in total. On the third day, amid a particularly calm stretch, Abel and I, sharing a canoe, had opened up a lead on the others by a distance of some two hundred yards. Abel decided to stow his oar and turned to me.

"Allstar," he said in that typical way, "I've been wanting to discuss something with you."

"What is it?" I asked, both concerned by Abel's tone and annoyed that I was now forced to power the canoe by myself.

"It's about Paul."

"About Paul," I repeated. "What about Paul?" Of the eight, Paul was the most mysterious to me. He was a chubby boy, a decently skilled, though lazy, athlete. He excelled only at tennis, mostly by means of his powerful serve and forehand.

"Have you noticed he's been leaving the bunk in the middle of the night?"

"No, I haven't noticed. I'm sure he's just going to use the bathroom. There's nothing strange about that."

"A couple of nights before we started the trip, I woke up when Paul was leaving. I didn't really think about it, or I thought the same thing as you, that he was headed out to the green house to use the bathroom. I tried to fall back asleep, but I also needed to take a piss and left the bunk maybe three minutes after he did. When I got to the green house, Paul wasn't there. I checked under the stalls for feet. No Paul. I was curious about where he went."

"Maybe he just pissed in the woods and went back inside while you were on your way to the green house."

"That's what I thought, but when I got back to the bunk he wasn't there. I tried to wait up for him to come back but eventually fell asleep."

"That's it?"

"Wait. Let me continue. I concluded that he wasn't leaving the bunk to use the bathroom."

"Maybe you just missed him under one of the stalls. It was the middle of the night."

"I followed him the next night."

"What happened?"

"This is what happened, Allstar. Paul, without a flashlight, went down the long path to the field and then turned down the hill to the lake."

"To the lake?"

"That's right, to the lake. Right before he got to the water, at the edge of the lake, he stopped. He stared out into the black lake for about twenty minutes, possibly longer. Then he turned around, went back to the bunk, and went to sleep."

"Are you joking?"

"That's what happened. I swear."

"And that's it?"

"Why do you always ask, 'That's it'? Actually, it's not 'it.' The next night, the night before we left for the Allagash, I followed him again. Same thing: to the field, then to the lake, twenty or thirty minutes of looking out, and back to bed."

The story unsettled me, but I couldn't figure out why. I wanted Abel to make sense of it for me. "Why do you think he does that?"

"No clue," Abel said, "but it's worth thinking about."

"Will you ask him about it?"

"I might."

Abel took up his oar again and turned away from me. In the meantime, the rest of the canoes had almost caught up with us, and I turned to the left and saw Paul paddling away, with Walt in the front of his canoe. What was wrong with Paul Freeman? I wondered as we continued around a lazy bend in the river. Why would he get up in the middle of the night to stare out at the lake? It made no sense to me at the time. I never asked Abel about it again.

I shook my head, trying to shake off the residual sleepiness. I slumped down in the chair in order to get my feet closer to the stove. I saw Paul again in New York a year ago, for the first time since camp ended. He had contacted me through university email and a short and stiff correspondence had ensued. I was about to terminate the whole thing when Paul mentioned that he had "received a strange letter from Abel the other day." "It motivated me to look you up," he said. I was curious about the letter, of course—doubly so because I hadn't received word from Abel in a very long time. My pride was wounded. Why hadn't Abel written me that strange letter or any letter at all? I quickly typed back, "How about lunch at our place on Riverside on Saturday. I'll introduce you to Sophia and the kids. Bring your family."

On Saturday, Paul Freeman, his wife Audrey, and their son Freddy arrived at noon. Sophia had baked pizzas, though it turned out that Freddy was lactose intolerant. She quickly threw together another one without cheese.

Paul seemed nervous as our families sat around the living room eating pizza and talking. He kept barking out directives across the room at Freddy, who was pursuing his two-year-old curiosity to investigate all objects he could get his hands on. He was especially keen on getting a baseball from a bookshelf just out of reach. The ball had been autographed by the former Red Sox slugger Jim Rice. I repeatedly tried to assuage Paul by letting him know that Sam and Sybil had already broken anything of value. This didn't have much effect, and after a while I told Sybil to take Freddy to her room and to show him her toys. She took his hand and led him down the hall.

After lunch, I opened a couple bottles of beer and invited Paul into my study. Paul agreed to join, though with a clear lack of enthusiasm and only after exchanging some sort of look with Audrey. When we got to the room, I gestured for Paul to have a seat in my leather armchair, while I sat behind the desk.

"Paul," I said, trying to sound casual, "it's been a very long time."

"True," said Paul, scanning the room full of books. "It's difficult to think of you as a professor."

"Why's that?"

"You never seemed very bookish, at least compared to some of the others, like Ethan or Walt or even Tex. You hardly read anything at camp. You spent all your time working on those baseball stats. I would have thought you'd end up an actuary."

"If I didn't get tenure, being an actuary was my backup. What about you, Paul? I have no idea what you've been up to."

"Me? Well, you can see it for the most part. We have Freddy now. Freddy is a lot to handle."

"Freddy seems no harder than most, certainly no more to handle than Sam or Sybil. Probably a lot less."

"I appreciate that," Paul said.

"What do you do for work?" I asked and immediately felt like I had moved the conversation onto fragile ground. Paul shifted uncomfortably in the chair.

"I used to be a financial portfolio manager. I quit after my clients lost a ton of money in the '08 crash. I could have stuck it out, I guess, but the whole thing was shit, Ezra, real shit. The hours were shit, the people, the work. Look, we're exactly the same age and I have already lost half my hair. You have a full head of hair, good thick hair like you always had. You're not even graying yet."

"I think hair loss is just genetic, Paul. I don't think it has to do with work."

"It was the stress. I had a lot of stress. I was taking both blood pressure medication and anti-depressants. Now I'm off both and into yoga."

"That's great," I said. He tipped back the rest of his beer and placed the bottle on the desk's blotter.

"I don't want any chips in the game, Ezra. I lost the instinct for greed. I'm too lazy for it. You remember how fat I was as a kid."

"You were chubby, not fat. You look good now."

"I'm actually aiming to put on a few pounds. I don't feel good, skinny like this. I tried for years to lose the weight. Then I lost it and got greedy and drove myself into the ground. I'm not a thin guy at my core, Ezra, if you know what I mean. It's hard to believe it lasted so long. It's amazing how badly we misread ourselves. Remember that summer when I suddenly started playing good tennis. We were thirteen and somehow everything seemed to click. I beat Kaplan that year for the first time, remember?"

"That was a big win, the first time Kaplan went down."

"I thought I was on my way to playing professional tennis. When I got home in the fall, I convinced my parents to sign me up at the local club. I entered six tournaments that year and never won a set. I got crushed, in other words, and I realized that I actually wasn't any good."

"At least you get to spend more time with your family now, with Freddy."

"That's the whole point, Stern. I'm aiming to get us out of the city, maybe move upstate somewhere, if Audrey can find a job. I've been here for way too long. I need a break. In that sense, I don't blame Abel for packing up and leaving like he did."

I was happy Paul had brought him up. "Yes," I said, "you mentioned that you heard from him."

"Got an odd letter, like I said in the email."

"I know that's what you wrote, but what do you mean by odd?"

"I mean odd," Paul repeated. "You know, odd."

"Yes," I said. "You already said that. But in what way was it odd? On some level Abel is always odd."

"This was different. You're right, he's always beyond the norm somehow, but this was something else."

"I don't understand what you mean by that, Paul." I was getting irritated, but was trying to hide it behind some sort of professorial affect.

"He seemed out of touch with reality. Abel's an outsider, I guess, but I always thought of him as a particular type of outsider, not so dreamy, not so indirect. He was always direct to a fault. He could be a real hard-ass. Could cut at the perfect spot. Always the precise spot. I'm sure you, of all people, know what I mean."

"I see," I said, though I still didn't get what Paul was talking about. It was clear that Paul didn't want to offer much, and I didn't feel much like pushing him. Paul looked down at his watch. "Did you write back?"

"Write back? I haven't written a damn letter since camp, and I'm not going to start now. Plus, it didn't really seem like Abel wanted any response. It wasn't that type of letter. He didn't even ask about Freddy."

"That's not his style."

"Fuck his style," Paul said. "We aren't kids anymore, Stern. We can't just go around talking about ourselves all the time, living in a world of one, a world of our own egos. That's what I learned in '08. That's what everyone should have learned in '08. Of course, nobody learned a thing. I used to see him once a month before he took off. It was always the same, just like at camp. I'll admit I was getting sick of it, sick of his narcissism."

"You saw each other that often?"

"That's right, at least until I met Audrey."

I would have liked to steer the conversation back to Abel's letter but couldn't find an elegant way to do it. Paul didn't seem forthcoming, or perhaps, I considered, as I bent down to throw another log in the stove, he was purposefully concealing something.

"We should get the kids together more often," I said, giving up hope that the conversation about Abel would lead somewhere. "Freddy seems like a really good kid."

"He's fantastic."

It took more effort than I thought it would, but I finally pushed my way off the sofa and into a standing position. I peered into the Casco morning. The sky was pinkish gray. It looked like a winter's morning, the type I had experienced thousands of times growing up in Vermont. I turned on my phone to see if Sophia had called. She hadn't. I flicked off the screen. She was expecting me later that day for dinner with Ellen and Dave. Sam had his basketball game the following afternoon.

Why hadn't Abel written me an odd letter? Maybe Paul had been mistaken. Maybe the letter wasn't odd at all. It could have been well within Abel's usual style, and in truth, that style could vary dramatically from one letter to the next. It could be that Paul received only a few letters from Abel over the years and was in a poor position to judge. It could be that Paul was simply a clumsy reader who couldn't find his way through a complicated text, and on some fundamental level Abel's texts were always complicated. I, on the other hand, had received hundreds of letters over the years and would have been in a unique position to judge this "odd" or "strange" letter against the history of our correspondence.

"Why," I said to myself as I gazed into the pinkish trees, "didn't I ask Paul to see that letter? Why didn't I sit down and write to Abel right away?"

I went to the kitchen and prepared a peanut butter sandwich. A peanut butter sandwich was what I had made every Wednesday at camp—Trip Day, during which all the campers were cast out to mountains, lakes, and other natural wonders throughout the state of Maine. Outside of camp, I almost never ate peanut butter and despised the combination of peanut butter and jelly. It could be that this was my first peanut butter sandwich in twenty-five years.

I ate it mechanically, working pieces of sticky matter away from the upper palette and washing them down with a glass of milk. There was no way around it, I concluded, I would have to call Sophia and tell her that I needed another day. It wasn't a big deal. We saw Dave and Ellen fairly often and it wouldn't be a problem to reschedule. The matter of Sam's basketball game was another story. I could either leave very early on the following morning or would have to make it up to the boy, take him to see a Knicks game or a circus or something like that.

I flicked on the phone. It was nine in the morning. I flicked it off. I would call Sophia later, I thought, when I wasn't in such a muddled state of mind. I drew some water from the faucet into the kettle and placed it on the Franklin stove. A few minutes later the water was at a boil and I poured it directly over a few large spoons of coffee grounds. I took the coffee upstairs to the office. Outside, the trees were covered with snow. It was the same forest I grew up with in Vermont. The nature beyond the house seemed both familiar and foreign. Or perhaps it was Nature with a capital N that felt foreign, a Nature with a spiritual essence, a soul of its own that was much greater than the collective soul of humankind. I had lived for too long, I thought, in a realm denuded of Nature, a realm out of balance, an only-human realm.

I took a stack of papers out of the top left drawer and sat down in the rocking chair. I peeled off the first pages, set the rest of the stack on the floor, and read.

The Visit

I have fled into the wilderness for one purpose, to escape.
I have no idea what I want to escape from or if I have
succeeded. I doubt very much that I have. Many times I have
thought that it would have been better if I had stayed
where I was.

Example: During my first spring and summer I attempted
to cultivate a vegetable garden. Nothing much came up and
what did the rabbits quickly nibbled away. I lacked focus.
I lacked the will to garden. There were too many days when
I laid down my hoe early and ventured into the field and
woods to pick berries. There was no need to lift a hoe
when such delicacies grew in the wild. As such, my hoeing
became a sort of pantomime. In the end, I can't say I blamed
the rabbits. They were doing the smarter thing, foraging
instead of growing. I was a rabbit among the berry bushes
and the fruit trees and could get whatever else I needed at
the General Store.

But this is a prelude to the main topic. I am writing,
in any case, only for those rabbits and squirrels, my most
regular companions, and I have no doubt that after I am gone
they will break in here and nibble my pages to oblivion.
The main topic is this: after two years of living here I had
my first visitor.

Juliet came to the house during the last week of June.
I was in my office when I heard a car pull up the path and
stop outside. A car door opened and then slammed shut. I got
up immediately and went into my bedroom to see what was
going on. There she stood, next to her car, in a pair of blue
jeans and a snug-fitting gray T-shirt. I watched from the

window as she looked around. She brushed some hair from her face. She reached into her shoulder bag and retrieved her phone, pressed a button or two, and then slid it away.

She came to the door and knocked. Did she know that I was watching her? She looked good, fresh, like an apple tree in bloom, its fruiting season some months away.

We had met at the end of the previous summer at the General Store, a few days before she had left Casco to return to suburban life. She was talking with Carl, Warren's assistant. It was some casual talk about not much, nothing that moved beyond noise for me as I did my shopping and waited for Warren to bring out a freshly butchered chicken that I intended to roast that night. I had recently gotten into the habit of roasting a chicken every Wednesday. The following day, I'd make myself a couple of chicken salad sandwiches and go on a fifteen or twenty mile hike. She saw me loitering over by the meat counter, broke off her talk with Carl, and came over.

"Correct me if I'm wrong," she said in a warm voice, "but are you the new owner of the little gray cottage on Mayberry Hill Road, the one tucked back a ways from the road?"

"That's me."

"I thought so. I'm Juliet. Juliet Klein. My parents own the house on the other side of the McKenneys. My father is Donald Klein, maybe you've met him."

"I haven't."

"He hasn't been around much this summer. Work stuff. My mother drives to North Windham to shop in the big supermarkets, so you probably haven't seen her around. Her name's Dorothy. She drives the white BMW."

"Donald and Dorothy."

"You've been here a year?"

"A little longer."

"In the Fieldstons' old house. It's hard to imagine them gone."

"I only met their son."

"Bob."

"Right."

"We couldn't stand Bob, frankly. He always made incredible noise with his motorboat. My father wanted to sink the thing for years. Now he has his own boat, even bigger than Bob's. Luckily, he's not around much to drive it. I prefer a peaceful lake."

"I agree."

"Do you? Well, we'll wait to see what happens after a couple of summers. Your friends will start coming and pretty soon you'll get the itch to waterski."

"I doubt it."

"Well, you don't really look like the skiing type."

On this went for ten minutes, until Warren came back with my chicken. After he had bagged it for me, I went over and paid for the groceries.

"Hey," she said, "mind giving me a lift home? I walked here but now don't feel much like walking back with all this."

"Sure," I said. "No problem."

She hopped in and pulled on her seat belt. I couldn't help glancing down at her legs. They were tan and athletic. She wore a short pair of orange running shorts with two white stripes on either side. She had on ankle socks and turquoise running sneakers. Her T-shirt was sky blue. Her brown hair was pulled back into a ponytail. As we got into the car she reached up and let it loose. It fell down over her shoulders in feathery bunches.

"I can't believe it's almost time for me to leave here," she said. "I always have to leave at the absolute best time of year, right when everything is perfect. What a drag. But a girl has to get back to work, I guess."

I thought of asking what she did but then didn't. I didn't want to know.

"My sister and I are going to make a batch of raspberry jam this afternoon. Can I bring you some when we're done? You'll need it to get through the winter - nothing better than the preserved taste of summer raspberries."

"Okay," I said and then added, for the sake of some inner petulance, "though I prefer my berries fresh off the bush."

She never came with the jam.

Juliet pulled up in an old blue Volvo station wagon. Rust rimmed the wheels. The paint job was faded. There was something wildly sexy about how she stood there, hesitant, in front of the house. She knocked on the front door. I hesitated, just as she had. For a moment, I considered hiding in my office until she went away. Since I had moved in, two years before, my house had felt only my footsteps. In the end I didn't hide. Her siege had already breached the outer walls.

That's ridiculous, of course. There were no walls but rather some dense patches of trees and bushes, and no siege was necessary. She had likely been in the house before. She knew the Fieldstons. The thought unsettled me. The Fieldstons - Lawrence, Betty, Bob, Emma, Susie - were ghosts that haunted my sleepless nights.

She had a firm knock - once, twice, three times. She waited for a moment and did it again: knock, knock, knock. As it turned out, she was not the type of person who accepted that her entry might be denied. By the second set of knocks I was downstairs and opened the door. I invited her inside.

The floorboards in the entryway seemed to creek and groan a little as she passed over them. During these two years, I had become a hermit and this house was now a hermit's abode. There was nothing welcoming about it, nothing homey. She looked around, fixing her gaze on one thing and then the next. She didn't say anything at first. Neither did I. The house was cool. The previous night the temperatures had fallen, and there was a chill in the air. I could see the gooseflesh rise on the rich skin of her arms. She wasn't as tan as the last time I had seen her, in August. She wasn't as relaxed or contented. I wondered what she had been doing all year.

I asked her if she wanted a cup of coffee.

"Yes," she said. "That's exactly what I want."

I went into the kitchen. She followed. I thought about asking her why she had come. I didn't. Too many perfectly fine moments, I thought, are ruined by giving away the game. The unknown often needs to linger, like a fine spirit on the lips.

The kettle grew to a boil. I poured the water through the filter, first for Juliet and then for myself. I gestured for her to sit down at the table, which was now in the eye of the late-morning sun. She crossed her legs and sipped her coffee. We exchanged a few lines, nothing interesting or important. They were meant to advance something completely else. There was a stone in the middle of the table, a piece of grayish-pink feldspar that I had found on a trip to Cape Cod with Hannah long before I moved to Casco. She picked it up and handled it tenderly, rubbing the smooth and rough surfaces with the palm of her hand.

The sun, in the meantime, had thrown Juliet's shadow on the floor. It was long and graceful like a branch of a willow tree. I felt an impulse course through me but didn't linger on it or try to define it. I allowed it to fade away like the strike of a piano key. I had been deep in work in my office when she arrived and now was struggling to regain footing in a conversational world. The willow branch swayed with a gentle breeze. It was just past the solstice and, I thought, the beginning of a long descent into winter. The rise and decline of summer - it was an epic Casco story, repeating each summer and eternally the same.

The combination of coffee and sun was warming me. I un-buttoned and took off my thick flannel shirt. I was wearing an old camp T-shirt underneath, a shirt I had worn since I was fifteen. It still fit. Its rich forest green had faded over time, but it had only become softer and more comfort-able. I wore it as often as I could.

Her expression changed when she saw this shirt. She smiled. She might have been amused that a grown man was wearing the clothes of a boy - I can't say for sure. Juliet turned out to be much more complicated than I imagined. But why? Was my imagination that limited, that brittle?

The story cut off. I flipped through the stack—the rest of the story wasn't there. Or maybe Abel hadn't completed it. What happened, I wondered, between my friend and Juliet? The piece struck me as odd. Abel seemed overly lusty—tan legs, running shorts, falling hair, hesitation, "wildly sexy." Much was missing here. There was too little of Juliet to say anything for sure. She wore a gray T-shirt and jeans, sure, fine, but what else? Did she have a spark of genius? I thought of Hannah, Abel's ex-girlfriend and perhaps his greatest love. She had possessed more than a touch of genius, and it had been this genius—I had thought back then—and not first and foremost her sexiness, that had attracted him. I had been drawn to the sexiness, the outer beauty. Abel operated on another level.

Abel—he must have pulled off that gray T-shirt and put his hands on her skin. That's right, I thought, Abel knew how to make love. I had heard Hannah's moans of pleasure from the other room during the year we shared a small apartment on Amsterdam Avenue. I would be on the sofa trying to read or study as her moans came through the wall—her deep moans, moans generated by the full expanse of her chest. It would be another decade before I had sex like that, before I inspired a moan as deep and full-bodied as Hannah's. Was this what Juliet wanted, to moan like Hannah? What did she think would happen when she came to the house in the woods that day? She knew that it had become a house of solitude. It was a beautiful early-summer day. Strong fragrances of summertime floated in the air. The wisteria on the side of the house was enflamed with color. Abel led her upstairs and into the office. He was going to share with her a vignette or poem, perhaps an aphorism or two. Abel had thousands of pieces. Juliet wanted to know what he was working on. Which one did he pick? I flipped through the stack.

05/15/2008

I come upon a fallen cedar,
Perfuming a glade.

```
    I sniff, and sniff,
    And sneeze.
```

Or this one:

```
                                    05/16/2008


Within an hour I had hooked a lake trout. It was twenty
inches and had a good weight. I grasped it in my bare hand
as it squirmed and writhed. I considered letting it go. The
choice, however, was between this fish and one I would buy
at the General Store, and I decided that this one would do
just fine for lunch. Back on shore, I cleaned it and grilled
it over an open fire. It was an average fish with little
flavor.
```

So many options: a budding and blossoming flower, a germinating seed, the leap of a squirrel. Abel was a master of image and sentiment, and a master of conversation when he felt inspired to participate.

They embraced. He moved her against the wall, holding her by the waist, guiding her. His lips found her neck. "Juliet," I whispered, "who are you? Juliet, where are you now?" I should find her, I thought, and complete this story, follow the story from that wall to the hallway and finally to the bed. I closed my eyes and imagined my friend pressing against her smooth, slender body.

A memory came to me of a Saturday morning in September during our sophomore year in college. Abel had woken me up at 5 AM. It was still dark. I hadn't gotten to bed until two or three the night before. "We're going on a trip," Abel said, "a field trip."

"Now?" I managed to say. "Where?"

"The lake. I want to have a swim."

"You're joking? Go back to sleep."

"It's no joke. Get dressed and pack a bathing suit and towel."

"How'll we get there?"

"I've borrowed my father's car. It's already parked outside. Come on, before it gets ticketed." Reluctantly, I moved from bed and put on the same clothes I had taken off only hours before. "Well done, Allstar," Abel said and gave me a firm pat on the back. "Let's go."

Outside, on the street in front of the building, was Abraham Prager's black Mercedes.

"How's your driving?"

"Under normal circumstances, it's fine," I said, "but I've only had a couple hours of sleep."

"I'll drive then. You can sit back and relax."

We got in and started on the way. Though it was still dark outside, the air was warm. The summer had been a cool one. September, by contrast, had been much warmer than usual. Perhaps it was this Indian summer that had Abel fixated on a lake.

"Where are we going?"

"The lake, as I said. You know, Allstar, *the* lake."

I shook my head in disbelief. To drive seven or eight hours to take a swim was nonsense, of course, but as Abel crossed the bridge on the way out of the city I surrendered to the inevitable. We were going to Maine. Neither of us had seen the lake in years.

"Ezra," Abel said after we had gone about an hour, "I know this seems impulsive to you, but I've considered it carefully. Lately, I've been thinking about a few things. First, our friendship is becoming habitual. We need to experience something with depth together, like a good swim in the lake. Second, life has become too fixed on books for us. I've been that way my entire life. My mother and grandfather saw to that. You've grown more bookish over the years. I'm not sure this is a positive development. It could be that it's interrupted your natural disposition toward something else. Maybe I'm partly to blame. Third, and most importantly, we need experiences that are full, not partial. I want something complete. We need to vow together that we will aspire to fullness today. Don't undermine this, Ezra. Embrace it. Take it all the way."

I nodded. I was too tired and muddled to respond with any coherence. "Sure," I said.

I leaned back in the rocking chair and tried to remember what we had talked about on that long drive to Maine, but nothing came to mind. I remembered that the sun rose at some point in Connecticut and that we stopped around Hartford for breakfast. I remembered that I had fried eggs, bacon and rye toast.

We arrived at camp early in the afternoon. Abel parked the car on the road and we cut through the woods and into the campground. We were trespassing, but neither of us cared. In some ways it felt like going home. Camp was out of session and no groundskeepers were in sight. As if campers again, the moment we reached the hill we broke out into a sprint toward the water. I felt a rush of excitement when the lake came into view. It was an autumnal color, a color I'd never seen it before. Around us the bunks sat empty of kids. Memories oozed from the structures like sap from a birch. I couldn't suppress it. I laughed in a way that I hadn't in a long time as we ran toward the lake. It was a spontaneous, manic laugh.

When we reached the lake, Abel peeled off his shirt. I did the same. Our shoes and socks came off next. Our pants came down. Our underwear came off. We had both forgotten our suits in the car. There we stood, naked, gazing at the lake like pagans.

Abel led the way onto the dock. He braced himself, bent his knees and then dove in. I did the same. The water was cool but perfect, as it is always was. We were suddenly in another world, a timeless space that strung together sensations separated by years like beads on a necklace. I felt myself at once nine years old and nineteen. I floated on my back for a few minutes and then, like I had as a child, twisted my body and dove down into the depths. I emerged with a mussel I'd pried loose from the muck and rubbed it between my fingers.

"Let's swim out to the island," Abel said. I agreed and we started off toward Turtle Island, some quarter mile away from the docks toward the far corner of the lake. The lake was empty. Abel had willed it that way, I thought, and so it was. Abel had a Nietzschean way of bending the world to his will.

We soon reached the island and waded onto the pebbly beach. Abel sat down on a patch of moss at the edge of some firs. The sun was shining, but it was slowly losing its warmth. The temperature had already started to drop. It didn't matter. Our youthful bodies seemed impervious to chill. I stretched my body toward the sun and then stood arms akimbo and peered back at camp as if gazing back through time. Abel, in the meantime, had reclined and lay with his eyes closed. I turned to him.

"What're you thinking about?"

Without opening his eyes, Abel said, "I'm thinking about the civilization that was here for thousands of years, one that's vanished with barely a trace. I never thought about it much when we were campers. Remember when Ethan found that arrowhead on the Penobscot trip?"

"Sure."

"I wonder how many people lived up here, lived on this very lake. There's no way of telling. They molded trees into cities, rivers into roads. There was a real relationship between the people and the land. The people knew their place. They knew what to take and what to leave alone. They would've never dammed a river, for example. The whole point of a river, in the Indian mind, was to find the sea. Can you imagine the feeling these people had when the invaders came and dammed up the rivers? The Kennebec—remember that trip?"

"I remember."

"The Penobscot worshiped a god called Gluskabe. Have I told you about it?"

"I don't think so."

"Gluskabe came to the people during a period of drought. A giant bullfrog had come and swallowed all the water. The people were dying of thirst. Gluskabe commanded that the bullfrog release the water, but the bullfrog refused. The god took his axe and cut down a yellow birch that had been growing for a thousand years. He lifted it and smashed the bullfrog. The bullfrog's stomach burst open and the water poured out. The water that flowed down the main trunk of the birch became the Penobscot River. All the limbs and leaves transformed into streams and lakes. The people rushed into the river to quench their thirst and were transformed into fish, crabs, lobsters, and whales. The myth connects it all together—the people, the forest, the rivers and lakes, the ocean. The idea of the bullfrog is a simple one. He's the hoarder of all that should be communal. He thinks he can contain the whole world within himself."

"I like that," I said, "the bullfrog, especially."

We got up and waded back into the lake. It was the time of day when the temperature of the lake was higher than that of the air. As I submerged myself, I had the sensation of being wrapped in a warm, wet blanket. We swam back toward camp. Occasionally, I would roll over and look up at the sky. A bank of clouds approached from the west. When we were about halfway back, we heard the wail of a loon in the distance. The loon expressed the exact sentiment I felt at that moment inside myself. It was a combination of melancholy and fulfillment. It was the safe, coddled melancholy of a child.

We left the lake and drove to Susie's Diner, the traditional stop for campers and their parents on the way out of town. Abel had come after the first two summers but never again after his mother died. I, on the other hand, had always looked forward to this first contact with the outer world after eight weeks of camp life.

I ordered my usual roast beef sandwich with horseradish mustard and a ginger ale. The sandwich came with a half-sour pickle spear and a generous handful of potato chips. Abel took a tuna melt and an orange soda. This was exactly what he had ordered when he was nine.

At some point, I said, "Maybe we should crash out somewhere and do the drive tomorrow. You must be exhausted. I know I am."

"On the contrary," Abel said, "I feel like I just woke up from being asleep too long."

By the time we were on the highway, the sun had started to set. As we drove over the bridge separating Maine and New Hampshire the sky was resplendent with colors—orange, deep yellow, pink, and red. I struggled to stay awake. The leather seat was warm and soft. I sank down into it. I wanted to complete the circle with my friend. I felt like the closing of the circle was important to Abel. The sunset was my last vision of the trip. I drifted off and slept deeply. When I woke up we were back in the city.

I rocked back and forth gently in the rocking chair and pulled the blanket tighter across my lap. It was cold now. I would have to make a fire in the office. Could it have been something as simple as the wail of a loon that brought Abel back here? Did he come out here to live or to die? "To die," I whispered. That made no sense. Abel was precisely the type who would drive sixteen hours in a single day just to dive naked into a pristine lake. This was living. This was vitality. I couldn't think of anyone more vivacious than Abel Prager. I had never considered for a second that Abel might take his own life. The loon wailed for a reason—it was a call of love, a wild call that filled the space with haunting echoes. Abel could wail like that. His life was a wail like that, but that was living, not dying.

I rubbed my face. It all felt too much for me. Outside, the snow was falling again. I thought about the car and the plowing. Not today, I thought—there was no chance of leaving today. The basic question remained unanswered. How could I connect those two dots? The first dot was the young man, Abel Prager, diving into the lake on that September day in 1990. There were hundreds or thousands of first dots. The second dot was a man of forty purposefully eating a handful of poisonous mushrooms and dying alone. Connecting the dots. A to B. There was no line that brought them together.

The phone rang. I had left it downstairs next to the Franklin stove and didn't feel like getting it. I realized that I had no idea what time it was. The sky was no help. Thick clouds had rolled in during the morning and the whole day had been grayish white. A snowy November, I thought. These were occurrences the likes of which my parents talked about with soft enthusiasm, this year compared to that, this year in relation to the history of others. The snowiest years of childhood: 1973, 1977, 1982, the great white year of 1985. The cold years: 1980, 1986, 1976. The warm winters full of rain and fog: 1978, 1981, and my high school graduation year of 1989, when the real Vermont winter never came.

It was September 1988, a day or two before Labor Day, when I got a short note from Abel, typed, like all the others, on the Remington.

"Dear Allstar," it began, "I've decided to stay put next year—to stay in New York. I'm going to apply to Columbia and I think you should do the same. I hope you do. It's high time we bunked together again."

Before I got this letter, I had planned to follow in my sister Judith's footsteps and attend the University of Vermont in Burlington. It was a logical step. My sister would be a senior when I was a freshman. Both of my parents had graduated from there. The costs were relatively low and it was likely that I could earn a scholarship. Besides, while I had been a solid student, or even a very good student, I never considered myself excellent. In truth, my grades were quite good. I had captained the school's basketball team (to a dreary 2-12 record) and pitched middle relief for the varsity baseball team. I had written for the school newspaper and published, together with two friends, a monthly literary broadsheet, which we sold for ten cents a copy.

The monthly release of the semi-satirical *Common Sense and Nonsense* took place in the café of a local bookstore, the Book Barn, and was organized together with the shop's owner, the transfixing Julia Pinecrest. The monthly release was a highlight of my final two years in high school. At the release parties, the featured authors would get up and read something aloud. One of the other editors or I would act as master of ceremonies. Julia Pinecrest worked the espresso machine and sold homemade snacks. The Book Barn became a destination, its café the intellectual center for the area's serious boys. This was in no small measure due directly to the person of Julia Pinecrest, whose intellectual sophistication, combined with her wild red hair, snowy skin, and ample bosom, served as a beacon, especially during the winter doldrums. I spent whole afternoons in the Barn's café, reading, studying, and watching the bookseller out of the corner of my eye.

At times, I would write a short editorial note for the broadsheet, but mostly I stayed in the background, preferring to choose and present others' works rather than my own. My own writings were full of blush and coyness, or were, perhaps, merely meek and flaccid. In mid-November of my senior year, a week after Abel and I had both received our acceptances to Columbia, two poems came in the mail from my friend. The following week, I brought the poems to the other editors, Angela Roth and Jenny Turnbridge, and made the case for their inclusion in the December issue. After some debate, I convinced them. They were, in truth, some of the best work we ever printed.

The night came for the December release. I stood up in front of all the guests and, full of passion, read Abel's poems aloud. After the readings were over, Julia Pinecrest approached me. It was hot in the Book Barn and her face was flushed. Because of the heat, she had undone the top button of her blouse, exposing the heave of her chest to the air.

She said, "Tell me the truth, Ezra Stern. There is no Abel Prager in New York City, is there?"

I felt a rush of inner tumult, the type one feels before telling a magnificent lie. But I didn't lie—not directly. I responded, though my eyes and being said the opposite, "Abel Prager does exist." In my mind surged the thought, "I am Abel Prager."

Her look expressed that she understood what I meant perfectly, that beneath an utterly normal façade, Ezra Stern/Abel Prager was extraordinary. She ran her hand along my cheek. It was as hot as I imagined it would be. "That's what I thought," she said and with a wink turned back to her duties behind the espresso machine.

How easy it had been, I thought, to erase my friend on that winter night at the Book Barn. It had been a mini-homicide of sorts, an identity murder. Abel once mused, years later and with no connection to the Book Barn or Julia Pinecrest, that what we called ultimate desire was the state of needing what we cannot possibly obtain. But then, he said, as if by miracle, that unobtainable object suddenly appears in reach. We lunge at it with all we have, not knowing that it's a mirage. With this lunge into the abyss of our own delusion, we obliterate all that lies between the self and the desired object. That's not all. By lunging, we obliterate both. Did I, even for a split second, think that I could actually become Abel Prager and possess, as Abel, Julia Pinecrest? Indeed, it seems I did. And the moment felt good—really good. It felt good even as I sat there in Abel's house and thought about her flushed face, open blouse, and hot fingers on my cheek.

The phone rang again and this time I went downstairs to answer it. I expected it to be Sophia and was surprised when the name Maxwell Hammond appeared on the screen. Hammond was a colleague, a professor of British Empire. Hammond was a marginal departmental figure, but this marginalization only seemed to encourage him to scheme from the periphery about any number of matters. For reasons I didn't quite understand, Hammond often looked to me for backup.

"Not now, Max," I said to myself and flicked off the phone. I was irritated that the call had taken me from the office, from my memories, from the touch of those fingers. I went to the kitchen and made another peanut butter sandwich. Twilight seemed to be approaching. A deeper gray had settled in. There must be something that would explain everything that had happened here, I thought—something I felt far from discovering.

I flicked the phone back on and called Sophia.

"It's Ezra."

"Where are you?"

"Still in the house. It started to snow here again. It looks like I'll have to spend another night."

"I know. I saw the weather report this morning. I had hoped you wouldn't try to make your way through it. Don't do anything dangerous."

"That's what I was thinking. What about Dave and Ellen?"

"I've already canceled with them. Sybil came down with a fever this morning."

"Is it high?"

"It's light, but she's been clinging to mommy all day."

"I'm sure she is," I said and felt a rush of warmth for my wife and little girl.

"I have to get back to her," she said. "Be safe, Ezra."

"Sure."

I flicked off the phone. It was good to hear her voice. It reminded me of a life that seemed distant from this place, from Casco. As I kept my thoughts, for another moment, on Sophia, Sam, and Sybil, I noticed a calendar hanging on the opposite wall, next to the pantry. I went over and took it off the nail. The calendar was entitled "Scenic Maine Villages," and judging from the image on the cover—Boothbay harbor at sunrise—it promised to be nauseatingly bucolic. The calendar had been issued in 2007, but Abel had blacked out the days of the weeks with a marker, making one year no different than the next.

I flipped through each month. There was almost nothing written in it. An entry, the only entry for January, penciled in on the second of the month, read, "Settle up with Warren at G.S." February also contained just one entry, "Mom," written on the ninth. March had a single mid-month entry: "J. returns?" The twenty-first, for some reason, was crossed out entirely. April, May, and June were empty. July: "Wood" on the fourteenth and a small question mark on the twenty-seventh. August brought Stonington into view and another question mark on the third, a star on the fifth, the tenth crossed out, another question mark on the eighteenth. September 1st—Blue Hill in spring bloom—"Send letter." October empty.

November featured a scene of Rangeley, a village caught between the mountains and the huge lake beneath them. No entries. December: nothing.

I used the bathroom and then boiled another kettle of water on the Franklin stove. I made coffee, unfiltered like before. As the coffee cooled, I went out to the woodpile and brought in a few loads, one of which I carried up to the office. I went back downstairs, took the pitcher of coffee, a cup, and three sticks of moose jerky, and climbed back up to continue sorting through Abel's papers. I prepared a fire and lit it. The flames leapt to life. No sooner had I settled back into the rocking chair than I realized it was getting dark in the room. I went back downstairs and took two candleholders. One I set on the small table next to the rocking chair and the other on the built-in window seat. I sat down with a large stack of papers on my lap. The coffee was stationed on the table next to the candleholder and the moose jerky. I would work late into the night, I told myself, and then tomorrow morning, first thing, I would call the Reynolds boys, get the car plowed out, and head back home. I glanced outside. The snow fell steadily.

I grabbed a bunch of papers and started to read. No title.

She appeared in the field in mid-August as I was filling a pail with blueberries. The sun was high in a cloudless sky. My fingers were stained deep purple. I was at the edge of the forest when she came around the side of the house. I had been out in the field all morning, reaping a significant harvest. This was my second pail of wild blueberries. I had no such luck with anything I actively tried to grow. In mid-July, I made the decision to abandon my garden and surrendered it to the rabbits. They were kind enough to leave me some carrots and a lettuce now and then.

She wore a thin blue dress and knee-high stockings - perfect, I thought, for walking through the long grass. When she was about halfway across the field she stopped, bent over, and plucked something from the ground. She held it up between her thumb and forefinger for me to see: the last wild strawberry of the year. I thought I had picked the field clean weeks before. She popped it into her mouth and continued toward me. If I close my eyes as I sit here now, I can see the scene with heightened clarity - perhaps too much - a type of hyperrealism that blends at its edges into the surreal, like a field melting into forest. And what can I make of the opposite scene that ended in disaster? Or is disaster putting it too strongly? Is "opposite" putting it too cravenly? Failure - for sure failure, principally mine but also hers. Or maybe the failure was ultimately neither of ours but of a higher order - a failure of the fates. A summer day, a winter night, thesis and antithesis - can there be dialectical resolution of August blueberries and a frozen lake?

Thoreau wrote, "Our moulting season, like that of fowls, must be a crisis in our lives. The loon retires to solitary ponds to spend it."

She came over and glanced down into my pail.

"It's been a good summer for berries," she said.

"Or for the picker of berries," said I. "I doubt the berries have an opinion on the matter." She shot me a look.

Had I been resentful that she had not returned since June and now the summer was coming to an end? During my time in Casco I had tried to get rid of expectations, but the years out here had not been enough. I was still half-civilized. She got to me. I felt a wave of intensity that I didn't like. I wanted equipoise - not tumult. "Take a handful," I told her. She reached into my pail. Her thin fingers wrapped around the fruit. She watched me as I watched that hand.

"I guess this is going to be my last summer here for a while," she said as she ate the berries.

"What do you mean?"

"I start a new job next week. I'll have to work summers. Two weeks vacation, that's it."

"That doesn't sound promising," I said to her and held up the pail for her to take more berries.

"No thanks," she said, waiving it away. "I actually can't stay long. I wanted to invite you to dinner tonight. My sister's cooking. It'll be Leah and I, you, I hope, and a few other friends. My parents are back in Connecticut already. How about it?"

I set my pail down and looked at my hands and arms. My arms were scratched up from moving in and out of the bushes. I tilted my head toward the sky and closed my eyes.

"I'm not trying to torture you," she said, "just to invite you for a pleasant evening."

"Fine," I said, "what time?"

"Come around seven. We'll eat out on the deck at sunset. I'm glad you're coming. I've been meaning to introduce you to my friends for a long time already - and of course to Leah. It's ridiculous that you haven't met her yet."

I lifted my pail again, plucked another clump of berries, and deposited them with the others. From the moment I had seen her come around the house I had sworn that I wouldn't say what I said next. "I had hoped to see you after that day in June."

"You knew where to find me."

What kind of games was she playing? Find her? I had already found her right here in this house. Then she disappeared. Her retreat back into the Klein house was a disappearance behind enemy lines. She was the emissary. I was not. She knew very well that I wasn't going anywhere near the Klein fortress. Donald and Dorothy - no, my world was not compatible with theirs.

"I saw you once as I was canoeing on the lake," I said. "You were putting in the sailboat with a young man."

"Probably Rick. He'll be there tonight. Rick Hagerson. The Hagersons are old friends. He's a terrific sailor."

"He's a good-looking guy," I said. "Good physique."

"He was a high school wrestling champion," Juliet told me, "but that was years ago."

"He doesn't look like he's missed a day at the gym since his championship season."

"You can ask him about it tonight if you want."

I thought about asking her about the other expected guests, but then didn't. Rick Hagerson was enough. Rick Hagerson, with his ropy arms and legs and washboard abs - he was more than enough.

I arrived at seven, after a long afternoon of work at the Remington. Three lengthy letters to the usual people - all unsent and stored away in the attic. The other guests were already there. It seemed as if most had been there the whole afternoon, sunning themselves on the Kleins' private beach and enjoying the company of the sisters.

Juliet greeted me at the door and offered me a glass of champagne. I hadn't had a sip of alcohol since coming to Casco and had sworn it off but I felt those horrible pangs of social obligation that not only get people to do something they don't want to do but inspire them to do it with more enthusiasm than under normal circumstances. I drank the glass in practically a single tilt. Leah came around with the bottle and refilled it immediately. The second glass was gone as fast as the first. I felt the familiar tremors of tipsiness prickling at my mind.

Leah Klein. I have to linger here. She was darker than Juliet - not only in terms of complexion, but also in other ways, psychological and emotional. Leah. She had dark brown hair that bordered on blackness. She had it cut in a vintage housewife style with a large, graceful curve running from the center of her forehead to her right ear. Her face was similar to Juliet's but less perfect. Her nose was more bent, like mine. After inspecting a family picture that hung outside the bathroom, I saw that it came from her father. Poor daughter with a father's nose, I thought. She had a penny-sized mole just below her left temple, nothing disturbing to look at, but somehow it upset the face's symmetry, which in turn compromised the symmetry of the whole. Her eyes were also blue, like her sister's, but contained a tint of green. They were deeper, more mysterious, perhaps more beautiful - certainly beautiful in a different way. The bodies were nothing like each other. Juliet was slender and athletic. Leah was plump - not fat, but soft and squishy. While Juliet gave off the impression of discipline and abstemiousness, Leah conveyed a sense of indulgence and indolence. While Juliet was fastidiously dressed and primped, Leah was disheveled. It is not fair to Leah to say this - in fact, it is grossly unjust. While alone she would have seemed perfectly normal, next to her sister one could not help but think of Leah as ugly, or uglier - the uglier sister.

Juliet circled back around. In the meantime, I had noticed a large painting on the wall of the open area that comprised the downstairs of the house. Kitchen melted into dining room, dining room into living room. A hallway led off into two smaller rooms in the back, but it would be some time before I would step foot in either. The painting - yes, it was large and fairly chaotic, a work of contrasts and conflicts, colors clashing with colors, brushstrokes with brushstrokes. Harmonious movements came to disharmonious ends. The overall composition was a study of discomfort. It was like a painting done by a child who for the first time realizes someone is looking over her shoulder.

"Leah painted that," Juliet said as she found me gazing into it.

"There's something utterly horrifying about it."

"Don't let Leah overhear. She's very sensitive about these things. Come on, let me introduce you to the others."

"Where's the wrestler?"

"Out on the deck. Come on."

We walked across the room to a group of four gathered in front of big sliding glass doors that led out onto the deck. The lake, in all its splendor, came into view, and I couldn't help but feel a pang of remorse that I hadn't spent the evening in my canoe or building a fire in the fire pit at the end of the forest path.

"Pardon me," Juliet said, interrupting the conversation, "I want to introduce you to our new neighbor on the lake. This is Abel Prager. He bought the Fieldston place down the road. Abel, this is Connor Johnson and his wife Megan. The Johnsons have a place on the other side of the lake, right next to the camp." Nods, smiles. "This is my dear old friend Dahlia and her boyfriend Craig. Dahlia's parents have a place on Thompson Lake. It's Craig's first visit to Maine."

A round of pleased-to-meet-yous and a barrage of the usual questions followed. Leah came around and asked what I wanted to drink. I requested a beer and she brought me a bottle of Stella Artois. As I drank it and listened to the conversation around me, I noticed that the wrestler stood alone out on the deck. I moved by the group, slid open the glass door, and stepped out onto the large wooden deck. Set up about three hundred yards from the lake on a rise, the house provided a stunning view. The air outside was perfect - cooling, crisp, fresh. Rick Hagerson was also drinking a Stella.

"You must be Abel," he said as I approached. He stuck out his hand, exposing the ample muscles of his right arm. I had a sudden fear that in a split second he could twist me into a ball and hurl me the some thirty feet to the ground and a near certain death. My hundred and fifty pounds would have seemed a bag of feathers to such a man.

"I am."

"Rick Hagerson," he said, "friend of the girls."

"The Kleins?" I said for no particular reason.

"Who else? Juliet says you're over at the Fieldston place."

"That seems to be the common way of describing it."

"What a lake - what a scene. Am I right, Abel?"

Though I felt averse to discussing the aesthetics of the lake with him, I said, "It's gorgeous." He took this as a proper occasion to slap me on the shoulder and clink his beer bottle against mine. I interpreted this as a sign that he was also (most likely successfully) pursuing Juliet.

"Let's get right down to it," he said. "What would possess a young single guy to move all alone to such a place? Don't get me wrong, I've always loved it here, but in summer. In summer."

"I think of it in reverse," I said. "If you love it here in the summer, what are you doing the rest of the year?"

"Simple. I'm living. I'm working. I'm engaging. I'm putting it out there."

"What are you putting out there?"

"Myself. My drive. It's only natural that we want to see what we can do among other people, especially among the best."

"And what do you do when you're putting it out there?" There it was - I had done it. I had opened that door into the magical theater. I should rather have faked illness and fled from the house.

"I'm a foreign policy analyst. Energy and security is my specialty. I'm at State."

"I see," I said.

"Prager - just between us, I know you. I've read your stuff on water policy. That is, if you are the Prager who worked at the GPI."

"That's me."

"I don't get why you would take yourself out of the game. Speaking as a friend - or a friend of a friend - you were playing with the big boys. There were people at State gunning to take you down. It was actually news when you left."

"I doubt that I figure much in their thoughts," I said, "considering all else."

"I wouldn't be so sure. Anyway, I'm only speaking of State. Who knows what's going on over in Langley."

"How long have you known the Kleins?" I asked, hoping to get off the topic.

"All my life," he said. "We grew up together in Greenwich. Our parents had houses up here until my parents sold a few years back. They spend most of their free time in Aspen now. I don't blame them. There's nothing like the West. I was in Leah's class in middle school before I went to Andover. Juliet and I overlapped at Georgetown when she was an undergrad and I was getting a masters. We got pretty close during those years. It's a shame she moved back to Connecticut. I'm still trying to lure her back down to DC."

The door opened. Connor Johnson came out from the house.

"What an evening," he said, breathing the air deeply. "Leah's preparing a feast in there."

"Connor," Rick said, "did you know that this young man who owns the Fieldston place is actually a communist spy." Connor laughed. "But seriously, Prager, what would you call yourself? Not communist, I guess. After all the Cold War is long gone. I'm sorry I missed those days. It would've been fun to be in State at a time like that. You're no hippie. Maybe a Chomskian."

"And what are you?" Connor asked, clearly used to Hagerson's bravado.

"A proud Neocon," said Hagerson.

"Then you're an endangered species," Connor said.

"Come on, Connor, you're taking the short-term view of it. We'll see how things look in ten years, in twenty. What about it Abel? A new geopolitical reality?"

"That goes without saying," I said. "Things change."

"They change when one takes action. Change happens in certain ways for certain reasons."

"But we seldom know what they are," I said. "It's like Tolstoy says: the more we strive to account for events in history rationally, the more irrational and incomprehensible they seem to us."

"I agree with that," said Connor. "Well said, Abel. It's good to see someone finally giving it to Hagerson."

"I answer Tolstoy with Machiavelli," said Hagerson. "All armed prophets have conquered and unarmed ones failed."

"Then I remind you what Machiavelli said of Cesare Borgia," I rejoined, "If his measures were not successful, it was through no fault of his own but only by the most extraordinary malignancy of fortune."

I am embellishing, of course, but the conversation did go in this general direction. Hagerson seemed to enjoy it. I also might have found pleasure in the lakeside sparring, though I felt cheapened afterward - especially as Hagerson downed the rest of his beer and flashed me a toothy smile. Juliet came onto the deck and refreshed the beers. Hagerson quickly pulled her over and made some comment about inviting anarchists to dinner. Juliet, maneuvering out of his grasp, announced that the dinner was almost ready.

I helped Hagerson and Connor pull the picnic table away from the wall and into the center of the deck. Dahlia and Megan appeared with a tablecloth, dishes, and silverware. The Klein sisters came out with platters of food. We ate. I drank three or four more beers and woke up the next day with a major headache.

The next day I recalled my tete-a-tete with Hagerson. It brought to mind a scene from Walden. I searched back through my notebooks and found where I had copied it down. I read: "One day when I went out to my wood-pile, or rather my pile of stumps, I observed two large ants, the one red, the other much larger, nearly half an inch long, and black, fiercely contending with one another. Having once got hold they never let go, but struggled and wrestled and rolled on the chips incessantly. Looking farther, I was surprised to find that the chips were covered with such combatants, that it was not a duellum, but a bellum, a war between two races of ants, the red always pitted against the black, and frequently two red ones to one black."

Alas, I was still an ant after three years of solitude.

"I am naturally no hermit," Thoreau wrote, "but might possibly sit out the sturdiest frequenter of the bar-room, if my business called me thither." Yes! How I had loved sitting in New York's downtown bars! He writes, "I had three chairs in my house; one for solitude, two for friendship, three for society." I am much less systematic than he is. I am also not entirely sure who is friend and who is foe. If I could go back and ask David Henry - before he became Henry David - I would have liked to know if there had been a chair for love, a chair for desire.

Juliet came. "Why did you leave so early?"

"I was drunk," I told her. "I didn't want to fall off the deck, or be thrown off by Hagerson. It would have spoiled your sister's exquisite meal."

"Rick wouldn't do such a thing. He's an aggressive talker, but that's about it. The wrestling taught him discipline."

"It also taught him how to manipulate a weaker human body into a misshapen mess."

"So you left the party early because you were afraid?"

"No," I said instinctively, but then corrected myself. "I mean, yes. I was afraid."

"Of Hagerson putting you in a headlock?"

"Yes, you could put it that way."

"I don't get it."

"Look," I said, "I don't know what you want from me. I'm not ready to join your club. I don't want to be a part of any club right now. I want to be out here away from it all. I want to discover something new, something higher than what I was able to find back home. That's it, Juliet. The party was nice, but I wasn't going to find anything there. I thought I might find something out in the field with you yesterday, but you were too busy. I don't want that. I think you should leave."

She was silent. Then she smiled. I was agitated, maybe a bit angry - angry, perhaps, that Hagerson was the faster and stronger dog on the hunt. I don't know. I didn't even realize I wanted anything from her until she appeared in the field that morning. She took a step closer and put her arms around me. No words. She kissed me. Had Hagerson tasted this mouth the night before? I wondered. I wondered what the rules were in Juliet's mind. What was permissible? What was morally suspect? Was it better, I wondered, to be loved or feared?

The sex was rough, full of aggression, as if we were long-time enemies settling scores. I wondered where it all came from - this violence inside of me - but there it was. And hers was also there, ripping at me, tearing at me, biting me. Hagerson probably would have drawn less blood.

She left Casco three days later. Hagerson drove her back to Connecticut on his way to DC. I probably heard the car speed past from my office. I was back at work on some-thing, something hidden away. She got to me. I had tried to disentangle myself from relationships like this - self-destructive ones, which for me seemed to be all of them, but here I was at the end of summer. I felt alone - alone for the first time in my solitude. Three chairs - solitude, friendship, society. I had one chair of loneliness. I gazed out into the night as the fireflies burned like a thousand distant torches.

I set the papers on my lap and closed my eyes. It was a momentary pause to try to connect to Abel—to his ghost, to those past feelings of despair that were now suddenly present again in the room. I fell asleep.

Day Four

I opened my eyes and shifted in the rocking chair. My body ached. Outside, a faint light welled up from some distant source. I got up from the chair, which now seemed to me like a sort of medieval torture device, and slowly and laboriously straightened my bent back. On the floor, papers were scattered everywhere. Images from my dreams came back to me like fractured memories of a long-forgotten past. A nightmare had woken me up from my uncomfortable slumber. It had been about Sybil. I had taken her to the park on a warm summer day and gone to buy an ice cream from a vendor nearby. I struggled to find my wallet. I searched my pants pockets and then rummaged through the pockets of my light summer jacket. I must have forgotten it at home, I thought, and then turned to look at Sybil. She was gone. I wheeled around to find her. The vendor demanded his $2.50 and held out the frozen cone wrapped in plastic. I turned to the left, no Sybil, to the right, no Sybil. I was in a full panic. The vendor was shouting at me. The customers in line behind me were losing patience—come on, man, get a move on, hurry up, get out of the way. My little girl had been snatched from under my nose. I let out a scream.

I sighed and rubbed my face. What time was it? I glanced around for my phone, wondering where I'd left it. I went downstairs, found the phone on the table and flicked it on with my thumb. 7:03 AM. I pressed a couple of buttons, first to check email. A message appeared that the battery was low. I cleared it away. The screen went black. I pressed the power button a half dozen times in quick succession, in hopes of squeezing another minute or two out of the device. No luck. I tried to recall whether I had tossed the charger into my bag as I was leaving the apartment but then remembered that I had decided not to because I had one in the glove compartment that plugged into the car. The car was dead, like the phone. I would need the phone to call the Reynolds boys. I would need the car to use the phone—a ridiculous situation.

My morning actions were becoming almost routine: wood from the woodpile—a load downstairs and one upstairs—fire in the stove, kettle with water, kettle slowly creeping to boil, coffee. As I waited for the coffee to brew, I felt a familiar tremor and then a sharp knifing pain in my gut—constipation. I hadn't taken a shit since I had arrived. I focused attention on the tectonic movements in my intestines and bowels. There was no point trying it now. It would come after the coffee. To help speed the process, I grabbed two apples from the kitchen and took them, together with the coffee, up to the office. I lit another fire there and gathered up the pages from the floor. I was anxious to get back to Abel.

I sipped my coffee. It was strong and tasted good. After a few sips, my gut was already rumbling. It would come.

"The loon retires to solitary ponds to spend it." When I told Ethan Weiss I was coming to Casco he asked if I was searching for Walden Pond. "I don't know," I told him, "but I know I need to get the fuck out of Concord."

Here I am. The summer has ended. It ended with Juliet driving south with Hagerson. For a few days afterward I felt relief. There was no question of anything with her. She belonged in Connecticut doing who-knows-what with who-knows-whom. I didn't care. A Promethean mood gripped me. I cut down a beech tree and chopped it up to dry. It was a week of hard labor using a handsaw and axe.

At the end of the month I got a note from Juliet. She said that she planned on coming to Casco for Columbus Day weekend and asked if I would be here. The weekend came and

went without her showing up. I wrote her a long letter and
stored it, unsent, in the attic. In early November she wrote
that Leah was having "issues" and that's why she was unable
to come. I ignored the letter. The next week another letter
came. "Why don't you just get a phone?" she said by way of
introduction. The sentence was underlined twice. "Leah and
I are coming to Casco. She's having problems - my parents
can't deal with it. I'm going to drive her up to the house
around Thanksgiving. I'll stop by and see you then."

"Whenever it is a damp, drizzly November in my soul."
November. I wondered about Leah's whale. That is, if she
had one. Or was she, like me, an Ahab without a whale? In
other words, did Leah exist or not? Juliet, it was plain to
see, knew little or nothing about the "watery part of the
world," as Ishmael puts it. Juliet was a land creature - a
young deer, perhaps. At times a lioness.

Solitary ponds.

It was a wet, rainy November. It was muddy along my forest
path. It rained four days out of five. Despite this, I have
to conclude that my soul is not one of drizzly Novembers, no
matter what meteorological conditions exist beyond the win-
dowpanes of my small cottage in the woods - the Fieldston
place, as it is commonly known. My soul is one of Februarys
and Julys.

A rainy day, a frozen rain fell. The wind slapped against
the house. The fire roared in the stove. She knocked.

I came down from the office to let her in. She had apparently walked from her house without an umbrella and was
now soaking wet.

"Sit down by the fire," I said and pulled the chair over for her. "It's giving off a nice heat now. I'll make the coffee."

I confess (to the squirrels and rabbits) that I was in a stormy mood when she arrived. I had spent the morning with a warm washcloth on my aching head and had only half an hour before made it to the Remington. I was in the middle of a letter when she knocked.

"I'm happy you're here," she told me.

"I'm always here."

"I mean here, living in this house."

"Where's Leah?"

"She's opening up the house. You know, getting the heat on, the water and electricity going."

"You're not helping?"

"I was anxious to see you."

"What's going on?"

"It's awful. Leah had a breakdown. She started drinking a lot, maybe some drugs. We don't really know. She was depressed - or something. She refused to see someone. Her friends started calling me and telling me they thought she was in trouble. My parents went into the city to try to get a sense of what was happening, but my mother had a huge fight with her - a typical Dorothy versus Leah blowout. I guess this one was worse than usual. That was a month ago. No, almost two months ago by now. My father still talks with her but my mother just can't deal. Now Leah's on the verge of flunking out of her painting program. She's supposed to be finishing this year. It took her four years to get in. Her friend Timothy told me that she's barely doing anything and already missed a major critique. That's when

I went to see for myself. I got a friend of mine, a psychologist, to write a letter to the school on Leah's behalf and they agreed to give her a leave of absence until the spring. It's clear she needs a break. I pushed her to move here for a month or two - to recuperate here. She can heal and build up her strength."

"Do you know what caused it, what caused the breakdown?"

"She won't say. Or maybe she can't say. Maybe she doesn't know herself. I'm not even sure there is a 'thing.' I'm just relieved she's here."

"And you think it'll be better for her to be alone in the woods?"

"It's not the woods. The house is a place of positive associations and good memories. Safe, childhood memories."

"For you or for her?"

"For both, I would say."

"But you aren't sure?"

"Yes," she said, "I am. I am sure."

"How long will you stay?"

"A few days. Maybe a week."

"You should stay for the winter. You should look after Leah."

"Don't say that. I would do it if I could. I just got this job and I can't lose it. I can't quit now. It was enough just to get this time off."

I felt repulsed by this statement but still drawn to her - to her, to the human being beyond or beneath these words. What drew me? It might have been her wet, fragile body. It might have been the way her hand trembled when she spoke about her sister's condition. I don't know. I still can't figure it out. I enfolded her in my arms and felt her cheek - cool and damp - on my neck.

"I need this," she said. "I need you here. I don't know what I would do otherwise."

We sat by the fire for fifteen or twenty minutes and drank coffee. She needed to go. She didn't want to leave Leah for too long. She asked if I would come to dinner that night. I declined.

I spent the remainder of the day outdoors, wandering through the woods in the rain. I sat gazing at the lake as the sun set. In the evening, I worked in the office, composing three long letters. During these days I wrote almost nothing but letters. I felt the impulse, increasingly so, to address someone real, someone out there in the distance.

She returned early in the morning. She didn't knock this time but simply pushed the front door open and entered the house. In a sort of half-sleep I heard the faint sound of the hinges squeaking. I sensed that she was coming, penetrating into my dreamlife. I didn't get out of bed to greet her. Her steps resounded on the stairs. She appeared in the doorway. I rose slightly to gaze at her - a figure from the murky depths of consciousness. Was she real? Perhaps all of it - Juliet, the house, Casco, Hagerson - was a dream, a transposition of things. She unzipped her jacket and let it fall to the ground. She slipped under the blanket. There was none of that late summer aggression this time. All that had faded into context, background for a tender embrace.

We fell asleep and slept for a couple of hours. It was nine in the morning when we woke up. It must have been five or six when she came up those stairs. We showered and ate breakfast. It was the first clear day in a week and we went for a walk, ending at the lake. The water was high. The wind rippled the surface.

Over the next three days Juliet came when she could, an hour here, a couple of hours there, another morning slip under the blanket. On the fourth day she was gone. Gloomily, I turned back to my solitude. I felt it - a sense of my oneness, my loneliness and despondence. I had come to depend on Juliet for something, for body heat or eye contact or softly spoken words. I don't know. The house felt colder than usual. I burned log after log to keep myself from shivering. The squirrels and rabbits seemed less playful. The rain fell with more resolve.

There need not have been despair. Two weeks later I had, for the most part, cleared away these gathering clouds. The storm had passed. My mind was clear. I tried to focus on the last days before the real winter came. I wandered around in the woods.

It was a dark night, a starless, moonless night. Leah came. She brought a bottle of whiskey with her. In truth, I had been hoping that she wouldn't come. I feared it. I feared her. I felt repulsed by her problems, whatever they were. I didn't feel like I could endure them. I was still, years after leaving Concord behind, recovering from a life in town.

She had lost weight, a lot of it. She must have lost between fifteen and twenty pounds, or more. She looked sickly. Her skin was pale. Wide, dark circles surrounded her puffy eyes. Her jeans, sized for her former proportions, sagged badly from her waist. Not even her turquoise belt, itself a hideous thing, could keep them in place. Her sweater, robin's egg blue, fit poorly over her shrunken bosom. Overall, her body appeared to have shifted without regaining a natural equilibrium.

"Do you want to get drunk with me?" she asked as I took her coat and hat and hung them on the rack.

"No," I said.

"At least have two drinks. Or one," she pleaded. I agreed and fetched the glasses.

We sat in the living room, I in the armchair and she across the room on the sofa. We held our glasses up to each other and gave a little nod without clinking them. Clinking would have been too much for me. I was trying to figure out what role to play. The role of friend didn't seem right. We were not friends. Therapist was beyond my ability. Neighbor, perhaps - neighbor sleeping with sister. Or neighbor in love with sister. No. Not yet. Or? Neighbor infatuated with her sister who has left town. Maybe.

"How's life so far in Casco?" I asked as I peered at her across the room. The question caused her to shift uncomfortably on the sofa. She crossed and re-crossed her legs. She sipped the whiskey. I sipped mine.

"It's good, on the whole," she said. "I mean, it's a little lonely, but I have a lot to do. I have to get my portfolio in shape for the spring. It's quiet. Maybe too quiet for me."

"I also used to feel that way. You'll get used to it. It's a lot different here this time of year."

"I hope I don't get used to it. I'm leaving in a month and then what would I do?"

"That's right," I said, "I forgot that you were staying for such a short time."

"Are you ever afraid out here in the winter?"

"Afraid of what?" I asked.

"I don't know. Afraid of some criminal, I guess, like some insane hunter with a big gun and a drinking problem and an unfaithful wife. There's nobody around - just you and the hunter. For some reason he's after you."

"I'm not afraid of that," I told her.

"Maybe you're afraid of yourself."

"What for?" I said, annoyed by the comment.

"Any number of things," she said. "Don't you ever feel some fury or rage or depression? Come on, why else would you be here? You're a young guy. Rick even called you something of a big shot. And Rick doesn't say that about many people."

"I don't think I'm afraid of myself, though I was afraid of what was happening to me."

"What was that?"

"I was being emptied out, drained, dried up. Like the Aral Sea."

"I don't know a thing about the Aral Sea."

"I don't want to get into this now," I said and poured Leah and myself another round. "I'm not interested in thinking about these things. It was a long time ago."

"How long?"

"A few years."

"That's not that long."

"Long enough," I said. Damn, I thought, she was conjuring that most dreaded feeling: nostalgia. It fluttered through my chest. I quickly drank the glass of whiskey. Juliet didn't press me this way. She knew the value of discretion.

"This is some resurrection story, I suppose," Leah said, "some born-again type of deal."

"Type of deal?" I hissed. "It's not a type of deal. It's a reorientation. One life among the billions."

"You're irrelevant, in other words. Come on, Abel. Don't be a coward. Why don't you just tell me plainly what's going on? Then I'll tell you and then we can finish the bottle of whiskey, vomit, and pass out. That's a successful night - that's how to build a friendship. Don't give me any of this metaphorical bullshit about the Aral Sea. You're fucking my sister after all."

"It's actually far from bullshit. Do you really think that it would be better if I sat here and told you some psycho-babble about myself, some narrative that I made up to justify my own actions? I prefer a good water-related metaphor any day. In any case, would you really believe it if I told you why I was here? If so, you'd be making a big mistake. There is no trusting anyone who tries to explain himself. The result isn't metaphor but lie."

"You're lying to me."

"Approximating. That's the whole point."

We drank another round, then another. In the meantime, I had added more wood to the stove, and the room grew hot. Leah removed her sweater. I took off my flannel shirt. She looked better without the poorly fitting garment. Underneath the sweater she had on one of Juliet's T-shirts. She must have recognized that I noticed this.

She looked down at her chest and said, "Can you imagine? I fit into her clothes. That's never happened before. What do you think?"

"It suits you."

The talk became easier. She smiled and peered at me with wide eyes. I might also have smiled, though I tried not to. It was clear that Leah was a radical force, that the lack of equilibrium in her appearance reflected a broader disequilibrium surrounding her. I felt off-balance, sitting there by the fire. It could have been the whiskey. It could also have been that T-shirt. I would have liked to see Juliet. I hadn't heard from her since she'd left. Most likely she was making the point that I needed to get a phone. She had too much to do, she said, to write letters. I had written and mailed her a letter a week before.

I don't know what we talked about for the rest of that evening. At some point late at night Leah announced that she was going home. I offered to accompany her and she agreed. We put on our jackets and shoes and went out into the night. The road that led from the house to the street was unlit - but the light from the house guided our way. Once on the road there were no street lamps and it was slow going as we passed by the McKenneys' place - abandoned now for winter. We turned onto the long winding path that led down to the Klein house. Leah grasped my arm for balance. I focused in order to provide it. It didn't take long to arrive at the house. It was unlocked, like most houses in Casco, and Leah entered ahead of me.

"Would you like to come in?"

"No," I said.

"Then goodnight, Abel," she said and shut the door.

I turned back and walked up the hill to the road. "Goodnight, Leah Klein," I whispered to myself. "Goodnight."

I felt the rumble in my stomach. I waited and focused on it. There it was again—gravity was doing its work. I slowly stood up, knowing that this was the delicate moment. Things could either loosen or harden. It had been three days. My whole body longed for purgation. Again it came; this time movement accompanied it. The story had come to an abrupt end with Abel walking back up the hill to Mayberry Hill Road. The next pages in the stack were full of lists of trees, organized by type, location, and size of circumference. Leah, it seemed, had vanished in this actuarial forest. I moved through the hallway and slowly down the stairs. It was not quite there. A couple deep knee bends and a glass of water would do it, I thought, and went to the kitchen to fill a glass from the faucet. I drank it quickly, hoping it would help the gravitational force. Slowly, steadily, I bent my knees and squatted down. I flexed my stomach muscles. The movement inside continued. Another deep bend, then up, then another. There it is, I thought, the decisive line has been crossed. Another bend, then up—the movement was gaining momentum. I drew another cup of water and drank it slowly. Pressure started to form around my pelvis. I tried to relax and think about emptiness, nothingness. There it is, I thought—it's ready.

As I stood in the living room above the Franklin stove thinking of my body's disgusting acts, a flash of some obscure emotion passed through me. I paused to consider it—but then it trailed away. I didn't have the energy to follow it. There had been a year or two, some time ago, during which I had felt these peculiar impulses. I had thought I could solve the situation through work; somehow I needed to get deeper into it, to escape the surface of things. The answer, I kept repeating to myself, was in the texts—in the acoustical resonance of those beautiful words—*shekhinah, sefiroth, tohu, tikkun, en-sof*—which somehow, by some means, aligned with their meaning, a meaning that had seemed ungraspable to me, as if it was stuck on the other side of a thick pane of glass, visible but untouchable, close and yet impossibly distant. *Tohu*—chaos. This was it, I had thought back then—I needed to find my way from chaos to the restoration of harmony, from *tohu* to *tikkun*, without relying on rational answers, without logic.

The very rationalism my first book had celebrated—this is what I felt the need to reject. Why wasn't it enough anymore? Sophia and Sam—Sybil only a year old—and order seemed to be crumbling around me. Yet, I maintained order—I fought away the chaos, not by destroying it (how could one destroy chaos?) but by filing it down, blunting the sharp point of its speared end. And I'd thought at the time, this is how we live—we live with the filed-down shards of chaos lodged in our minds, minds adjusted to this reality—*this*.

Outside, daylight was starting to emerge from the darkness. The snow had stopped. The clouds had vanished under the cover of the night. I felt an urge to get out of the house and into the fresh morning air. It occurred to me that I should pack up some things and walk through the field and down the forest path to the lake. Abel mentioned a fire pit down there. I would build a lakeside fire and continue to read through Abel's papers on the edge of the snowy woods. Yes, that was precisely what was needed now. I went up to the office to collect some papers and began to sort through a large stack, scanning the pages in hopes of seeing the names Juliet and Leah. Could it be that Abel's fate was wrapped up with the Klein sisters? In the last analysis, could it be that some sort of sibling competition or contest had led to Abel's suicide? Was it really suicide?

Abel Prager. Abel. My mind turned to the story in Genesis. I thought about how the birth of Cain and Abel came directly after the scene in which God drives Adam and Eve out of the Garden of Eden. *Now that man has become like one of us*, God says, *knowing good and bad, what if he should stretch out his hand and take from the tree of life and eat, and live forever!* God, fearful of mankind, drives Adam and Eve from the garden. Eve gets pregnant: "I have gained a male child with the help of the Lord," she says. The child is Cain. Next comes Abel. Abel becomes a shepherd, Cain a tiller of the soil. Cain and Abel sacrifice to God. Conflict arises. A murder takes place. Punishment comes. Mercy comes. Later legends maintained that Cain was not jealous of God's love for Abel but was in competition with his brother for the love of a woman, and that it was this love—love between brothers and sisters—that had brought about the crime.

I sat down in Abel's rocking chair and put the wool blanket over my legs. The drive to leave the house had faded. Now I yearned to settle back in. I picked up a stack of papers and set them on my lap. For a while, I just sat there looking out the window and sipping coffee. I was trying not to think about anything, trying first and foremost not to focus on my aching lower back and stiff neck.

It was all mine, I thought. This house was mine. The desk and its contents were mine. The field beyond the window and the woods beyond the field were mine. That path down to the lake was mine. These were material things—an inheritance. There was much besides this. Here, in this house, the Prager line had come to an end. It had now merged with the Stern line. From me, the remains of the Prager line would pass to Sam and Sybil and then on to their children, my grandchildren. I wondered why Abel hadn't married. I wondered if Abel had ever given thought to having children of his own. It seemed unbelievable to me that I didn't know this. Then again, I thought, I had barely known that I, Ezra Stern, wanted to be a husband and a father. Sophia and I had not explicitly planned for either Sam or Sybil.

Sam was born not long before Abel left the city. The first memory I have that contains both Abel and Sam is of the bris. It was late June. The apartment on Riverside Drive was stifling hot. The mohel, Dr. Flagler, was visibly perspiring and repeatedly daubing his shiny forehead with a pale-blue handkerchief. I had felt a mix of emotions that morning, a surge of paternal pride when I greeted my mom and dad, a strange type of embarrassment when I caught a glimpse of Sophia's parents across the living room. They weren't Jewish and somehow, seen through their eyes, the whole process seemed to me barbaric and brutal. Mostly, of course, I was deeply worried about my son. During the last two brises I had attended a rising dizziness had forced me to take refuge in another room, far from the act. For Sam, I would have to hold it together. I needed to be there with my boy.

When the time came for the procedure, I could tell I was losing it. Flagler unsheathed the scalpel and removed the cap from the disinfectant. From the kitchen, where the caterers were busily working away, the thick scent of mini-quiches poured into the room. I scanned the crowd. Four members of the history faculty were there and, it seemed, were eyeing my every move. The dizziness started. My forehead broke out into a sweat. I searched the pockets of my pants for a kerchief but they were empty. Just as I was about to make a break for the bathroom, Abel emerged from behind my aunt Beatrice and put a hand on my shoulder.

"Allow me to hold a leg," he said. "I hear that Flagler has the truest cut in the business."

It was enough. Abel secured a leg. Flagler's assistant took the other. Flagler drew the blood and made the cut. Sam shrieked and turned bright red. Vaseline was applied. I hurried through the crowd, shaking hands and receiving congratulations on the way to the bathroom. There I spent a few minutes splashing my face with cool water. I thought of that hand now, Abel's hand. It was a small, sturdy hand. It had a certain girlish slenderness combined with a masculine amount of hair around the knuckles. I recalled the expression on Abel's face as he held little seven-pound Sam's leg. It had been a look of utter poise. It had steeled me for that critical moment.

Only months after the bris, Abraham Prager died. Abel appeared in my office doorway.

"Bad news, Allstar," he said, "the big guy died." He took a couple of steps into the office and put his hands on the back of the armchair where I invited students to sit for meetings. "He had a heart attack. He was at home by himself. Peterson from the bank called me because my father missed a big meeting. He said that my father had never missed a meeting before without calling in. Nobody could get him on the phone. I went straight home. He was lying on his bedroom floor."

"When?" I asked. Despite the intense heat coming from the radiator behind me, my body felt frozen.

"Two days ago."

"I can't believe it," I said, thinking of the strong and healthy man I had known since boyhood.

"Neither can I, Allstar."

"How are you?"

"No clue, Ezra. Somehow it hasn't settled in yet."

I took a sip of coffee and tried to focus on how Abel had looked at this moment, standing there in my office in Whitefield Hall. It could be that Abel was paler than usual that day, or thinner or less full-bodied. Or maybe not, maybe he looked exactly as he always looked. I reproached myself for my lousy attention to detail. I was a poor seer, a poor listener to words left unsaid. Sophia once told me that I didn't know how to hear the silence.

I couldn't remember what had happened next. At some point Abel left the office. I saw him again at the funeral. I looked on as my friend, standing apart from the rest of the group, watched his father's coffin descend into the ground next to the plot his mother had occupied for over two decades. Without another word with Abel, I left for a weeklong conference in Heidelberg.

When I returned from Germany, I felt spent. During the taxi ride on the way home, I chatted for a few minutes with the driver, a Belorussian, then slumped down into the seat. The Heidelberg talk had gone badly. An Israeli and a French professor both had grilled me. Professor Walker from Oxford, with whom I had worked during my year of research in England, had half-heartedly come to my defense. I had defended myself incompetently, always too slow, too late. I was no good at this verbal combat.

The taxi wove through the traffic. I peered out into the grim urban landscape between the airport and the city and had two related feelings. The first was how grateful I was for Sophia and little Sam. They anchored me. The second was one of shame or disgrace. It was something akin, I thought, to how a major league pitcher must feel when he gets shelled out of a playoff game in the early innings. Not only did the pitcher face the humiliation in front of the entire viewing world, a public humiliation; he then had to go home to his family to face a second, private one. For sure, Sophia didn't know anything yet about the Heidelberg conference, but I would tell her and make my quiet demands for comfort and support. She would provide it, as she always did, and as she did that night, with a glass of scotch and some strokes to my ego. Pathetic, I thought, pathetic.

I glanced down at the papers in my lap. I picked up the top page and read:

10.7.2006

Water freezes into ice and becomes a solid. It melts and becomes a liquid again. It evaporates into gas. It condenses and precipitates as a liquid. We are like water, constantly changing forms depending on the outside temperature. We think of mercurial as meaning capricious or unstable. We should rather consider it our essential state of being. The body, after all, is 70 percent water. Today my watery soul is frozen. Tomorrow it will be liquid. The next day it will rise through the air as steam.

10.8.2006

From the Tao:

"Nothing in the world is as soft and yielding as water. Yet, for dissolving the hard and inflexible, nothing can surpass it. The soft overcomes the hard; the gentle overcomes the rigid, everyone knows this is true, but few can put it into practice."

10.09.2006

My mother gave me a collection of Basho's haiku before my first summer at camp. It was a regular paperback edition, but she had bound it in leather. The leather had worn pleasantly over the years, lightening in places, darkening in others. This is the first time I have gone back to it since my arrival in Casco. My long walks have turned my mind to another wanderer from long ago and across the world, Basho.

Atop the mushroom -
Who knows from where -
A leaf!

I flipped through the stack and began to read again.

12.20.2007

Leo Schulz appeared in my dream last night. Unfortunately,
or perhaps mercifully, I woke up too abruptly to remember
what he wanted there. Leo is a character that infiltrates my
nocturnal landscape; he is a harbinger of dangerous times,
a bird of prey. Most of the time, when he appears I succeed
in pushing him back into the unconscious fairly quickly
(to cage him), but this time is different. It is nighttime
again and he is still here with me, perched on my shoulder
like a canary bird or a muzzled falcon. He is chirping his
demands in a language I don't understand.

12.22.2007

Leo Schulz

During our fifth summer, our tightly knit group received a
new camper, Leo Schulz. Groups at camp, it should be said,
find internal balance; after an initial period of testing,
members settle down into roles. Both this overall balance
and the relative positions of each variable were delicate
for us. Then there was the fourth dimension - the group had
a history by this fifth summer. We had canoed and hiked
together. We had lived through scenes of bed-wetting and
teary conclusions to visitors' day and much besides. We had
been punished together by the assistant director. We had
performed plays and competed in fierce competitions both
with and against each other. We knew who was good at what,
who was the best or worst at this or that.

Here, then, all of a sudden, was Leo Schulz. He was of average height and average build. His family lived in the Philadelphia suburbs. His father, it was said (and I later confirmed this), was a chemist at the University of Pennsylvania. To put the matter simply, Schulz combined what had heretofore been thought mutually exclusive. He excelled at everything in the domains of both body and mind, as if he had been cut from the cloth of some Greek or Roman demigod. As such, he was confident, even brash. He competed fiercely and nearly always won.

At baseball, Schulz outpitched Ezra. He swam faster than Adam. He shot a straighter arrow than Walt. He was a better soccer player than Tex. For the first couple of weeks that summer, an odd thing occurred. Everyone in our little group was somehow diminished. Schulz became a giant among us. I was the only one who wasn't shrinking - mostly because my athletic status was already abysmal. The result was that, through no act of mine, my status seemed to be elevating, for I alone had not been vanquished by the mighty Schulz, and it seemed that what talents I possessed fell beyond his ability to surpass.

Middle of July came and that meant the selection and organization of the August play. This was my domain. I had played the lead role in our group's productions since that first summer. In anticipation of this continuing, I had brought an idea for the play with me. While I had been reading a collection of short stories by Hemingway that spring, it occurred to me that it would be great to stage the story "The End of Something" as a one-act play. The story had one main male role, a main female role, and then another small, supporting male role, which I had assumed would be

filled by either Ethan or Walt (none of the others liked
acting). I proposed to the camp's director that we should
ask at the girls camp across the lake to see if a girl of
equivalent age would like to play the part of Marjorie
opposite my Nick Adams. The director categorically rejected
this idea but counter-proposed that we ask if the camp's
resident doctor, Dr. Solomon, would permit his daughter,
Rebecca Solomon (also age 13) to take the part. Dr. Solomon
loved the idea. Rebecca agreed and it was on.

That summer the camp's drama program was run by a guy
named Danny Weaver, an Amherst College student in his third
year. Weaver told me that even though the play was my idea
(and that he was quite taken with it) he would still have
to call for open auditions among the group for the parts
of Nick Adams and his friend Bill. "Everyone in the group
deserves a fair shot," Weaver said. In theory, I had no
problem with this, especially because I assumed I would be
the only one to audition for the lead.

Two of us, Leo Schulz and I, showed up in the camp's
assembly hall that afternoon. I auditioned first, as Weaver
sat in the otherwise empty assembly hall with a clipboard
in his hand, making occasional marks. Like Schulz, it was
Weaver's first summer at camp, a fact that started to unnerve
me a little as I worked through my lines. After I was done,
Weaver told me to wait outside, denying me the opportunity
to see what Schulz could do. When Schulz finished, he, too,
was instructed to wait outside by the door. Weaver took five
or ten minutes and then called us in. Schulz got the lead
role. He would be Nick Adams. I would be the friend and foil,
Bill.

To say that I was furious would not capture the full range of my emotional tumult, a tumult that was combined with regret and longing when I formally met the stunning Rebecca Solomon for the first time a week or so later.

During the next weeks the three of us rehearsed together under Weaver's direction. Despite my jealousy, I couldn't help but admit that Leo Schulz was good. He might even have been better than I was. His stage presence was solid. His delivery was sound. His emotional range was dynamic. His big problem, it turned out, was that he was, in a certain sense, lazy. He didn't focus that well. At times, he seemed hardly to be paying attention.

In fits and starts and with a fair amount of frustration, our little play came together. Rebecca was fantastic - and it was safe to assume that by August both Schulz and I were in love with her. We rehearsed two or three times each week, and each time I tried whatever I could to win a few minutes alone with Rebecca. I never succeeded. I started to suspect that Schulz was having better luck of it than I was and that they were stealing a moment or two here and there to kiss behind the curtain. Not that it mattered much. The real issue was that I had lost my standing among the group. By losing out to Schulz I had been reduced to almost nothing, to near zero.

The evening of the performance came. The previous re-hearsals had all gone well. Schulz had finally nailed his part. I had even started to feel a certain amount of pride in our collective undertaking. Then something unexpected happened. Schulz, it seemed, couldn't handle the pressure. At least three times during the performance he had to be prompted by Weaver standing offstage. His timing was off. His body language was stiff. The play was a failure.

The next day, after lunch, I caught up with Schulz as he was making his way from the mess hall to his bunk for rest hour.

"Hold up," I called. Schulz stopped and waited for me. "What the hell happened to you last night?"

"Fuck off, Prager," he said and turned to walk away.

I was aghast. After what he did, he was insulting me! I couldn't stand him any longer.

"I will not fuck off. You should never have gone out for the lead role if you couldn't handle it."

"And you think you would've done any better? You're pathetic, Abel, a pathetic, nerdy, awkward loser."

Before I knew it, my hand balled into a fist and I punched him as hard as I could in the shoulder. Just as suddenly, Schulz's fists responded. One hard blow landed on my face, splitting my lip open and causing blood to run down my chin. Another blow found my stomach. I doubled over in pain. A third blow struck my kidney and I fell to the ground in tears.

In all, it took approximately fifteen seconds for Schulz to beat the shit out of me. I stumbled to the green house, washed myself up, and then went back to the bunk. As I was lying there with my eyes closed Kaplan noticed my swollen face. He asked what had happened and I told him and the rest - Weiss, Tex, and Ezra - that Schulz had lashed out after I criticized his performance. They were shocked. We vowed that for the remainder of the summer none of us would utter a direct word to Schulz. He would be a pariah among us. What's more, we would spread the word until all in our group shunned him. It worked. For the last three weeks of camp Schulz might as well have been a leper. After a week or so of this, Schulz seemed to be breaking. He tried to reach out to one or another of us. We rebuffed him each time. At some point I saw him crying by himself. On departure day his parents were the first to arrive - no doubt to rescue their miserable son. He never returned. I never told anyone that I hit Schulz first.

I set down the pages and thought about Leo Schulz. I closed my eyes and could see scenes from *The End of Something* pass across my eyelids. It was a story about two relationships, the first an amorous one between the central figure, Nick Adams, and his girlfriend, Marjorie, and the other a fraternal one between Nick and Bill. The basic story went as follows: It opened with Nick and Marjorie fishing in Lake Michigan near the defunct mill town of Horton's Bay. The mill had long been closed and the industrial ruins formed the backdrop to their fishing scene. Rebecca Solomon was beautiful, far too beautiful to play the role of the drab Marjorie. This gave the play an uneven, unbalanced feel from the start.

It was coming back to me. Schulz was gazing at Solomon as she uttered her lines. There was a blaze in his eyes, like when a coal that has turned white suddenly and spontaneously leaps to life and starts to glow a deep red. No, Leo Schulz had not performed poorly. He had played the role quite well, albeit with a deep inconsistency, as the play was about the burning-out of love, while Leo himself was clearly in love with Rebecca.

The fish weren't biting. Marjorie and Nick pulled the boat to shore and planted their rods in the ground. Nick built a fire. Marjorie retrieved a blanket from the boat and spread it out. She sat. Nick joined her. She unpacked the dinner from the picnic basket. Nick waived it off. She pressed him. They ate. An argument about nothing ensued. They watched the moon rise. Nick said to her, "It isn't fun anymore." Then came the quintessential Hemingway line. I considered it now: "I feel as though everything has gone to hell inside of me."

I repeated the line. "I feel as though everything has gone to hell inside of me." At age thirteen, I had no clue what this meant. "Gone to hell"? What was this "everything" to which Nick referred? I remembered asking Abel about it.

"He outgrew her," Abel said, "or he had outgrown himself, his life. He wasn't ready for marriage, kids, and a steady job at a factory somewhere. But he doesn't see it as an improvement to be free of her. He doesn't see much hope in anything."

"What about Bill?"

"Bill is the world of men, the world of guns and booze."

"So Adams chooses guns and booze over love?"

"That's essentially it."

"Why?"

"Don't know, Allstar. Maybe because girls get too deep. Love means something a whole lot different and more serious than friendship. The stakes are higher when it comes to love. Nick couldn't play in such a high-stakes game."

Everyone agreed that the performance had been good. I remembered discussing it with Ethan Weiss. Ethan had praised it—and Leo Schulz, especially. And I trusted Ethan more than anyone besides Abel. If Ethan had been right, then why had Abel and Schulz gotten into that fight? And why would Abel construct such a fictional narrative about it all these years later, including a perhaps fictional sense of guilt? The group, it was true, had rallied behind Abel. At some point that summer, I had contemplated challenging Schulz to fisticuffs directly, but ultimately didn't dare to do it. I did, however, brush Schulz aggressively off the plate during the next baseball game. If Abel had wronged Schulz somehow, it meant that I had also wronged him. We had mobbed the boy as crows a threatening owl.

I started to read again.

01.01.2008

A feverish New Year's Eve day. Five long letters written and stored in the attic. For the past days and weeks I have slept either poorly or not at all. It is approaching midnight and I am back at the Remington. First things first, I turn to my copy of Walden. HDT - "This is a delicious evening, when the whole body is one sense, and imbibes delight through every pore. I go and come with a strange liberty in Nature, a part of herself."

Now that I have it open, I can't resist. HDT - "I find it wholesome to be alone the greater part of the time. To be in company, even with the best, is soon wearisome and dissipating. I love to be alone. I never found the companion that was so companionable as solitude. We are for the most part more lonely when we go abroad among men than when we stay in our chambers."

Those pesky reversals, which Emerson grew to hate.

Like pond and village.

Juliet was supposed to arrive from the village for a week at the pond. She wanted to see me, she said, and to check up on how Leah was getting along. She cancelled. Leah, she wrote, seemed to be doing fine, and her boss had asked her to attend some meetings in London, which she couldn't pass up.

For my part, I hadn't seen Leah in a week or more. It had been raining on and off, and I assumed that she, like I, was locked indoors in a pleasant mode of winter hibernation. What did it matter if I wanted to see her or not? The fact was, whether I saw her or didn't see her depended entirely on her. I didn't seek her out. I didn't seek Juliet out either.

HDT - "Our village life would stagnate if it were not for the unexplored forests and meadows which surround it. We need the tonic of wildness."

HDT - "We need to witness our own limits transgressed, and some life pasturing freely where we never wander."

Dear Henry David, Leah was such a pasturing beast. She roamed out of the woods to the pond's shore around dusk on New Year's Eve, holding a large picnic basket. I relieved her of it and set it down on the coffee table in the living room. It was raining lightly and I offered to place her jacket near the stove for it to dry. She removed it and revealed that underneath she was wearing a rather pretty dress. She had on nylons and high-heeled shoes. I was dressed in typical pond attire - jeans, T-shirt, and a flannel shirt.

"What's in the basket?"

"Dinner and dessert," Leah said. "I apologize if you have other plans. I don't mean to intrude."

"Not at all," I said.

"It can get lonely in Casco. The summers are so full of people. Hardly a summer day goes by without a horde of guests on the beach and in the guestrooms. I'd come to think of it here as a commune of sorts."

"Please, Leah, sit down and tell me what I should bring for the dinner."

"Plates and silverware and glasses. I brought a bottle of champagne to celebrate the New Year."

I got up immediately and brought the things. In the meantime, Leah unpacked the basket. She had made roasted lamb with a cranberry jelly and a host of other delicious things. It was packed up and still warm. I set out the plates and she carefully distributed the contents.

"How are you doing?" I asked as she spooned the cranberry jelly onto the side of the meat. Though she hadn't gained back any of the weight she had previously lost, she looked healthier than before.

"I'm just swell, Abel. I've been taking long baths, smoking a cigarette now and then on the deck, looking out over the lake. I'm feeling good. I think I might stay a little longer out here. Maybe into the spring."

"What about school?"

"I'll start back in the fall. I don't think anyone will care. I'll send some images of new work to my committee and that will be enough for them to leave me alone."

"You're working?"

"Wonderfully. I didn't expect it would go this well. I should thank my little sister for the idea."

"Have you heard from her?"

"No more than you have."

"I hardly hear anything. She's kept her distance."

"And you've kept yours. She's a busy girl, Abel. She's ambitious. Haven't you figured that out yet? She's not the type of girl to give up her life to come live in the woods with you. At most she'll spare a couple weeks in the summertime. But what you really want to know, I imagine, is if she is sleeping with someone else. You're out of luck. I don't know."

"I don't care."

"Do you?"

"No," I said.

"Do you like ambitious women, Abel?"

"I don't like ambitious people."

"You like my little sister."

"I do and I'm not bothered by that contradiction."

"Very well," she said, "but how do you like the lamb?"

"It's incredible. You're a great cook," I said and uncorked the champagne.

"Isn't the fire getting a little low?"

"Are you cold?"

"Not yet, but I will be soon."

I opened up the stove and threw in a couple of logs. "That should do it."

We sat there for a few minutes sipping the champagne in silence. I had left the stove's door slightly ajar and now the fire was blazing. I leaned over and closed it up.

"Juliet said that you had a bad argument with your mother."

"Don't bring that up," she said, "or you'll spoil everything. My god, where's your sense."

"I'm sorry."

"Don't be. I don't like apologies. Tell me, Abel, do you plan on living here forever?"

"For as long as possible."

"What does that mean?"

"In the words of Henry David Thoreau, 'I think the richest vein is somewhere hereabouts; so by divining rod and

thin rising vapors I judge; and here I will begin to mine.'
This is it for me. This is the best place I know. It's the
most favorable spot to discover the hidden secret of the
world."

"Do you really mean that? It's often hard to tell with
you when you're being serious and when sarcastic. Juliet
felt the same way."

"I mean it completely. I want to concentrate on what
surrounds me. I don't want to think of abstract things. I
want to be able to feel things, to smell them and touch
them."

"But you think of Juliet, and she's not here. And what
about your family, your parents?"

"My mother died when I was eleven, my father a few years
ago. But I don't think of them as abstract, especially my
mother. She's been gone for a long time, but I can imagine her
touch as if she just reached out and stroked me. My father
didn't touch me very often. Even though he died not long
ago, he's becoming increasingly distant. My mother remains
right there, just out of reach. And she comes to me in my
dreams."

"Describe it," Leah said. "Tell me what that touch feels
like. Tell me what you dream about."

"I'd rather leave those things where they belong. If
I tried to describe them it would muddle everything up.
Words just muddle most of the time. A touch is like those
underground springs that feed Pleasant Lake."

"Another water metaphor, goodness!"

"What do you have against metaphor? Or is it water that
you have a problem with? Is water too ordinary for Leah

Klein? Should I start using metaphors with champagne instead?"

"It's not water. I have a dislike of evasive tactics. I prefer direct statements."

"Didn't we go over this last time?"

"You're right, we should find some new territory."

"There's precious little of that left."

"I'm sure we can find some."

The champagne flowed. Evening crept toward night. At some point she kicked off her shoes. Her face was flushed from the heat and the champagne. I noticed during dinner that she hadn't eaten much and wondered if her thinning was a result of some conscious choice. I wondered whether this choice was a sign of a sick mind.

"Reach inside my basket and take out that tin box," she instructed. I did as I was told. "Go ahead and open it." I popped off the lid and saw two stacks of oatmeal chocolate chip cookies. My mother had made a similar kind. "Take one," she said, "I baked them this afternoon."

I grabbed one and brought the tin over to Leah on the sofa. She also took a cookie. I sat down next to her.

"How old are you, Abel?"

"Thirty-seven."

"Isn't that too young to give up?"

"Who's giving up? I'm just beginning. I have no intention of giving up on anything worth having."

"What about all the memories, the people, the past life? I barely see a trace of you in here. These are all the Fieldstons' old things. I remember this place from years ago. It looks exactly the same."

"Everything that I wanted to keep is in the office upstairs."

"Take me there. I want to see it."

"Not now."

"Then when?"

"I don't know."

"It's New Year's Eve, Abel. Tomorrow doesn't exist." For
some reason, I reached out and touched her knee. "Take me
to your office, Abel."

"It's cold up there. Let me first light another fire."

I went upstairs and started a fire in the office stove. I
thought about Juliet and how she had never stepped foot in
the office. At that moment it seemed significant to think
about. It was part of some larger morality play. A pang of
something fizzed through my blood. The fire was burning. I
stuffed it as full as possible. It was too much for such a
small room. In half an hour or so, I thought, it would be
way too hot in there.

And so it was. Sweat dripped off Leah's naked body and
mine.

"Read something to me," she said, and when I shook my
head she added, "Come on."

I reached over to the desk and grabbed some pages. It was
an entry I'd just typed on the Remington from my journal
- dated February 20, 2007. It described a walk I'd taken
across the frozen lake and an encounter with a peculiar
ice fisherman in his hut during the late afternoon. I read
it aloud to Leah as she sat in my lap, her face tucked
into my shoulder. She was much lighter than I imagined she
would be, even lighter than Juliet, who had greater muscle
density and probably thicker and healthier bones.

"There's something both brutal and beautiful about that story," she said when I had ended. "It's almost childish in places."

"That's exactly what I thought," I said as I stroked her rich, dark hair.

"You're kind of that way, Abel. You're kind of brutal and childish. The lake in winter, I like that."

We sat together in the chair for a while. The fire continued to burn. Silence fell upon us. At some point, we had sex again.

"Let's end the night with a drink," I suggested. She agreed.

I made my way downstairs and poured two whiskeys. When I came back to the office we found our previous positions. I sat in the chair. Leah climbed into my lap and pressed her face into my shoulder and neck. I don't remember the midnight hour. It passed as all minutes pass. At some point Leah got up and walked across the hall and fell asleep in my bed. I lay next to her as she fell asleep. Then I returned to my office, finished my drink and waited for the fire to burn itself out. Deep in the night, it must have been close to daybreak, I slipped into bed next to her. Sleep didn't come. Daybreak found me pounding away at the Remington. Brutal, childish is a sleepless mind at daybreak.

01.02.2008

Leo Schulz was back again. I saw him across the field as I was walking (in my adult form) from the archery range to the shed to check back in my bow and arrows. It occurred to me that I was alone. Other than Schulz in the distance, nobody was in sight. This was a rare state of things at camp. I paused to consider it. Then I removed an arrow from my quiver and set it into the bow. I aimed it at Leo, pulled back the string and released. The arrow cut through the air. It was on target, heading directly at Schulz's chest. For a split second I thought I had murdered Leo Schulz. The arrow lost its momentum. I hadn't provided it with enough force to reach him. It dropped to the ground some twenty yards short of the target. Leo was peering across the field at me. Though he was far away I could still somehow see his face clearly. It was a look of recognition. He knew what I had become: a criminal, a madman.

01.03.2008

Leo Schulz again. He is talking to the camp director. The director points a very long finger at me. It was a foot long or more. My father will be called. He is sitting in his driver's seat, silent and ashamed of me. Finally, he turns to me and says, "What would your mother have said about this?" Tears flow down my cheeks as I grope for an answer. Freezing rain slaps against the roof of the car. Leah sleeps beside me.

01.04.2008

Sleep is poor and short. It is still dark when I get up. If I don't wake her, Leah will sleep to noon or even later. I leave her to it. One of us must sleep. She claims that she hasn't had a dream since coming to Casco. This is nonsense. I suspect she is concealing her dreamlife from me on purpose, as I keep mine from her. The Remington is not an option now, as its noise is sure to wake her. Downstairs the fire has gone out. I quickly make a new one, wrap myself in a blanket, and sit beside it. By the first traces of light outside I am restless. It is fiercely cold out there. I head for the lake.

The ice-fishing hour beckons. I see, in the distance, the place where my ice fisherman has set his shack. Smoke appears to rise from the small pipe-chimney there. The ice beneath me is mostly covered with snow by now, with the exception of some windswept places where the ice has a faint bluish tint. I think of HDT again - "Why is it that a bucket of water soon becomes putrid, but frozen remains sweet forever? It is commonly thought that this is the difference between the affections and the intellect."

Daybreak streams in with pinks and yellows. After half an hour I am at the shack. The fire is out. The shack is empty. The last boreholes have long since frozen over, forming sapphire disks.

01.05.2008

No sign of Leah today. I consider walking over to the Klein manor but decide not to. I have too much to do. I would like to get started on my project about my grandfather, but for some reason I hesitate to bring the material down from the attic. The attic absorbs easily and is stingy when the time comes to give back.

01.06.2008

No Leah again, though perhaps she will emerge in the darker
hours. At times during the day I feel a strong longing for
her. Thoughts of Juliet punctuate these longings and then
fade. Let Hagerson have his way!

01.07.2008

No sleep, no Leah Klein. I try to force myself into slumber.
It's no use. I toss and turn until almost noon. I think again
of HDT's putrid bucket of water. I feel a deep freeze coming
on. It was a mistake to stoke the fire and overheat the room.
My bucket melted. The lake thawed and the loon wailed. I
remember the first time I heard the loon wail. Ezra Stern
told me what it was. Is this the reason I love and need him
as I do?

01.08.2008

Ice crystals form in my bucket. I still cannot sleep more
than an hour or two here and there. I am afraid of Leo
Schulz. He is haunting me. I have been forced to write him
a long letter and have sent it special delivery by pigeon,
which I launched from the dormer window in the attic. I
see him in a dusty corner, backstage of the camp's assembly
hall. His hands and arms are slithering up Rebecca Solomon's
shirt like garden snakes.

01.09.2008

From Simone Weil:

"I did not mind having no visible successes, but what did grieve me was the idea of being excluded from that transcendent kingdom to which only the truly great have access and wherein the truth abides. I preferred to die rather than to live without that truth. After months of inward darkness, I suddenly had the everlasting conviction that any human being, even though practically devoid of natural faculties, can penetrate to the kingdom of truth reserved for genius, if only he longs for truth and perpetually concentrates all his attention upon its attainment."

01.10.2008

Sleeplessness has turned day into night, night into day. The ice is frozen again in the bucket. Dirt has fallen on the surface from some unknown source, perhaps a bird alighting from a branch above. Squirrels dart across the roof. The fiery inferno of my Franklin stove burns below. Fire and ice - this winter world is becoming increasingly elemental. Civilization fades away into a medieval winter. My body hair is growing thicker. My thick beard covers my face and neck like an Old Believer. The Fieldstons left behind a long mirror in the upstairs bathroom. I peered into it this morning and was sure that I am shrinking in size. I am about two-thirds my former self. Could it be? My appetite has increased because of my lack of sleep and lack of dreams. I eat and eat, and yet the proof of my shrinking

is right in front of me. Where is Leah with her picnic
basket? Nowhere in sight. I walk instead across the frozen
lake to the General Store. I buy a duck, presumably shot by
Carl, and roast it. With nothing but my hands, I consume
the whole thing. Grease drips down my arms. Now I must be
able to sleep - a whole duck will surely weigh me down
into a greasy pool of slumber. Hours pass without it. In
frustration I hurl a full glass of water across the room
and watch as it shatters against the wall. I cut my finger
picking up the shards. I am unable, therefore, to pound
the keys of the Remington and must write this with pencil
instead. Worst of all, I am already hungry again!

01.11.2008

She opens up her picnic basket and takes out two thick, raw
steaks. I am seized with the need to grab one with my bare
hands and rip apart the meat with my teeth. I want red meat,
raw and bloody. Nothing else will satisfy my hunger now. I
resist but tell her to cook mine rare - "and I mean rare."
She does it, searing the outside but barely affecting the
middle. It is still cool inside. The meat is outrageously
good and I inhale the whole steak in minutes. She looks on
with an expression of disbelief. The steak weighed over a
pound, she tells me. She seems frightened by my appetite,
as if I am a wild beast who at any moment might turn my
wolfish gaze from the plate to her. In truth, she has every
right to worry. I cannot control my urges. My stomach calls
out for more. I leap at her. The taste of steak is still in
both our mouths. She pushes me away. I circle back again.

How does she sleep so soundly? I want to wake her up and ask her about her dreams. Was she also dreaming of raw meat?

01.12.2008

The ice melts. The dirt that had fallen on the top of the bucket now sinks to the bottom and forms a substrate. A cold spell comes and freezes the water again. The ice is once again pure. The muddy bottom is concealed. This is how a bucket silts up.

01.13.2008

Thirteen hours of consecutive sleep last night. I wake up refreshed and rested - and relieved. Dark clouds have passed. I decide to hunt again for my ice fisherman - as I feel in need of his mantic talents. His method of divination through scratches on the surface of the ice has proven singularly effective. I trust him almost completely.

Though there are two relatively recent holes, he is not there. Instead of walking back to my forest path, I head over to the Klein property. The house is perched on the hill above the lake like a castle. I decide to seek out Leah.

I knock. She comes to the door. She's wearing the same clothes as days ago. Her hair is a mess.

"What's the matter?"

"I'm not in the mood to come out and play today, Abel," she replies in her droll way.

"May I come in?"

"No," she said, "I'm working. I don't want to be disturbed now."

"Take a break. It looks like you could use one."

"If I take a break I'll never start again."

"Sure you will."

"You don't get it, Abel. Not today. Not now. Leave me the fuck alone."

She shuts the door. I am bewildered and walk slowly back up the path to the road. Once home, I try not to think about Leah. It doesn't work. Instead, I tell myself that I need to give it up. Leah has intruded too deep into my Casco life. I came here to search for solitude, to find a wild seed, a kernel of the untouched, the transcendent, the truth. With thirteen hours of sleep under my belt I feel like I can find anything. I will rise above it, I tell myself - above her, above Juliet, above the sisters Klein - and spin and spin through those magnificent reddish golden clouds.

Another squirrel runs across the roof. Leah sleeps in my bed. She came to me full of remorse. She has an underground reservoir of sadness. I am pulled toward it. My divining rod bends over such a sweet spot as this. It is the lachrymose well of an aching soul.

01.14.2008

I am canoeing on Pleasant Lake. In the distance I see a loon flying low over the water, flapping its wings madly to gather speed. It makes a wide arc, and now it is headed directly toward me. It seems to be in an attack mode. In the dusky light I perceive its red eyes glowing with what I can only assume is a preternatural hatred or evil. It is coming to avenge long-forgotten wrongs that I have committed. I seize my Morehouse paddle in self-defense and station it behind my shoulder. The loon is coming straight at me now, approaching with incredible speed. In a flash, I swing my paddle and strike the bird from the sky, killing it instantly. It falls into the lake and I scoop it out with my fishing net. Its neck and left wing are broken. Its red eyes have faded into a dull gray, as if the blow from my paddle has popped the internal bulb that animated them. A premonition grips me that I will clean and roast the bird and eat it for dinner. The ice fisherman's voice resounds from the deep, "You have become a cannibal." I look down at my plate and see Ezra's face peering up at me from a severed head. Leah lets out a whimper and rolls over onto her side. She sleeps.

01.15.2008

A snow squall hit Casco with the suddenness of a thunderclap. Massive clouds appeared. Snow fell and fell. By evening my solar power was empty and the lights went out. I felt no impulse to activate the back-up generator and instead lit a few candles. The light shifted into a seemingly eternal and deep grayness before fading away into black. Vision. Surely vision, our primary sense, did not hold sole purchase on the tracking of the passage from day to night. In clearer skies we give over to it completely. Today vision was all but useless. It was easier to close my eyes and to let the darkness soak through my pores and enter my blood. If only this darkened nighttime blood would have brought weariness with it! The opposite occurred. Candles burst into flame within me. I sit here now with these fiery teardrops burning stronger than ever. It is deep into the night now.

Sleep remains far away. The shadows of my internal organs move with the slightest breeze.

Leah is not here. I hope that she has not been overtaken by the sudden squall. It is not the night for wandering in these woods. The lake has surely become a yawning gap in the Cimmerian landscape. Tomorrow, when the storm passes and the skies clear, the lake, with its newly fallen blanket of snow, will become a frozen paradise. Thus it will remain until the lakeside dwellers emerge and scar its perfect face with their cross-country skis, snowshoes, and snowmobiles. This nighttime stage for a Nordic epic will become a scene painted by the elder Bruegel and full of children, dogs, and village houses in quiet repose.

An hour ago I thought I heard a knock on my front door and assuming that Leah had come, I ran downstairs to let her in. I opened the door and found nobody there. The squall was so intense that I could barely see five feet in front of me. I investigated the path beyond the threshold and discovered no fresh footprints there. It must have been noises from the storm, I concluded, unless the storm was powerful enough to cover one's tracks in under a minute. If so, this particular night was ideal for prowlers and thieves.

01.16.2008

I woke up to the sound of the Reynolds boys plowing out the path to the road. The Reynolds boys are not known to be this efficient and in truth, I would have preferred their usual lack of attention. The feeling of being "snowed in" is a strange pleasure lost to modern man. I suspect that Leah called them and since they were in the neighborhood

they decided to clear my path as well as hers. While not
efficient, the Reynolds boys are not purposefully or willfully inefficient either. Their business is more a product
of circumstances than entrepreneurial will. On the other
hand, it would take a great deal of will to dissolve it.
They are the only snow removal operation in the immediate
area. To this, one could add a dozen or so other services
they provide. Despite holding a veritable monopoly in mul-
tiple domains, the Reynolds boys don't give a thought to
exploiting their position. They seem unaware of how much
people around here depend on them, the summer people most
of all. Alas, I still feel I must be classified on the summer
side of the ledger.

01.17.2008

There it is again, the knocking sound. It comes at the same
time tonight as two nights ago: 11:04pm. My initial theory, that the noise was generated by the bending of tree
branches under the weight of newly fallen snow, has been
discredited by the recurrence. This night is clear of snow,
but the clouds have blacked out the moon and stars. Darkness! Evil lurks outside in this shadowless place. After
some minutes of hesitation, I go downstairs to investigate.
Another pause and I open the door. The cold winter air
breaks against me and drives me a step back into the house.
I move forward against it. For the first time since moving
to Casco I feel afraid, afraid of the woods, the darkness,
the night, the winter. It was nothing, I say to myself, nothing but the most ordinary knocking sound from some hidden
but altogether ordinary source. No footprints are visible

other than those of the Reynolds boys and my own. I recognize theirs at once. The Reynolds boys wear the same boot, differing from one another only by half a size. I am unsure which one has the bigger foot.

01.18.2008

I go to the Klein house. Leah lets me in. At first, I don't ask what she's been doing these last days since the storm, though fresh tire tracks reveal she has come and gone many times. She doesn't offer much, and after a few minutes I start to feel uncomfortable. I realize that it was a mistake to come. Leah looks tired and pale. It seems like she's squinting as she follows my pacing.

Finally, I say, "Leah, I know this will seem like an odd question, but I wonder if you came to my door last night and knocked. It would have been at 11:04pm. Was this you? And if so, did you also do this same thing two nights before?"

She gazes at me with a stony expression and a rather vacant look in her eye. At some point in the next minute or two I think I see a slight twitch of her nose, as if it has been tickled by dust.

"No," she says, "I didn't."

01.19.2008

Leah's condition is worsening. I don't know what to do for her. For the first time since New Year's Eve I write to Juliet. I suggest that she come to Casco and check up on her sister. Maybe I'm looking for a way out of this affair and figure that Juliet could fetch Leah and take her away.

It would be a convenient rupture. I suspect there is little likelihood of Juliet coming. She hasn't written in months. It could be that she knows what is going on here. The trees out here have eyes and ears.

01.20.2008

Two long letters written today. Most satisfying day at the Remington in weeks. I know now that I will outlast the winter. I must get out of the house and into the woods more often. Snow is no barrier. Sleep has returned. My dreamlife has settled down. Leah has not come in days. Leah is one face of winter and the glistening wet snow is the other. I returned to the house this afternoon in a full sweat and stripped down to my shirtsleeves. Today I feel like I have what HDT calls the "genius of sauntering."

01.25.2008

I was ill the last days and with no strength to record thoughts. High fever, delirium, intense sweats - cold and hot. I must have caught it at the General Store. The likely carrier of contagion is Carl, from whom I am certain I caught a nasty flu my first winter here. Of note is that Carl himself did not suffer from this virulent sickness. I'd seen him at work every third or fourth day for the past weeks. The same thing was the case that first winter. Carl is a transmitter - strong enough to battle back infection but not strong enough to kill the germs entirely. They move from the palm of his hand to a coin or bill, then to the hand outstretched to receive it, then into the mouth of the victim, and finally into the victim's bloodstream. After days of hardly eating, I feel my appetite returning. I long for Leah's picnic basket. I close my eyes and smell her freshly baked muffins. I am not yet strong enough to make it to the ice-fishing shack, though I would like to see my mantic fisherman. Augur and auger, the ice has shifted. His scratching is bound to reveal something new. I must return to him before the thaw, before the thaw!

01.26.2008

I am a camper, a young one, nine or ten. I see my small body from the shore as it stands on the dock, knees bent and ready to dive into the lake. At the same time, I am the boy, of course, peering down into the water. As I get set to spring forth, I start to notice something strange shifting below me. The lake is suddenly not its normal color. It has changed from a cobalt blue into a disconcerting brown. The lake water also appears to have thickened into a sort of putrid sludge. I look down at it in horror and watch as trash emerges from its depths: old rope, used up milk cartons, bottles, and a rusty bicycle wheel. My legs are still tense in anticipation of the dive. How can I dive into this? The brown muddy liquid, I conclude, is certainly a cesspool of feces. I feel sure that the shit is being pumped from the camp's green house into the lake. I wonder whether the lake has always been this polluted and I had simply failed to notice or whether this is something new. I vow not to dive. I will never dive into this lake again. How could I willingly submerge myself into such a substance? At the same time, I know both that I must dive and that I will dive. The dive,

in other words, is inevitable, and as I pull back away
and find myself viewing the scene again from the shore, I
realize that the dive has already happened. The boy on the
dock is my past self. Upon this realization I am overcome
with a feeling of dread. I quickly scan my body to see if I am
covered with the brown sludge. Thankfully, I appear clean.
I am the boy again. I peer down into the water. Something
is emerging from the depths. It is large and comes up slowly.
Yes, there it is, a swan, dead and festering, covered with
sewage and trash. On shore again, I see the young thin body
spring into the lake. Somehow I know he has (I have) gone
in after the swan. It is a hopeless attempt, I think, to save
what is already well beyond saving.

01.27.2008

Leah sleeps in the other room. After a week of sickness, I am
still not fully well. I wish now I hadn't mailed that letter
to Juliet. I should have stored it in the attic like the
others. It's quite certain she will not reply. I am caught
in a schoolboy nightmare. My only option is to wait for
morning.

01.28.2008

I'm following HDT into the primitive forest of Maine. "This
is what you might call a bran-new country; the only roads
were of Nature's making, and the only houses were camps.
Here, then, one could no longer accuse institutions and
society, but must front the true source of evil."

Another passage from a few pages back:

"Let those talk of poverty and hard times who will in the towns and cities; cannot the emigrant who can pay his fare to New York or Boston pay five dollars more to get here, - I paid three, all told, for my passage from Boston to Bangor, two hundred and fifty miles, - and be rich as he pleases, where land virtually costs nothing, and houses only the labor of building, and he may begin life as Adam did?"

To live as Adam, to face the true source of evil: the only reasonable conclusion to this paradox is that Thoreau believed the source of evil lurked inside the Garden of Eden. He was right - its source was the tree of knowledge. Or could it be that the tree of knowledge only made Adam aware of the evil - of the evil that lurked inside him? As such, the true source of evil in the Maine woods is also an internal evil - unmarked, unmapped by civilization. I must see the ice fisherman in the morning to discuss this matter and much besides.

01.29.2008

Snow again today. There was no chance of making it across the lake to the ice-fishing shack. The oracle there, a young man by the name of Jeremiah, claims that his education as a mantic ice-scratcher was the result of a long inward journey, one that lasted many years. I asked him once if he felt connected to his namesake, the prophet Jeremiah, but he claimed to be unfamiliar with the biblical story. I am not sure if he is lying or telling the truth. Either way, both my Jeremiah and Zedekiah's share the message of doom.

01.30.2008

I spent most of the day working on my piece about Jeremiah.
By noon the sky had cleared, and I made it to the General
Store to re-provision. No sign of Leah during these last
days. The night problems are starting to reemerge with their
typical pattern. I wake up after five or ten minutes of
sleep in a full panic, after some intense dream. It takes
hours to get back to sleep, and then I sleep poorly and for a
short duration - no more than five or six hours. This is the
first stage. Gradually, the periods of sleep will get shorter.
After that, I will have three or four nights of, basically,
pure insomnia. At the point of complete exhaustion and
breakdown I will slip into a long and deep sleep - twelve
hours or more. Once I slept for eighteen straight hours
without waking. This is the rebirth into the land of the
living - through the gates of ivory I will trot, like Aeneas.
The gates of horn have long since been torn away.

01.31.2008

The sleeplessness is shifting my perception. I am at that
point of considering whether to fight it or submit to it
- to try to follow this new mode of consciousness into
unexplored regions of the mind. A case in point: as I was
sitting at my desk working on the Remington a few hours ago,
I heard a voice. It was calling my name in a loud whisper.
"Abel. Abel," it repeated at a regular interval. Ktaadn comes
into view. I hear a knock. "Its summit is veiled in clouds,
like a dark isthmus in that quarter, connecting the heaven
with the earth." Horrible! Who is HDT? The knock comes again,

then the whisper. I slowly make my way downstairs. Nobody is at the door. But a discovery! I see prints from her boot. Leah has been at the door. I throw on my jacket and boots and head out into the night. Her boot prints continue to the road and vanish there into the darkness. It is slow going. "Leah," I say and get no response. "Leah, are you out here?"

I reach the Klein's path and head down toward the house. The house is lit up. From the distance, I see Leah move across the kitchen window. She disappears and then reappears a moment later. She moves away again. Her bustle seems odd to me, and so I decide that rather than heading straight for the door, I will retreat into the trees to get a perspective into the large downstairs space through the side window. When I do so, I immediately see that Leah is not alone. There is a man in the house with her. He is standing next to the table with a bottle of beer in his hand. Leah puts a plate down in front of him. He is eating from Leah's picnic basket! Leah wears a yellow dress. The man is young. He's dressed rather fashionably - too fashionably to be a local. He comes from the city - from Concord. His face is cleanly shaven. Leah holds a glass of wine now. She touches his shoulder with her hand. He sits.

I am overcome with feelings - despair, anger, shame, and humiliation. Cloudbursts of each let loose upon me until the unconcealed truth dawns on me: the man is Leo Schulz. There is no doubt. But how could this be? Schulz, it seems, has stepped out of my nightmare and onto center stage. When the curtain falls tonight he will be groping this new Rebecca Solomon. Rebecca/Leah, yes - it is the eternal pair. The ugly duckling has finally become a swan.

I rose from the rocking chair. The blanket slid from my lap and fell to the floor. There was much to process from this January 2008. It was one month of seventy-two or so that Abel had spent in Casco. Concepts tumbled through my mind: delusion, paranoia, and insanity. Or was it much simpler than that? Was it the result of a cumulative lack of sleep? Had Abel started to live out his dreams during the waking hours?

There was no sense speculating about this or anything else. I would have to test these hypotheses against other information, like I did with my scholarly work. Out of context, as this month was to me, nothing could be satisfactorily determined; anything could mean anything. Nothing was sure. Nothing beyond the walls of this house was definitively real. It was too late now to step foot outside and test whether this internal reality had a connection to an external world. I thought of that knocking, that whispering voice calling "Abel, Abel" on that January night. Flutters of nervousness passed through my chest.

I walked slowly out of the office and into the hallway. Pausing, I looked up at the ceiling and saw the cut-away rectangle that framed what I imagined was the pull-down ladder leading up to the attic. It occurred to me that all the material that I had worked through, all that Abel produced on the Remington, was somehow derived from what might exist above my head. The attic absorbed but didn't give back.

Weariness gripped me when I thought about what must be stored up there. How, I wondered, would I make my way through all this material? It seemed increasingly clear that a thorough examination of it would be the only possible way of making sense of anything. It would be the only way of understanding his life. My academic brain flickered to life. "A hermeneutical method is what's required," I said aloud. Tomorrow. Tomorrow. At the same time, I thought, I should really figure out a way to call the Reynolds boys and be on my way. Tomorrow was Sunday and on Monday I had classes. Thanksgiving break began on Tuesday night. On Wednesday the family was scheduled to leave for Putney to spend five days with my parents. Sophia's parents would drive down from Burlington on Thursday for the meal.

I went into the kitchen and fixed a sandwich. I gazed into the field beyond the window. Clouds covered the sky. Below them the light was slowly receding. I had no idea what time it was but thought that it must be late afternoon by now. "Out there," I whispered between bites, "out there, Abel died." "She found him," I said, "she—Juliet or Leah." Or maybe there was no Juliet or Leah. Maybe Warren or Carl or whoever it was at the General Store that day had made it up or heard it wrong. Out there, I thought, out there in the distance. I closed my eyes for a few seconds and when I opened them I thought that what I really needed was a glass of whiskey. I poured a few fingers and went to sit by the Franklin stove. The fire had gone out and I felt little impulse to rekindle it. It was a bad omen, I considered, that I had lost the will to carry out tasks necessary for my own survival. Was this how it had started for Abel? Such fear moved me to set down the glass and attend to the stove.

The wood crackled. The sound no longer seemed quaint to me but, in some elemental way, suffocating and menacing. I picked the glass back up and took a sip. The whiskey slid easily from the glass down my throat. Something must have happened between Abel and Leo Schulz that year, I thought, some secret thing that Abel had been harboring all these years. A secret. I tried to remember if I could recall anything peculiar from that summer. Nothing came to mind. Camp memory, it seemed to me, was of two basic kinds. There were those crystal clear scenes that were stored in the brain with a type of hyperrealism that seemed almost too real to be true. Then there were random still images—images with one point in focus and the rest as some sort of hazy background, lost in the blur of the past. They revealed one particular moment or part of a moment, one feeling or part of a feeling. I thought of a lunch I had had with Walt a few years back and remembered my surprise when Walt admitted to not having a single sustained memory from all those years at camp. "It's all blended together," Walt said, "into a soupy mass of campness."

Over the years, at one time or another, I had reconnected with all members of the final group: Abel, Ethan, Paul, Walt, Adam, Tex, and Danny. In the meantime, Tex, or Stevie Berman, had become Steve Berman, Danny Kaplan, Dan or Daniel Kaplan. Both Adam and Walt lived in New York, and I got together with them from time to time. Adam was a journalist who specialized in business and wrote for an online magazine called *Real Money*. Walt was also a writer, a novelist. His first and only novel, called *The Journey North*, took place in the seventeenth century and centered on a diplomatic mission by colonists stationed at a frontier fort on the southern Maine coast to discuss a peace treaty with the Native Americans, who had just launched a major raid on the fort and wiped out the surrounding village. The mission was undertaken in bad faith, for the military outpost had already called on Boston for reinforcements and was getting ready to get revenge and then some, information unknown to the "peacemaker," George Prescott, a deeply religious man whose worldview ranged from the utterly pragmatic to the deeply apocalyptic. It was a tremendous book, well-deserving of its many prizes. It had sold well, though not well enough to support Walt and his family for more than a year of Manhattan living—a pressure that Walt felt acutely, as he would describe to me during our thrice-yearly nights of binge drinking.

Tex, or Stevie Berman, lived in San Francisco, and I had last seen him in 2007, when in the area for a major Jewish studies conference being held at Stanford. I had been staying in Palo Alto and took the train into the city early Sunday morning to meet him. Stevie told me almost immediately that he didn't have much time. He seemed generally agitated or anxious. I asked a bunch of ordinary questions and got a string of evasions and vague statements in response. He was dressed in a baggy pair of khaki pants and a dark-green sport coat that looked to be a size or two too large. It wasn't just that the clothes were poorly fitted—they were also ugly and of bad quality. We had lunch, during which I caught Stevie checking his watch at least half a dozen times and his phone every ten minutes.

Ethan and Danny Kaplan. I closed my eyes and thought of the time I'd seen Danny Kaplan since we all parted on that rainy August day so long ago, lifetimes ago. I was standing in front of the statute of Jan Hus in Prague's Old Town Square when I turned and saw Danny snapping photographs. Sophia and I were in Prague on our honeymoon; Sophia was back at the hotel spa.

"Kaplan," I shouted in surprise," "Danny Kaplan!"

Danny approached and let his camera hang down against his chest. "Well, I'll be damned. Ezra Stern. I never thought I'd see you again. Other than Abel, I haven't seen or heard from a soul from camp in all these years."

"Not even Walt?"

"Nope. Not a word exchanged with Walter."

"You should contact him. I'm sure he'd love to hear from you. I see him from time to time. In any case, tell me what you're doing here."

"I was taking pictures of this statue, whoever it is."

"Hus," I said. "Jan Hus."

"Never heard of him. Great statue though."

"He was a sort of Czech Martin Luther, though Hus ended up being burned at the stake. It started a series of regional wars, the Hussite Wars."

"You sound like a historian."

"I am a historian."

"No kidding. Well, in that case I'll believe you. What about you? What brings you here?"

"I'm on my honeymoon. I just got married."

"I don't see a wife on your arm."

"She's back at the hotel."

"Problems already?"

"Not really. She wanted to use the spa."

"The spa, I see. Who is she?"

"Her name's Sophia. She's from Burlington."

"Good work."

"What about you?"

"It's a long story, Stern. I floated around Paris for a few years painting, taking pictures, and doing the art thing until my father cut me off. I found a gig teaching art at a high school in Rome. Got together with an Italian woman for a while. We broke up. It was pretty messy. I quit my job and moved up to Berlin. Got my stuff in a decent gallery there. You should come and check it out, take a little honeymooning detour."

"What brings you here?"

"A friend of mine in Berlin, Klaus, an Austrian, told me I should meet a friend of his—a woman. He met her at art school in Vienna, though she's from Budapest. I know, it's a geographic muddle. So it's a blind date. She's supposed to arrive in Prague later today on the train. No clue what to expect. That's it. There it is."

"Sounds promising."

"Not sure about that."

"At least exciting."

"To tell you the truth, Stern, I'm hoping for less excitement and more of the mundane shit. I've had plenty of excitement. I'd like to experience something else, something like stability. Where are you living now, with this new wife of yours?"

"New York. I've been there since college."

"I heard you were rooming with Abel."

"For two years, our first two."

"Did he ever tell you about the time he stayed with me in Paris?"

"No."

"I'm not sure how he tracked me down. I was pretty lost at that point, if you know what I mean. One day, I got this letter, typed on a typewriter, saying that he was coming to Paris and wondering if he could crash with me for a few days. The only way for me to respond was by mail, and so I mailed a postcard to his father's place with directions to my apartment. Two weeks later he rings at the door. That's it. There he was. He looked just like he did at camp. Same expressions. Same basic size and shape. Hairstyle, glasses, all the same. The only difference was the lack of the brown and green. He could have showed up in full camp uniform and I wouldn't have even blinked. For that matter, it's funny to see you, too, without the uniform. All grown up and with a wife waiting back at the honeymoon suite."

"We just have an ordinary room," I assured him. "Abel never told me about this trip, which is surprising. I would've assumed he would've said something about seeing you, one of the eight."

"Well, considering that he was far from open about what he was doing there, I'm not all that surprised. I mean, in some sense it was typical Abel. He's a real one-of-a-kind. I'm sorry that I've lost touch with him again. He sent me another letter when he made it back to

New York, a short note. The trip had something to do with his grandfather. That's what he told me. His grandfather had lived in Paris in the 1930s—and other places. He'd come originally from somewhere in the east."

"From Austria, from Vienna."

"Sure. You probably know more about it than I do. Abel said that he'd found something in the papers his grandfather left behind. He was trying to track something down. He didn't get into any detail. He was going on to Berlin and Vienna—possibly other places, but I can't remember now. It's all kind of a blur—too much substance abuse back then."

The whiskey slowly vanished from my glass. Abel had been in Paris searching for something about Herschel Prager. If Abel had found this missing piece, this key, it was likely to be in the house, in the desk drawers or up in the attic. I thought about the attic. I feared it, and I realized that what I really feared was my friend. I feared Abel—Abel's depth, his completeness, and all that was unknown, all that was essentially unknowable, all that was true.

Ethan Weiss. He had been an awkward boy. He was lanky and walked with a comical, duck-like gait. He had pinkish-white skin, which by midsummer darkened into a strange shade of orange-brown. Surprisingly, he was not a terrible athlete, at least relative to the physical prowess of the group. In baseball, Ethan was a contact hitter and rarely struck out. His swimming was solid, especially his butterfly, which was the fastest of the eight. At tennis he was average, below me on the ladder but above Walt. At soccer Ethan was terrible, on the basketball court he could hold his own—better on defense than offense. He was wily table tennis player, adept at various spins.

Ethan was also shy, and for the first summer and much of the second it seemed to me that he hardly said a word. He read a lot. He never spoke about home, never mentioned his parents, who had gotten divorced only months before that first arrival. Only Ethan's mother came on that first visitors' day—and all the others. I never once met his father.

During that first summer I grew increasingly intrigued by the quiet boy. It could be that my primary source of interest was the way Ethan meticulously cared for a stuffed bunny rabbit named Blackberry, which he made sure to tuck into his bed each morning after the daily round of bunk inspections. Ethan was often sick, and he and Blackberry would have two or three brief stays above the infirmary each summer. When healthy, though, Ethan was not weak. He could paddle a canoe with the best of them. Unlike Tex, Ethan never whined on hikes in the mountains. Ethan was fundamentally strong and weak, insecure and supremely confident, maddeningly aloof and incredibly tender and kind.

We reconnected in graduate school, Ethan having come to the city from Chicago to do a doctorate in clinical psychology with a heavily Freudian emphasis. He was still tall, six-one or six-two, and had grown a beard, which he kept neatly trimmed. He often met me wearing his round, gold-rimmed glasses, a checked flat cap and a tweed jacket—a costume that made him look like a Londoner circa 1910. Sometimes I would meet Ethan alone, other times together with Abel. At times I got the feeling that Abel and Ethan had met without me—that I had been excluded—a circumstance that would enflame a very specific type of gnawing jealousy.

I poured another shot of whiskey and sat down by the fire. I closed my eyes. A photograph emerged from the depths of consciousness. It was the eight of us filing across Katahdin's Knife Edge, the thin trail that led from Pomola Peak to the higher Baxter Peak along a dramatic path of strewn rocks. On both sides, the rock faces slanted steeply down. That day, the day we climbed Katahdin, was a gorgeous summer day, and the picture caught the perfect blue sky and yellowy sun. The group, despite its collective terror, agreed to stop along the dangerous trail and let Uncle Tom, as he was called, snap a photo for the camp's yearbook, the *Warbler*. This hike was the crowning achievement of camp, a test of character and a passage into manhood far more meaningful than any bar mitzvah. We descended from Baxter Peak each with a new sense of selfhood and with an invigorated feeling of unity. For a brief time, a day or two at most, this passage over the Knife Edge created bonds closer even than the bonds of blood. We were a unit—a compound forged in the crucible of shared fear, anxiety, and, ultimately, triumph. The photo marked the halfway point, a stage between childhood and adulthood. To have such clarity of purpose, I thought, to once again know that the goal was simply to make it across without falling off the side—such a feeling, such a feeling, I mused inconclusively. Yes, I had been absolutely terrified. Those impossibly steep slopes to either side, the narrow path ahead. At some particularly slim parts of the trail I had felt my legs stiffen, my knees begin to shake, my mind race in panic. I knew there was no turning back. To turn back would have meant turning the whole group back, the seven other boys, Uncle Tom and Uncle Eddy.

That night, as the Knife Edge was slowly turning into a memory of conquest, we sat around the campfire toasting marshmallows on sticks. Abel, always prepared, went to his tent and returned with a copy of Thoreau's account of his trip to Katahdin in 1846. "Simple races, as savages," he read, "do not climb mountains,—their tops are sacred and mysterious tracts. Pomola is always angry with those who climb to the summit of Ktaadn."

Pomola—the bird spirit, the spirit of the night, the guardian of the secrets of Katahdin. He would come for those who trespassed in his zone with his moose-like head and blazing eyes. "Eyes of icy fire," Abel called them that night, as he told his chilling campfire tales while poking his stick into the mash of coals beneath his feet. As I sat there listening to the coming of Pomola's vengeance, I felt the afternoon confidence drain from me. I worked the brown, crispy marshmallow from the stick and felt myself regress back into early boyhood. Despite conquering the Knife Edge, I was still afraid of campfire ghost stories—Abel's stories, Uncle Tom's nightmarish tales.

All these years later I could still see it, all of it. I could still feel it in my chest. Paul, Walt, Danny, Tex, Abel, Ethan, Adam, and Ezra Stern. Abel had killed himself with wild mushrooms. Was he mentally ill? Paul stared out into that black lake. Danny had pulled up all roots and was floating around Europe, meeting strange women in railway stations in Prague. When we were kids, we had had a poor vocabulary for talking about behavior. There were no words to describe disorder, only the age-old ones—weird, strange, odd, crazy. A kid back then had to create his own system for these concepts, with limited tools.

The morning after Katahdin was cool and dewy. Drops of water clung like diamonds to the poles of the tents. I woke up early in hopes of finally moving my bowels. When nothing was coming, I wandered around the campsite to gather branches for the morning fire. Uncle Eddy would be making buttermilk pancakes. I loved the way the butter melted on the hot skillet above the open flame. I loved to hear the sizzle and to see the pancake batter bubble and turn golden. I loved the moment of the flip, the scent and taste of pancake in the crisp, fresh air, and the maple syrup. I loved camp and my fellow campers, the whole thing, the whole myth. I cared about those boys, deeply so—at least it seemed that way at the time. What happened to that—to that empathy, to that boyhood love? It seemed to me that I had understood and felt more profoundly and completely than I could now. My love seemed meek in comparison, except for my love for the children—an anxious, worrisome, fatherly love.

Then there was Sophia. The fish and the fisherman—that irritating comment. Why had Abel said it? If only Sophia were here now, I thought. I would like to feel her, to gain support from her quiet resolve. Her small frame—insubstantial and yet strong. I first took full measure of her strength during the last stages of Sam's birth. It was as if her body mirrored the cosmic power of a world in perfect harmony. "Nonsense! Nonsense!" I said aloud. What sort of muddled thinking is this? I am a professor of medieval Jewish history after all, I reproached myself, not a schoolboy with schoolboy ideas.

I took my glass and walked into the kitchen. I stood there staring out into the snowy field. Tomorrow I would get in touch with the Reynolds boys. Tomorrow I would walk down and see the lake. Tomorrow I would go over to the Klein house and see if Juliet or Leah were there for the Thanksgiving break. Tomorrow I would go home.

The last traces of residual light drained out of the sky. All became black beyond the window. A mental numbness gripped me; I had thought too much today. My head began to throb. My stomach grumbled from hunger and constipation. The fire would need to be tended. Without thinking, my fingers uncorked the whiskey. I hesitated. Sophia wouldn't like it. It's enough, she would tell me. She had grown to dislike my drinking and my drinking moods. Perhaps, I thought, she had grown to dislike me—my increasing inwardness, my anxiety, which seemed to flame up unpredictably, my delicate and yet expansive ego. Often I sensed that my family functioned better without me around. The mood was lighter, more playful. I had been a great lover of childhood, and yet how could it be, I wondered, that I had so little of that child left inside of me?

Darkness surrounded the house. Night clapped against its windows and walls.

I went to the bathroom. I made a sandwich and ate it while standing in the kitchen. When I finished, I lay down on the sofa and closed my eyes. Inspiration, I thought—I would like to believe in that, in some higher power, a universal truth, a cosmological order. Children have such faith; I had had such faith back then. You can see it in a child's eyes: *belief*. What a cruel joke that a child's belief does not last, that it is replaced with a constant search for substitutes. But nothing can fill the void. I lacked what those medieval mystics had discovered: the vision of a child. This vision could transform letters into numbers, numbers into a mystical map that joined the soul with the universe. Rocks could give water; bread could fall from the sky. I had lived a full childhood. It was a childhood beginning on Pomola's Peak and ending atop the Promethean heights of Baxter. Leading me across that treacherous ground was Abel Prager. Abel was a bird in flight. I dreamed that I, too, was flying alongside my graceful friend. We swooped and swerved over the pointed treetops. We raced each other into the clouds.

Day Five

Much to my relief, it was light when I woke up, and as a matter of habit I picked up the phone on the table beside me and touched the screen. Alas, I remembered, the phone was dead. Outside, the sun was shining, and it came streaming through the windows. Icicles that had formed on the eaves were glistening.

There was no time to linger today, I thought, as I popped up from the sofa and began to run through my morning tasks: wood from the woodpile, fire, stoking the Franklin, water in the kettle, coffee. I made extra this time and took it upstairs to the office in a large blue pitcher, together with a mug. I vowed to have one last look, one final session before getting in touch with the Reynolds boys and starting home.

The office had not yet felt the warming influence of the sun, and so I made another fire there. Once this was done, I turned to the desk. I hesitated, considering whether I should continue on with the journal or dive into something else either earlier or later, something more directly on point, whatever point that was—certainly something about Leah or Juliet or, preferably, both. Maybe something about Herschel Prager. From the desk drawers, I took out everything and stacked the pages in large piles on the top. I was a historian and used to vast amounts of raw material in need of organization and a steady narrative hand. There was no use being intimidated by Abel's papers. Better, I thought, would be to take a walk and clear my mind.

As if overcome with resignation to the task before me, I grabbed a large stack of papers and sat down in the rocking chair. I flipped through the stack until the name Juliet caught my eye. The piece was not dated.

Casco Days

A white BMW pulled up the path and parked in front of my house. I came from the office to see who was approaching. Juliet, wearing her typical summer attire (jeans, sandals, T-shirt) got out of the driver's seat and came to the front door. It had been a long time since I'd last seen her. It had been since that January night, Leah's second winter here. I was surprised Juliet had come.

Her knock was the same as ever. I came to the door. We greeted each another. I ushered her into the kitchen and made some coffee. It was a warm, fresh morning, and I had been in my office thinking about the loon and HDT, specifically about a passage from the record of his trip on the Allagash and East Branch. "In the middle of the night," the line goes, "as indeed each time that we lay on the shore of a lake, we heard the voice of the loon, loud and distant, from far over the lake." It continues, "It is a very wild sound, quite in keeping with the place and the circumstances of the traveler, and very unlike the voice of a bird. I would lie awake for hours listening to it."

As I had suspected for a long time, HDT was also an insomniac. Upon conclusion of the Chesuncook, he writes, "Not only for strength, but for beauty, the poet must, from time to time, travel the logger's path and the Indian's trail, to drink at some new and more bracing fountain of the Muses, far in the recesses of the wilderness."

I wonder whether I have not spent my entire life searching for such a "logger's path."

"How long have you been in Casco?" I asked.

"I'm just arriving now," she said, "I left home early this morning. As you can see, my mother let me use her car."

"I haven't seen your parents all summer."

"They haven't been here once. This is the first summer I can remember when they won't be coming to the house."

"And you?"

"This is my first trip of the season."

"I thought as much."

"I'm not sure why I stopped by. I haven't even been to the house yet. I wanted you to know that I'll be here for a while."

"How long?"

"Three weeks, maybe four."

"What about work? I thought you only had two weeks off."

"Actually, I quit."

"That's good news."

"I wouldn't say it like that, or at least, I'm not sure."

"It's good that you'll have some time here. You've hardly been here."

"I know that, Abel. I wouldn't mind some help opening up the house if you're not too busy. Nobody has been up here since winter. If you're in the middle of something, don't worry about it."

"I was in the middle of something, Juliet, but nothing that I can't find my way back to later on. Hold on," I said and went upstairs to put on a fresh shirt. I'd been wearing the same one for days and could sense an acrid smell coming from the armpits.

We drove the short distance to the Klein house without saying much. The field in front of the house - on the other side from the lake - was in an atypical state of overgrowth, though for this reason far more beautiful than usual. Dandelions, lupines, and a few magnificent red poppies textured the grassy surface. I paused and wondered whether one could still find a few small sweet strawberries buried away from the rabbits and squirrels. I thought about asking Juliet if we could put our chores on hold and check the field but then concluded it would be best simply to go along with what she wanted.

We went into the house and turned things on, opened things up, got the water running from the well, wiped away the cobwebs, and swept up the dead houseflies. I shook out the large living room carpet and cleaned the ash out of the fireplace. Juliet worked in the kitchen. After that, I walked through the house to make sure nothing was amiss - no windows broken, no critters lured into the house for shelter during the winter months. All looked good. From above, Leah's enormous painting loomed over me. Leah loomed.

"Abel," Juliet said as she saw me staring up at the painting, "could you go and get a package of light bulbs from the closet in the little room at the end of the hall? The one to the left."

My heart leaped and my stomach clenched. The little room at the end of the hall on the left - how was I to go back in there? "I don't think so," I responded.

"Why not?"

"I don't know where the bulbs could be."

"On the shelf, above the hanging things. They should be easy to see."

"I'd rather not."

"What are you being so weird about? Just go get the bulbs so we can have some light in here. The LEDs."

"Fine," I said and walked slowly to the back of the house. I pushed open the door and entered. There was no sign of anything now, no sign that anything had happened there. Just a room, an empty room. I found the bulbs quickly and left, shutting the door behind me. Click, the door latched shut. The small space might as well not exist, such a small space as that. The only thing to recommend it was the side-long view of the lake it afforded - that frozen, moonlit lake.

She took the bulbs and replaced two in the kitchen. I used the third in the living room. I enjoyed watching her put in the bulbs, the way her body stretched out toward the ceiling like a dancer, the graceful arch in her back, the exposed midriff.

"Let's go for a swim," I suggested and she agreed. For the past few days the lake had been a perfect temperature, the water a velvety texture.

"Do you have a bathing suit under there?" she asked me.

"No," I said, "I'll just go in with my underwear."

"Go get my blue suitcase from the trunk and I'll change into my suit," she said.

When I brought the suitcase back inside she unzipped it and found a yellow bikini. To my surprise and delight, she casually stripped off her clothes and changed right there, realizing, I suppose, that I could not peel my eyes from her.

We walked down to the lake and to the end of the Kleins' dock, where Juliet executed a graceful dive. I followed her immediately. The water felt cooler than it had on the previous days, though perhaps it could have been that my skin was hotter, more aware and alive. We swam out a ways to get the view of the lake beyond the jetties. In the distance, a few motorboats cut through the water. Sailboats moved back and forth in front of the girls camp across the way. It was a summer scene, a scene of everyday life. A dragonfly flew close by my hand and I waved it away, though was soon sorry for it because I realized it was a Violet Dancer damselfly, no common sighting, and tried to follow it for as long as I could as it zigzagged away. Eventually its thin body and diaphanous wings vanished into the blue.

Juliet swam up next to me and was treading water. I moved closer to her and put my hands on her waist. We kissed, and as we did, our mouths sank below the surface, giving us a drink of lake water, which was nothing bad after all.

With that, Juliet was back, back in Casco, and I was happy she was back. It had been a long time. Summer had finally returned with the last gasp of wild strawberries.

We drove to Naples for dinner that night, my first dinner in a restaurant since leaving New York. I found the experience ridiculous and wondered why I had sought it out with such gusto in the past. At the same time, I enjoyed it, enjoyed being out with Juliet and not inside my house with Leah's picnic basket. After dinner we took a walk along Sebago Lake. Juliet told me that Hagerson was set to arrive the following day. The confession upset me and I spoke in an uncharacteristically strident way.

"Are you kidding me?" I said. "Why is he coming? Can't we have some time without the wrestler?" I paused and then added, perhaps unwisely, "Or anyone else?"

"Rick comes every summer," she said calmly. "He's like family."

"Family," I began and then checked myself. The wrestler, I thought and then stifled it. Juliet looked away and out to the lake. An old riverboat ferry was moving into dock and the buzz of night revelers could be heard aboard. We started again on the path and Juliet bought an ice cream the flavor of blueberry cheesecake, which I found radical and repulsive. I took lemon sorbet.

She drove me home. I asked her to come in. She hesitated and then agreed. When we got inside she asked what I had been working on.

"Two things," I told her, "a piece about my grandfather and another piece. Something I don't want to get into now."

"When I told Rick I was coming up here he asked if I was going to see you."

"That's what he said, 'to see'?"

"Yes."

"What did you say?"

"I said I would see you."

"What did he say?"

"He asked why I would do that."

"And?"

"Nothing surprising. I told him I wanted to, that's all. Later in the day he sent me an article you wrote for the Global Affairs Journal. He said it was the last thing you published before you went into hiding, before you gave everything up." I looked at her blankly, not knowing what to say. "I read it," she continued. It seemed like she was going to say something more but then stopped herself.

When it seemed like she might continue I said, "Don't say anything about it. Please don't. Not now. You just arrived. That's a topic for another time and place. I wrote it a long time ago. Leave it in the wrestler's world."

"Fine," she said, "but I hope we can come back to it some other time. Not tonight. I understand. Not now. And to your books, too. I have them all back in Connecticut."

How can I describe the feeling of making love to Juliet again? It was like reaching the summit of a mountain and finding that perfect perch on a warm, smooth rock. I fell asleep soon after she did. Deep in the night I might have heard the loon's call.

She had to go early the next morning in order to get to the store and make sure everything was in proper order for the wrestler's arrival. He was due into Portland by noon and at the house by mid-afternoon. I had grown accustomed to a short northern summer - but this short? Less than a day? None of it made sense, none of it.

No word that night from Juliet. Perhaps the wrestler had pinned her down. The thought bothered me a great deal. My night was restless and sleepless. The following day, I was canoeing on the lake when he pulled up beside me in the Kleins' kayak.

"Prager," he said, "enjoying the weather?"

"What's there not to enjoy?"

"True enough. It's great to be here. Too bad we couldn't make it until now. I missed this place."

"I bet."

"Still hiding?"

"If you want to call it that," I said and made some soft strokes with the paddle. "I prefer to call it living."

"On a day like today I sure as hell can't blame you. And now, after the election, who the fuck knows what's going on. Not that it wasn't expected. It was clear to see from a mile away. You didn't need to be an intelligence operative to know that Obama would win, right? On the other hand, I doubt it will matter much in the end. The good guys are still good and the bad, bad."

"Are you sure about that?"

"Pretty fucking sure. But hey, maybe it's time you got back into the game. Juliet asked me if there was anything I could do to help you out. You know, to maybe pull you out of here for a while. I told her I could make a few calls if you wanted. It's a good time for you, Prager, your team has just taken the field."

"I don't have a team," I told him, "I wrestle alone."

"With whom are you wrestling, may I ask?"

"Myself."

"In that case, how about coming by for a game of chess later? We'll play out on the deck. Do you play?"

"Sure," I said, "I play."

"It's settled. Come by after you're done on the lake. Juliet is going to pick up some sandwiches at the store. Should I call her and tell her to get you something?"

"No thanks," I said.

"I've got some beer, so don't worry about that. A drink and chess on the deck this afternoon, then. See you there," Hagerson said and darted off.

That afternoon, I found him sitting on the deck sunning his body and reading a history of Kissinger's China diplomacy.

"Beer?" he asked, as if he were completely at home in the Klein house, which I guess he was.

"That would be great," I said, though I didn't know if this were true. Even such details were muddled up by the unfolding situation.

"Perfect," Hagerson said and retrieved a large bottle
from a cooler stationed beside him. "I picked up some Chimay
on the way out here. You can't find much worth drinking at
the Casco store. This is the best stuff you can get. I got
used to it when I lived in Brussels. They sent a young gun
like me to get slapped around by the Europeans over Iraq,
if you can believe it." He poured two glasses of the coppery
liquid and handed me one. "Tell me what you think?"

I sipped it. "It's really good," I told him.

He took out the chessboard and placed it on the table.
We set up the pieces and chose sides. I started with white. It
had been a long time since I'd played and even longer since
I'd played steadily. My father taught me after my mother
died. It was an activity we could do together without saying
much, perfect for those next few years.

When the game with Hagerson began I suddenly felt incredibly nervous and realized that I really wanted to win.
No, I badly needed to win. This was an unsettling realization, as I hadn't competed like this in years and had previously thought that the competitive bloodlust was socially
determined rather than instinctual. I played an aggressive
opening, challenging Hagerson all over the board, trying to
provoke early conflict and capture. But the wrestler didn't
take the bait. He played calmly and confidently. Then, all
of a sudden, he shifted into attack mode. My whole plan
unraveled. My advanced line of pawns broke apart and he
picked them off one by one. There was no preventing full
collapse now. His major pieces sprang from their redoubts
and pressed me back. I tried to pretend that I was still in
it. I sipped my beer and considered each move, at times holding or stroking my chin. All it took was a slight lifting

of his eyes and a little curl of his lip for me to know that he knew that I knew that the game was over. I was finished. We played a second game and he again beat me decisively. It turned out that I didn't have it in me to grapple with the wrestler. He was the stronger player, the better tactician, the more powerful mind.

"You know, Prager," he said after the conclusion to the second game, "if you don't mind me saying, I'll tell you what your key problem is."

"What's that?" I said and slurped some of the creamy head from my newly filled glass of beer. In truth, the Chimay was fantastic.

"You get fixated on one line of attack or one point of defense, whatever the case may be. Even when it's bound to fail or destined for gridlock, you don't abandon it but instead keep orienting around it. Meanwhile, your opponent, in this case me, starts shifting the game somewhere else, taking over the direction of the board. Before you know it, you're being flanked on one side or another."

"You're saying I lack vision," I said in an attempt to sum it up.

"You could put it that way. I'd say that you have a hard time letting go, even when you know your situation is hopeless. It's a typical type of human - especially male - stubbornness. Men have some basic desire to play out an ill-fated hand. You knew early on, for example, in the second game that you were not going to win the center with the structure you had in place. Yet you continued with it. Why? Because you didn't want to think of an alternative? Because you'd rather try to maintain strength, albeit a slowly diminishing one, than embrace chaos? You have no faith in your tactical mind. That's what surprised me."

"Sorry to disappoint," I said peevishly.

"Don't get sour, Prager. Chess is chess, after all. And life is life."

Juliet came out of the house wearing her yellow bikini with a white T-shirt over it. I suspected it might have actually belonged to Hagerson, as it hung down to her mid-thigh area. She handed the wrestler a sandwich wrapped in wax paper and he quickly unwrapped and began to eat it. The bloody roast beef made me start to salivate like a dog. "Thanks babe," he said, with his mouth stuffed full. He slapped her on the back of the thigh below the T-shirt. The sound was jarring and it, combined with the beer, sun, and mental exertion started to make my head spin. I needed to retreat and lie down.

I stood up and thanked Hagerson for the game.

"Hope to see you soon, Prager," he said and added, "Come by anytime."

"I'll walk you back," Juliet said and slipped on her sandals.

When we were about fifty yards from the house Juliet said, "What's your problem? Rick is being perfectly friendly. What more do you want? Why don't you try to relax and have a good time?"

"How long is he staying?"

"I don't know. Two weeks, I guess. I think he's going to leave on the Sunday after Casco Days. He wants to be here for that."

"The carnival? He's staying for a small village carnival?"

"He's attached to it, like I am. It's part of our childhood. We loved it as kids. And it's actually still nice to go, to see people, to be part of the little community here. Have you ever been?"

"Not once," I said.

"That's a shame. We'll have to change that this summer."

"I'm not big into carnivals."

"Come on, Abel. It's fun. We'll eat some hamburgers and waste some money on games. You can try to win me a stuffed bear, one of the really big ones. That's what local boyfriends do."

"Then maybe the wrestler can try it."

"Please, don't be petulant, not after all that's happened. It's summer now. We're going to enjoy it."

We turned off the road and onto my path. When we got to the house I invited her in.

"Just for a bit," she said, "Rick is going to take me sailing this afternoon."

"Is that so? Well, then," I said and kissed her forcefully.

"You're much less tame when there's another wolf prowling around," she said.

"Is that why you invited the wrestler?"

"Maybe it is," she said. "It's nice to see the man in you."

"What do you usually see?"

"A boy," she said, "a sensitive boy frightened by the world."

"That's completely wrong. I'm not afraid of the world. I'm embracing the world for the first time in a long time, for the first time since I was a boy."

"Maybe Rick should sail alone today," she whispered.

She stayed the whole afternoon. When she left I couldn't help but think of Thoreau and his older brother, John, both of whom, as young men, fell in love with the same woman, a seventeen-year-old girl named Ellen Sewell, who in the end rejected their proposals. The infatuation came at the same time John and Henry David made their trip together down the Merrimack and Concord rivers, an account of which Thoreau published as his first book. Not long after the river trip John cut his left ring finger while shaving, a cut that gave him tetanus and killed him days later, as he lay in his brother's arms.

For the next days I was gripped by incredible energy. My story of Herschel Prager started to gain form. His Berlin days, those strange Berlin days, started to come to life for me. The world was at the brink and he stood at the center of the chaos and disaster - and he saw all of it. And yet what a flawed and despicable man he was. But aren't all prophets so flawed, so despicable? Yet, I loved him, and at times I even thought I loved him more than my own father.

In a state of heightened sensibility and ebullient mood, I confronted the wrestler again over the chessboard. Again, he defeated me easily. Again he spoke about getting me some leads in DC, and I was becoming alarmed that by hook or by crook he was going to drive me out of Casco. Casco was the setting of his childhood myth, after all, and I was the intruder. Nonetheless, I was developing a certain fondness for him. I even confessed this to Juliet one night after making love. She laughed, slipped out of bed, and went downstairs. I followed her. She went into the field in the back, which was full of fireflies, and walked through the tall grass until she reached the middle of the field. I looked on as the moonlight fell upon her. Her whole body seemed to glow in the darkness like some fairy spirit.

She called out that we should go to the lake. We walked down the path without a flashlight, the moonlight being enough. When we reached the lake we saw that a gentle breeze was stirring the water and that the crests of the small waves caught the silvery moonlight. I'd never seen the lake in such a state of fantastical perfection and sidereal beauty. Amid this scene we peeled off our clothing and waded slowly in from shore. As the water reached our necks, there it was! In the distance, right on cue, the loon. The loon!

A week later Juliet spent the night again. I woke up early, about two hours before sunrise. When dawn finally broke I climbed up the stairs and looked in at her. The night had been warm and she had tossed the cotton blanket away and now slept half-covered by the sheet. I sat down at the edge of the bed and gently roused her from slumber. She looked at me with tired, glazed eyes and then tucked her head back down into the pillow. I told her she should get up, that I was about to leave on a trip and wanted her to come with me. She asked where we would go and I told her that we were headed to Mount Blue State Park to hunt for golden chanterelles and it was key that we arrive early, before the day's bustle began.

Juliet sat up in bed and gazed at me. After a long silence, she agreed, got up, and pulled on her jeans. I was happy for it and told her that I'd prepared some toast and a thermos of coffee for her to have on the way; we needed to leave at once. When I added that I'd made us chicken salad sandwiches for lunch she didn't object.

As we left Casco the morning dew was lifting and the air was misty and fragrant. Juliet put her hair back in a ponytail and sipped at the thermos. After a few sips she said that she didn't know I was into mushroom picking.

I had been mushrooming since I was a child, I told her. My mother had learned the art from her parents, who would take her and her two sisters into the forest most weekends during the summer. It was one of her great passions, great among her many passions, and she could identify almost any mushroom we came across, edible, toxic, or otherwise. She trained me by example, though of course I could never have acquired such a thorough knowledge as a boy. I'd have to resort to books when I got older to fill in the blanks, those many blanks. She had a dictionary of mushrooms - my mother did - written in Russian and published in 1904. Though my mother spoke Russian, she never taught me. I had to learn it at school and did so primarily to read the dictionary of mushrooms she left behind. I was always drawn to the delicate drawings it contained, done in India ink.

My mother would come for me early in the morning, often before dawn, and we would take the car and drive out of the quiet city with our empty baskets and picnic lunch. On the drive into the countryside she would tell me stories about her childhood. She was always calm on these trips, always relaxed, and I never got the feeling, as I did at home in the apartment, that she would rather be doing something else.

After she died, I didn't go mushrooming for a while. At camp, whenever I would spot a good one, I'd just keep it to myself and whisper something for only her to hear. It connected me back to her, to her hands placing the mushrooms into the basket, to the way her face and especially her eyes looked when examining a fine specimen for worms or rot.

When I was older I went into the forests again. I first started with Hannah when we were seventeen. We would spend whole days hunting. Nights sauteing the results and drinking wine by an open fire, hoping that we hadn't made a gross error in identification. She trusted me - she trusted my judgment completely, surrendering her life into my hands, for mushroom hunting and mushroom eating was a matter of life and death. As I spoke, Juliet was staring out the side window, silent, perfect.

My mother loved the hunt and she loved the mushroom. Non-edible varieties she appreciated as if they were rare and precious flowers. She would bend down and inspect them: the cap, gills, ridges, flesh, stem. I, too, came to love it, to love the mushroom and its power, the mushroom as life-force of the forest, its mycelia forming an endless, labyrinthine network deep beneath the forest floor. It is a network of communication and symbiosis beyond our ability to comprehend. If we want to find nature's secret, I said to Juliet, we need to follow the path of one of those thin threads that journeys into the humus of the infinite.

But this life force, I said, also has an inverse: disintegration, death. While mushrooms like the chanterelle promote life, its cousin, the jack-o'-lantern, survives by eating away at its host, speeding rot and decay. Others kill - not trees but humans. The Roman emperor Tiberius Claudius, I told her, was murdered by his wife Agrippina, who fed him a dish of poisonous mushrooms, the "death cap," the Amanita.

My mother had no interest in the death associated with mushrooms, only in their life and beauty, even the beauty

of the greatest killer of them all, the Amanita. To her it
was a flower, deadly but beautiful. Six or seven milligrams
of a-amanitin, the death cap's toxin, will bring down the
average human. Such incredible potency, the ability of a
mushroom to destroy the human liver within days.

I paused and could see such issues were upsetting Juliet.
It was not, after all, death that I was interested in
but life. It was a day to celebrate life, a perfect summer day. I was in a great mood. The conditions were ideal
for chanterelles - a wet spring and a moist, warm July. That
day, the third week in July, was sure to see the first major
chanterelle eruption.

How long it had been since I had searched for the golden
trumpets, I could not remember. For sure, I'd found many
along the path to the lake or bordering the washes that
ran down the hill through my acres of forest, but these
were spontaneous discoveries, not orchestrated mushrooming.
I hadn't had a basket with me to store my treasure. Instead,
I would carefully pluck the chanterelles with my fingers,
careful not to crush the fleshy stems, and wrap them up in
my handkerchief. In truth, since moving to Casco I almost
exclusively sought out the Boletus edulis, the King Bolete,
the porcini. I am addicted to it by memory, memory of my
mother's passion for what she called the belly grib, the
"white mushroom." For years I had ignored all others: morels,
of course, and chanterelles, oyster mushrooms and sulfur
shelves, in my quest for the belly grib. It wasn't until I
was seventeen that I came to know it by another name.

There we were, amid the insane vibrancy of summer, driving along the tree-lined roads, the grasses at the edge
defying the speed of the riding mower. I thought about how

I had never talked about this side of my mother with Leah during her two winters in Casco. We had only discussed those long, dark February days. She knew nothing of my mother's life, and what a life she had led - a life, a life! How she had lived! New York was not as alive as she was. No other city in the world could have contained her, and I learned to love and live in the city through my love of her.

We came to the park and found the trail. I'd been on the trail a year before and thought it a ripe spot for the golden trumpet. I suspected that someone else had gotten to them before me. Not this year, not today. The conditions were right. The soil and the trees were right. The cosmic order was properly aligned. Sure enough, as it had to be, after some fifteen or twenty minutes of walking, we came upon the first of our harvest around a large cushion of moss beneath a stately white pine. I lowered myself down and picked the trumpets at the bottom of the stems. I looked on as Juliet did the same.

We continued along the trail, reaping a bountiful harvest. At some point on the trail I had a premonition. I asked Juliet to wait for a few minutes and turned into the forest. I must have walked for ten minutes before stopping. I looked around and there, standing some distance from any other tree, was an oak in the prime of its life. Yes, the oak seemed to me the emperor of these parts, a lord among vassals of birch, spruce, and pine. There beneath the oak sat two of my mother's belly grib. They were young and healthy, without the slightest imperfection. I bowed my head down to my Forest God who had led me to this spot and carried my treasure back to Juliet. In the meantime, she had progressed a ways up the path, and I caught up to her at the base of Mount Tumbledown. She asked me what I was doing and I told her about the porcini and removed the cloth from the specimens for her to see and smell the wonder. A glaze of emotion flared across her eyes. Or maybe it was my eyes that flared.

We ascended Tumbledown with heavy breath. As we got higher, the trees gave way and the hot sun bore down on us. We were sweaty and happy as Juliet spotted another cluster of chanterelles, her first pure find, and bent down to gather them in. We were traveling along our way, The Way, and I thought about how I'd been studying the Taoist classics for years, comprehending little and always battling against my own rational impulses, but all of a sudden, as Juliet took my knife and pruned the ends of those chanterelles, a first ray of understanding had glimmered from the blade.

We carried our baskets over the rise and into the mountain's bowl, where there was a lake between Tumbledown's many peaks. It was afternoon now and in our weary and hot state the sight of the lake suspended high in the air produced a feeling of euphoria. From my backpack, I took out our bathing suits. We changed, set down and covered our baskets, and ran for the lake. The water was cold, crisp, and even purer than that of Pleasant Lake. Deep, cold, and clear - this was a mountain lake. We swam a little but mostly just floated, letting the sun beat down on us, refreshed by the cool water.

We hiked to the top of the next peak and looked out over the alpine vista. We made our way to an outcropping and there, at the edge, with the forest sweeping out in all directions, we unpacked the sandwiches and ate our lunch.

There was no hurry today, no talk of the wrestler. When we were done, Juliet folded her sweatshirt and set it down as a pillow. We lay back and I closed my eyes. When I opened them a few minutes later, I saw that Juliet was looking over at me. I asked her what she was thinking about. She told me that it was the first time she had ever seen me resting like that. It made her happy, she said, to see me at peace.

After looping around, we found ourselves back on the trail heading down the mountain. We had already collected our fair share of mushrooms and my mind had now turned away from the hunt. About halfway down we stopped to drink some water. Juliet noticed a cluster of mushrooms and directed me to them, wondering if we should also gather them. The cluster was clinging to a mossy and rotting log. Their petite size, brown caps, and small annuli, together with the brown coloring on the lower stems, gave them away at once as the Galerina autumnalis, a mushroom, I told Juliet, that contained the same toxin as the Death Cap, a-amanitin, and could satisfy the desires of any modern day Agrippina.

She asked me which emperor came after Tiberius Claudius. Nero, I told her - Nero who fiddled while Rome burned.

We drove back to Casco. In the back sat our baskets of trumpets and those two gorgeous porcini. Juliet, the wrestler, and I would feast that night. I cut the porcini into long, thin slices and cooked them with herbs and butter. The taste was earthy and magnificent. Even the wrestler, deeply suspicious of all that was "wild" in this life, could hardly contain his delight.

One chair for solitude, HDT said, and two for friendship and three for society. Or how about this: one for loneliness, two for love, and three for treachery? As I thought about these "chairs," I gazed out from the Kleins' deck onto the lake and realized that this had been a real day, one of two or three complete days I had had since childhood. Over the water flew my misty Fata Morgana, whispering softly to me as the evening breeze whispers in the trees.

A day later - or two, or three - I received a letter from Leah. Its appearance surprised me, and though I was alone in the house, I took it into my office and closed the door before opening it.

Dear Abel,

Let me first say that I am sorry about January. What happened was not what I would have wanted, though I know it seemed otherwise to you at the time and maybe still does. Might it have been what you wanted? That is unfair. Never mind, the winter is over. The spring has come and gone. What water metaphor would you insert here? Something about a river washing itself clean. Don't frown. I don't know anything about rivers and it could be that they don't wash themselves clean. In that case the irony would be clear. Memory is no river. A lake? A frozen lake? See, your insidious way of thinking has gotten to me. I'm no longer capable of saying the plain truth. You would probably say that this is actually closer to the truth, and so be it. I received your letter. Thank you for what you said. Thank you for what you didn't say. Who do we blame when things go wrong, when they spin out of control? Ourselves usually - and usually we are right. I'm sorry to say that I

won't be able to make it to the lake this summer.
The director says that I need to finally start
back in the fall or I'll lose my place. In the
meantime, I need to focus on my work and there's
no possibility to work at the lake at this time
of year. By the end of the term, though, I am
sure I'll need to escape to the woods. Look for
me, then, when the first snowflakes start to fall.
Wait by the stove for me.

Leah

I put the letter back into its envelope and took it with
me to the corridor and then into the upstairs bathroom,
where I retrieved a stepladder from the closet. I used it to
pull down the drop-ladder and climbed into the attic. The
space was hot and smelled of a combination of cedar, pine,
and dust. The dust seemed worse that day than in the past,
and I immediately broke into a fit of sneezing. This was the
first letter I'd received from Leah, and I had not written
her an unsent one, which meant that she did not yet have
a designated box. I briefly considered combining Leah with
Juliet, but then thought better of it. That wouldn't do.
Leah needed a box of her own.

After filing the letter away, I sat there for a while,
thinking of many things and of nothing - listening to the
squirrels scampering across the roof above my head. Though
the letter had been difficult to read, it also brought some
sort of relief. Yes, I was relieved by it; I might even say I
was liberated by it. I tried to take a few deep breaths. It
was summer, I whispered to myself. Juliet was here. I had to
seize hold of these summer days as Thoreau would have. It

was time, I told myself, to follow that logger's path and to stake my claim in the wilderness of the heart.

A few days passed with relative ease. I felt good, exceedingly good, in fact. Those days I sprang up at dawn and was in the canoe on the lake as the pinkish light shimmered down on the world. I was in the woods, on the Klein's deck, in bed with Juliet, in the fields picking berries. Without any effort on my part, the cosmos had found order.

Then it began to pull apart. The first cracks appeared, as they usually do, at night. The pattern began - the sleep decreased. I was pulled back to the Remington at all hours. One day I paddled over to the Kleins' beach early in the morning and from the distance saw two forms there, Hagerson and Juliet. Were they embracing? Copulating? I needed to know. I wanted to catch them at it and finally put an end to it. No, I didn't. I needed Juliet. They must have seen me coming because by the time I pulled my canoe on shore they had disappeared back into the house. When I went into the house and told them I'd seen them on the beach, they denied being there. They just got up, Juliet said. Look, she said, the coffee is only brewing now.

I drank coffee with Hagerson on the deck. He was reading the newspaper from a mobile device.

"You know, Prager, it's amazing. I work every day on foreign policy issues and get briefings from people all around the world. I'm constantly reading the shit, for like eighteen hours a day. And you know what? I still open up the paper and say, 'Man, I didn't see that coming.' It's fucking nonsense."

"Don't start with that," Juliet said. "We're trying to lure him out."

"The longer I'm at State the more I think I understand Prager's point of view, though in the end I still find it self-defeating. You think you can walk away from all this shit," Hagerson said and held up his device, "but Casco is just a short drive from civilization. It can't exist without New York and DC, without the strip malls in North Windham where everybody goes to buy their crap. There is no beauty without ugliness."

The loon retires to solitary ponds to spend it, Thoreau said. I was caught between opposing instincts, to advance or retreat. In the background, as during all Maine summers, winter loomed.

The weekend of Casco Days arrived. Hagerson and Juliet had gone together both Thursday and Friday. It was Saturday evening now and Hagerson was set to leave the following day. I showered and put on a fresh pair of pants and a clean short-sleeved shirt with a collar, something from my New York days. I pushed my gray sneakers aside and rummaged around my closet until I found a pair of brown leather shoes. I wiped them with a damp towel to remove the dust. What did I want? Perhaps to feel for a second that I wasn't in Casco, as difficult as it is to admit. But didn't Thoreau now and then - and in fact fairly often - need to leave the Pond? There was more. I wanted to forget the winter, to forget that January scene and that horrible February when I was eleven. That was part of it. Forgetting. The other part was Juliet. I wanted Juliet.

I drove around the lake and parked on the hill below the village. Darkness had just fallen and the carnival lights could be seen whizzing and flashing from the distance. The Ferris wheel's golden outline slowly revolved through the nighttime sky. Music was playing when I arrived. A rather pedestrian faux-Bavarian band was on stage. Around me, people were playing carnival games, winning prizes, losing contests, eating cotton candy and candied apples, and drinking vats of soda and bottles of beer.

It didn't take long to find them standing at the edge of the tent. Both Hagerson and Juliet were dressed in non-lake attire. Juliet had on a pair of diamond earrings. I felt like surrendering myself to the festive mood and was even happy to see the wrestler. January had been cathartic, in a way.

I bought the three of us a round of beers and we stood talking for a while about nothing much. We joked a little bit, the type of familiar razzing that friends do. We. I. I laughed heartily and freely. Did HDT ever laugh like that? It doesn't matter. Hagerson was drinking pretty heavily and after three more beers broke away from us to talk to a woman across the way with whom I had noticed he was exchanging looks. She wore a blue dress and red lipstick.

Now that Hagerson was gone, I could focus on Juliet. Her hair was free of her ponytail and fell nicely over her shoulders. She had on a pink summer dress that ended above the knee. Her legs looked long and gorgeous - just as they had on that day many summers ago when she got into my car for the first time. She had on more makeup than usual. Her nails were painted pink.

We walked through the carnival, now and then stopping to play one of the foolish games. Even though I had a terrible fear of it stemming from childhood, I suggested that we ride the Ferris wheel. Juliet liked the idea and we climbed in. Slowly, we rose above the carnival, above Casco village, high above Pleasant Lake.

As the wheel turned us up toward the stars and our little bucket swayed back and forth in the air, in my mind's eye I glimpsed the Fata Morgana - my mother was walking down the hill at camp toward my bunk on visitors' day. She vanished. My father appeared. He was lying on the floor of his apartment, alone and lifeless. And there was my friend Ezra Stern leaning over a copy of the Hebrew Bible in our college dorm, trying to discover meaning in this world.

"Juliet," I said, "I want you to stay in Casco."

"I guess I could stay a week or two longer."

"No," I told her, "not a week or two longer, all year. I want you to stay with me."

She looked at me with a frightened expression, or lack of expression. "Stay here?"

"Yes."

"Abel, how could I?" She turned away for a few seconds. Our bucket reached the top of the wheel and the whole structure came to a halt. We swayed back and forth in the night air. She turned back to me. "Abel," she said, "I'll stay with you."

The wheel started again and we rode back down in silence. When we got off I spotted Hagerson in the distance, leaning in and whispering something to the woman in blue, flexing his considerable charm.

A while later fireworks exploded over the little village and faded almost immediately out of sight. The carnival was over. Another Casco Days had come to an end.

The story broke off. I put down the pages on the window seat and gazed over at the huge stacks on the desk. Behind them sat the Remington, its black lacquer now catching the late-morning sun. August 2009, I thought—it was over two years ago. The lawyer's letter came to mind again. "Abel Prager," it said, "requested that you be able to access the house without delay." *Without delay.* I shook my head. There was no order here—no sense. It could be that there had been an original order and that I had disrupted it when I took the papers from the drawers and began moving them around. It could even be that they remained in order now, though organized around a principle that I could not see and did not understand. My stomach rumbled. It was hunger, I thought, combined with the irritation of drinking too much coffee on an empty stomach. During the past hours I had consumed the whole pitcher without giving it any thought.

Though I would have preferred to keep on reading, I knew I needed to get some food to settle my stomach. As I stood up, dizziness gripped me and I suddenly felt like I might vomit. Hurriedly, I ran into the bathroom and gagged a half-dozen times, my body convulsing in a seeming prelude to the ultimate disgorgement. Instead, I brought up only a few mouthfuls of coffee-colored phlegm, which I spat into the sink and rinsed down the drain. When I lifted my head from the sink, after splashing my face with cool water, I saw myself reflected in the mirror for the first time since I had arrived. The image took me aback. The unshaven face, the eyes, red and swollen from the convulsions, the messy, greasy hair, and a smudge of stove ash on my forehead combined to form the impression of a being quite alien to me. It had been five days since I had last bathed. It felt good, I thought, to be dirty.

Nonetheless, it was clear that I should leave this place immediately. I should call the Reynolds boys, get my car out of the snow, and make it home in order to be able to teach on Monday. These last few days before Thanksgiving were some of my favorite of the year on campus. The energy felt right, the air was perfect. The students seemed inspired to work a little harder, to think a little deeper, by the promise of the break, by the earlier darkness.

I went downstairs and into the kitchen. Nothing appealed to me. While I stood in front of the modest provisions, I grabbed a couple sticks of moose jerky and began to gnaw on one of them. The flavor, at first wildly exotic, was now familiar. I followed the first stick of jerky with a cheese sandwich. The combination of jerky and sandwich upset my stomach again. The first mild constipation cramps were forming, but I knew that the process was nowhere near its endpoint. All told, it was rather closer to the beginning—a thought that mildly depressed me. I sensed that the next time was going to be a horrible struggle—and that these negative thoughts and untoward expectations would make it much worse. When I focused on it, I could feel my entire rectal system clamping shut like the tightening of a vise. Sophia had told me many times that the whole thing was psychological—especially in light of the fact that changes (even radical ones) in diet did little to affect it—and suggested that I discuss it with Dave after one of our weekly racquetball games. I didn't feel close enough to Dave for that. Once I tried to discuss it with Ethan Weiss but then pulled back in fear of the Freudian implications of the problem.

Medieval Mediterranean—I was scheduled to lecture on the rivalry between the Italian city-states of Venice and Genoa in the fourteenth century. If I missed this lecture, it would mean pushing back the lectures on the Ottoman Empire, which, in turn, would mean postponing or even cancelling outright the final lectures on the *Reconquista* and the creation of imperial Spain. The course was scheduled to end with the year 1492. Somehow I needed to make it there, to tell the story of the incredible rebirth of the Mediterranean in the late Middle Ages while gesturing toward its decline in the Age of Exploration. Medieval Mediterranean—it began with the Muslim conquests and ended with Columbus, with the fall of Granada, with the expulsion of the Jews from Spain. From the eighth to the fifteenth century, an epic story of war, wealth, and the incredible mixing of faiths and ideas. Medieval Mediterranean—it was this world that produced humanism and the Italian Renaissance, those great pillars of modernity. The sea's death was Europe's life, I thought and suddenly was seized with the desire to stand before my students again.

I paced back and forth in the kitchen, eventually picking up the chunk of feldspar on the table and rotating it around in my hand. There was no doubt that I was getting closer—closer and closer to that moment of death and the meaning of death that would also inversely provide the meaning of life, a life, Abel's life. With feldspar in hand, I went back upstairs and into the office. During the past hour, clouds had rolled in and covered the sky with a blanket of gray. I wondered if it would snow again and keep snowing until springtime. Day after day it would come until the house was buried in whiteness.

I peeled a stack of pages from the top of one of the stacks.

HDT Journals

April 1839

Drifting in a sultry day on the sluggish waters of the pond, I almost cease to live and begin to be. A boatman stretched on the deck of his craft and dallying with the noon would be as apt an emblem of eternity for me as the serpent with his tail in his mouth. I am never so prone to lose my identity. I am dissolved in the haze.

July 6, 1845 [third day at Walden Pond]

I wish to meet the facts of life - the vital facts, which are the phenomena or actuality the gods meant to show us - face to face, and so I came down here. Life! who knows what it is, what it does? If I am not quite right here, I am less wrong than before.

May 31, 1850

I love to see the domestic animals reassert their native rights, - and evidence that they have not lost their original wild habits and vigor.

November 16, 1850

What shall we do with a man who is afraid of the woods, their solitude and darkness? What salvation is there for him?

November 16, 1850

Some of our richest days are those in which no sun shines outwardly, but so much more a sun shines inwardly.

November 16, 1850

I have no more distinctness or pointedness in my yearnings
than an expanding bud, which does indeed point to flower
and fruit, to summer and autumn, but is aware of the warm
sun and the spring influence only. I feel ripe for something,
yet do nothing, can't discover what that thing is. I feel
fertile merely. It is seedtime with me. I have lain fallow
long enough.

June 13, 1851

As I climbed the hill again toward my old bean-field, I listened to the ancient, familiar, immortal, dear cricket sound
under all others, hearing at first some distinct chirps;
but when these ceased I was aware of the general earth-
song, which my hearing had not heard, amid which these
were only taller flowers in a bed, and I wondered if behind or beneath this there was not some other chant yet
more universal.

June 15, 1851

After walking by night several times I now walk by day,
but I am not aware of any crowning advantage in it. I see
small objects better, but it does not enlighten me any. The
day is more trivial.

July 2, 1851

Today the milkweed is blossoming. Some of the raspberries are ripe, the most innocent and simple of fruits, the purest and most ethereal. Cherries are ripe. Strawberries in the garden have passed their prime.

July 6, 1851

Already I gather ripe blueberries on the hills, the red-topped grass is in its prime, tingeing the fields with red.

July 16, 1851

I think that no experience which I have today comes up to, or is comparable with, the experiences of my boyhood. And not only this is true, but as far back as I can remember I have unconsciously referred to the experiences of a previous state of existence. My life was ecstasy. In youth, before I lost any of my senses, I can remember that I was all alive, and inhabited my body with inexpressible satisfaction; both its weariness and its refreshment were sweet to me. I remember how I was astonished. I looked in books for some recognition of a kindred experience, but, strange to say, I found none. With all your science can you tell how it is, and whence it is, that light comes into the soul?

July 19, 1851

My spirit's unfolding observes not the pace of nature. The society which I was made for is not here.

August 1, 1851

The question is not what you look at, but what you see.

I flipped through the pages. On it went, fifty, sixty, seventy pages full of quotations. What point did this copying serve? Clearly, reading it was getting me nowhere. It was true that I felt some sort of close comfort in tracing Abel's mind at work, thinking about Abel thinking about Thoreau. But a thorough analysis could wait until I was back in New York, until I found myself once again in the safety of Whitefield Hall. I moved back to the desk. There was so much, too much. I paused and set my hand on one of the stacks. An inward shining sun, the light of the soul, and the unfolding of the spirit. What choice did I have but to tunnel down toward my friend? The image of the molting loon crystallized before me. I knew enough to know that the loon molted its breeding plumage at the end of the summer and grew a drab, brown coat for the winter months, and then in late winter, in preparation for spring, it molted again, this time trading its worn-out suit for formal mating attire. I also knew that during the two molting periods the loon was weak and vulnerable. The molt, in other words, carried the danger of death from disease or predator. The loon was unable to fly during the molting period; a lack of only a couple of feathers rendered it unable to lift its weight into flight. Migration patterns were another thing: the lake in summer, the ocean in winter, the loon returning to its birthplace to mate and breed.

I stood there with my hand on the stack of papers as if swearing an oath on the Bible. Unwittingly, I had placed my other hand against my heart and could feel it beating with abnormal rapidity.

The end of our second year of living together came to mind. It was a warm day in May and we sat in the apartment on Amsterdam Avenue with the windows open, letting in the clamor and rush from the street below. The semester had just ended; the second year of college was behind us. On the coffee table in our small living room sat forms from the landlord to renew the lease, which expired at the end of the month. They had arrived in the mail some weeks before and had sat neglected while we took our final exams and wrote our term essays. I had a couple of weeks off before the start of the summer session, during which I planned to take an intensive Hebrew course as well as a course in biblical translation. My advisor, the historian Kaufman, had told me earlier in the year that if I held out any hope for a future in medieval Jewish history I had to get my languages in order and my knowledge of the Bible in respectable shape. On top of that, Kaufman told me, I would soon have to add Arabic and Latin and German and possibly medieval Spanish and Ladino. I knew that staying in school basically as a full-time student would be an extreme burden on my parents. But what other choice did I have? I could have gone back to Putney and worked in the grocery store for a few bucks an hour—but that was a dead end.

"What do you think about this?" I asked Abel and slid the envelope over to him.

Abel took the pages out and glanced at them before tossing them back onto the table. "We're going to have to let it run out, Allstar," he said in a certain tone, with a certain something. For some reason, these words, or the way he said them, made me feel like crying. Maybe Abel sensed this—much always remained unspoken between us, perhaps too much. "You see, Allstar," he continued, "I'm moving back in with the big guy. He needs me there. He hasn't been doing well on his own these last years. It took me a long time to realize it, and maybe it's because I don't see him that often, and with him, everything is a matter of the slightest degree. But it's clear to me now. He's not doing well, and I was just ignoring, choosing to ignore, what I didn't want to see."

I moved to the window and looked out into the snowy field. Abel would live with his father until Abraham Prager died in the winter of 2005. Fourteen years. Fourteen years together. As far as I knew, Abraham Prager never thought of marrying again. Never once did Abel talk about a woman having been in the apartment or his father going out on a date. After Lillian, nothing could measure up. It was the burden of that otherworldly beauty.

It could be that the physical separation of our living spaces actually reanimated our friendship. Suddenly, a relationship that had grown rather humdrum blossomed again with spontaneity. We spent many evenings that summer taking long walks in the park, talking about everything imaginable. Two weekends were spent hiking in the Adirondacks. Things with Hannah were badly frayed at that point, but Abel didn't speak of it much, for it was on those two weekend trips into the mountains that I learned about Abel's growing obsession with the subject of water. This seemed to me a bizarre and unexpected shift. I had always imagined Abel would be a novelist, playwright, or poet—or some rogue intellectual like Walter Benjamin. Water, environmentalism, policy, and politics—all this seemed far beneath my gifted friend.

In typical Abel fashion, he was ahead of the game. He began work on his senior thesis project during his junior year. It would be a study of three major African damming projects—the Aswan in Egypt, on the

Nile; the Volta River dam in Ghana, on the eve of its independence; and the Inga dam project on the Congo River in the Democratic Republic of Congo. During the summer between junior and senior year he won a university research grant to study in all three places. The results were predictably impressive. His thesis was honored as the best of the year, with one professor calling it the strongest undergraduate work he had ever seen. His work on the dams got Abel a job at an environmental NGO, though I can't recall the name, probably because Abel quit after less than a year. He spent a year or more writing a book exclusively on the Aswan dam situation, which was published in 1996, the same year he took a job at the Institute for Environmental Policy as a research fellow. A year later, he was forced to resign on account of critical editorials he wrote about Egypt's New Valley Project—at least this is what he suspected at the time. He traveled again after that—going back to Ghana, then traveling throughout the Nile basin states, about which he wrote a long article for *The Atlantic*, and then to Russia for his first journey to the Aral Sea. Another book appeared in 1999—*Water and Power*, a study of the geopolitics of water resources in various crisis zones.

The book led to a new job as a member of the United Nations' Millennium Ecosystem Assessment Team, which was charged with making fresh water projections for Africa and the Middle East. In 2003, Abel quit the UN team and went to work at the Global Policy Institute. I thought back to those years after 9/11—the war in Afghanistan, the run up to the war in Iraq— politically charged years during which I was practically buried alive in documents from the British Library.

Abel and I drifted in different directions, into different worlds. Intellectually, we seemed to have ever less in common. Professionally, Abel was far ahead. Socially, we were spending less time together. A divergence, I thought, a slow and steady divergence. My path led to the bosom of academia and family life—to Sophia, Sam, and Sybil. Abel's path led to this, to Casco, to his death. For most of his life, I considered Abel the only person, besides Sophia, whom I could really trust. Now I wondered if this were true. It could be said that I had lost faith in the friendship somewhere along the line. With fading trust, empathy also somehow might have faded. Judgment might have crept in. Rejection lurked in the shadows. Or maybe this was some sort of rationalization, some self-serving analysis after the fact. It is hard for me to understand the history and trajectory of my thoughts about Abel. Certainly, understanding Abel's thoughts and feelings about me were far beyond this. I'm not even sure I wanted to know. Everything suddenly seemed covered by a thick peel of something. Ego, I quickly concluded. Male identity. Adult male identity and ego. This seemed true in my case. But what of Abel? It could be that for Abel it was something else. Depression. Paranoia. The onset of some sort of psychosis. Schizophrenia. If only the communication had not broken down as it did. This connecting tissue was a fragile substance, no stronger with Abel than it was between me and my parents or my sister Judith or even Sophia and the kids. Sophia was still there, though it seemed strained and fragile with her as well. Perhaps I was making too much of it, perhaps these thoughts were a product of something else, like the gray day or the snowy field or the stories of Abel, Juliet, and Leah Klein.

I turned my back to the field and went into the bathroom to urinate. Then I continued into the bedroom. The bed was made and draped with a plain beige cover. I had always admired my friend's fastidiousness—and indeed, Abel produced by far the tightest hospital corners of anyone in the group. Vague thoughts, vague regrets, drawn from a murky pool of memory.

Concrete. There were also many moments that were utterly concrete, I thought, in order to brace myself against slipping into an increasingly languid and useless state of mind. For some reason, these things were harder to pull upon, slower to crystallize, more demanding to recall. But that wouldn't do. The relationship had been very concrete and those first, crucial years most of all. There was much more than what Walt had called a "soupy mass of campness."

Concrete. The time we saw the snapping turtle in the camp's swimming area was one example. We both refused to dive, in fear of the Leviathan. Eventually Uncle Jim, the head of swimming, tossed both of us from the dock. I could remember the feeling of being seized by Jim's hard, hirsute arms. That was concrete—those arms. Or there was the time when Toby, a boy in the group one year above us, blasted a soccer ball directly into Abel's face during an interdivisional match. The shot mangled Abel's eyeglasses and left a deep cut across the bridge of his nose. The game stopped. I ran over to him. Tears streamed down Abel's face, but he wasn't issuing a sound. It was the first time I experienced Abel's silent method of crying. Or there was the time we spotted the dead moose carcass floating in the Allagash River, followed by a cloud of black flies. Or the time on the Moose River trip when Abel dove into the water one morning and emerged with a leech clinging to his back between his shoulder blades. Or later, there was the first walk in Central Park during the first week of living together in the dormitory, during which we met Hannah and her friend Steffi just days before Hannah left for school in Boston. There was the first trip downtown to the East Village and my first time drinking out in a bar. First experiences, these were the experiences that gave friendships their ultimate durability, if they were, in fact, ultimately durable.

My eyes scanned the room. Abel's bedroom was plain, furnished only with a Shaker-style bed and two matching end tables, most likely, I thought, left behind by the Fieldstons. Handsome pieces, though cold and austere. This was no time for any of this, I reproached myself—for this or any other nonsense, like self-pity, jealousy, or insecurity. No more, I vowed, no more. Nothing more! I vowed again even more vehemently as I ran my palm along the grain of the wood on the bed's headboard. As if jolted, I quickly left the bedroom for the warmth of the office.

Juliet and Leah; Leah and Juliet. I scanned the pages for these names. The hope of finding the path to enlightenment, that secret about my friend, I thought, lay here. "Leah" appeared and I pulled some pages from a stack.

12.10.2009

"I discovered a strange thing," Leah said after taking a sip of whiskey. The winter had blown her into Casco a week ago.

"What's that?"

"It's about your Jeremiah."

"The ice fisherman."

"One day I was in the middle of painting and I suddenly stopped and had the urge to look him up on the computer. I searched for 'Jeremiah' and 'Pleasant Lake' and 'Maine.' I don't know what I was expecting, maybe nothing, but then one of the first links was to an article in a paper called the Sun Sentinel - some local newspaper, I guess. The story was about a young man named Jeremiah who apparently made his home on the lake every winter. He wasn't from around here and so nobody knew much about him, except that he was known to have caught the three largest fish ever drawn out of a Maine lake. Here's the list - I printed the article: a 35 lbs 2 oz northern pike, a 34 lbs 8 oz trout, and a 33 lbs 10 oz muskellunge."

"A beast of a thing," I said.

"Here's how the story ends: 'The legend of this young Jeremiah has only grown over time in fishermen's lore since he vanished as the ice broke up after the winter of 1933 and, as far as anyone knows, never returned to Pleasant Lake again.'"

Leah set the page on her lap and looked at me with some sort of anticipation. There was a long silence and then she asked me if I planned on commenting. I said I didn't.

"Don't you see the issue here?" she asked.

"No," I said.

"Tell me, Abel, what I was looking for on the lake that night. Why was I out there in the cold and darkness? What were you doing out there all those times?"

"I don't understand what you mean," I said.

"Don't fuck around with me. We both knew the rules. Then you deceived me."

"I don't know what you mean by rules," I said. "You talk like we were playing some game."

"Weren't we? Aren't we?"

"No," I said.

"What about reality, then? I thought you were being real with me."

"I've been nothing but real," I said, at which point Leah slugged back her remaining whiskey, slammed her glass down on the coffee table, and left the house.

12.21.2009

HDT: "I am thankful that this pond was made deep and pure for a symbol. While men believe in the infinite some ponds will be thought to be bottomless."

01.08.2010

The lake froze. The snow fell. A terrible spell of cold weather has seized Casco, making by far the most comfortable spot my little office with its own stove. In there with the door closed and the fire raging I can still work in a pair of jeans and short-sleeves, while throughout the rest of the house, even by the Franklin downstairs, I have been shivering away in a thick wool sweater. A brutal cold, some ten degrees below zero.

Today, however, the cold spell breaks and the sun shines with unusual vigor for this time of year. I decide to break out of my office and go for a hike, my first since early December, if not before. I prepare two chicken salad sandwiches for the journey, a thermos of coffee, my canteen, and a couple of oranges. The plan is a simple one - I will walk down to the lake and ski across it to adjoining Parker Pond. I will continue across the length of this smaller cousin until the end, at which point I will abandon the skis and polls and hike a couple of miles to Rattlesnake Mountain. There I will climb to the lookout point just below the true summit and take in the view of the surrounding lakes, which are strung together like a bracelet of frozen jewels, Sebago to the south, Long Lake to the west, Pleasant and Thompson Lakes to the north, and Crescent to the east.

The walk down to the lake is easy. The snow, while deep, is uneven, and I am able to wind my way over shallow paths until I reach the road through the woods, which has been spared the heavy snowfall by the canopy of evergreen branches overhead, now drooping in on me from the weight of the snow. By the time I reach the lake I am warm and decide to strip off the sweater I am wearing beneath my jacket. I slip on my ski boots and click into my father's old cross country skis and slide onto the frozen lake. The sky is a pale blue and the reflection of the sun against the snowy and icy surface of the lake is nearly blinding. I am forced to wear my sunglasses, another item that used to belong to my father. As soon as I am moving, I feel a wave of energy course through me. I quickly find my rhythm - not fast, not slow, a respectable, steady pace. I am happy for the time being not to go by the Klein house, for I am headed in the opposite direction on my way to the mountain. Mountain indeed! The Rattlesnake is but a hill, even if it is the highest point around.

I lose myself as I ski and think of absolutely nothing but the back and forth of my legs, the slide and catch of the newly waxed skis on the snow, the extended leg and the thrust forward, the body as precise machine. I am no great skier and have not noticeably improved since I learned in Switzerland as a boy, when my father boarded me for a month in the mountains while he saw to business in Zurich and Geneva. I feel this Swiss education now, this Swiss precision, as my legs thrust and pump back and forth.

The trip across the lake goes quickly and I glide under the low bridge that separates Pleasant Lake from Parker Pond. The pond is quaint by comparison and I am soon across it. At this furthest point, I pop out of my skis and stick them and my poles into the snow. I exchange my ski boots for hiking boots and set off toward the Rattlesnake.

The next part of the trip is the least pleasurable, as I am forced to make my way a good distance along the side of a country road, which has been narrowed by snow banks on either side. Each time a car races by I feel my life imperiled, though luckily the day is light on traffic. At last, I wind my way by Coffee Pond and head into the forest and, without the help of a trail, to the base of the Rattlesnake.

The distance isn't far and the thick cover overhead has prevented the snow from gathering with much depth here. Soon, I am at the base and start the ascent. No more than half an hour later and I find myself at the best lookout point, where I stare out into the blue, white, and green distance and eagerly eat both of my sandwiches. After this lunch, I recline in the soft snow. The day is warm enough to make me think of summer and I wonder what Juliet would have thought about Casco and the seasons had she also made this short climb to this pleasant clearing. Some ponds are bottomless, I muse, and some seasons, like summer, are both all too finite and, at the same time, infinite or endless. Juliet needs to find that endless element of summer, I conclude, and close my eyes. She sees only what is limited, circumscribed, determined. Leah. Leah arrived with winter. She had been wearing Juliet's clothes again that night in December, the last time I saw her. Her hair, though darker than her sister's, was now styled similarly. Leah had not gained back that weight she had lost that first winter - and perhaps she had lost even more. She was now as thin or thinner than Juliet.

My sleep has been uneven and I am not surprised that, under this gentle sun, I have dozed off and slept for an hour or so. I awake somewhat flustered and a bit startled and immediately drink the remainder of the coffee. I take out my copy of Walden and turn to the end. "Only the day dawns to which we are awake. There is one more day to dawn. The sun is but a morning star." Yes, there he is, the less clever but bolder writer - a robust man striving to break the chains. I don't want to think about these things now and vow instead to carry on and to look for some fruits of winter on my way back to the road.

In the woods, I collect a bouquet of rose hip and winterberry branches, a fine peace offering, I conclude, for Leah Klein.

My skis are where I left them. It is now growing dusky and cold. The sun set but minutes ago and the sky is still rich with the color of deep, reddish copper. Again I focus on the movement of my legs and utilize the tracks I cut on the way out. They have frozen in the meantime and my pace is much faster as a consequence. Soon I am climbing the little hill that leads from the lake up to the Klein house. Through the window, I spy Leah working on a painting in the large room downstairs. Her hair is pulled up and set on top of her head - a new arrangement for her, at least something I have not seen before.

She lets me in and tells me to wait while she finishes what she's doing. I sit at the table and look on as she moves her brush from palette to canvas. As always, I find myself perplexed, confused, and even horrified by Leah's willfully congested works, works that seem to go to great lengths to be without harmony of any kind. I consider asking her about

it and then hold back. In retrospect, perhaps it would have
been better to strike at the issue directly. Something tells
me, though, that this is not the direct issue but a symbol or
a mask for the issue, an issue much larger than the contents
of her portfolio.

Beside the stove I see Leah's picnic basket and it occurs
to me that something delightful is cooking in the oven. I
ask her if she has plans to dine with someone tonight. My
mind flashes to the image of Leo Schulz sitting in this
very spot. She tells me that she is roasting a goose and had
planned to bring it over to the Fieldston place, but since
the occupant of that place was now here, they might as well
dine at Klein Manor. I request that she still deliver the
food to the table in her picnic basket. She agrees to play
along.

Leah goes to change her clothes. She returns in a rather
smart dress. I think about her talk of games and rules and
suddenly feel as if I am in the middle of a performance.
I grow uneasy but have no desire to leave. She brings the
meal over in the basket and serves me a large portion of
meat together with dumplings and red cabbage. She takes
only a very small portion for herself. I notice that she
is wearing a lot of makeup, hastily and sloppily applied.
I feel myself in a mock version of the 1950s household,
ordinary and deranged.

The meat is greasy, and after I spend some minutes hack-
ing at it with my fork and knife Leah tells me to just
eat it with my hands. That way, she says, I can get at the
most tender parts by the bone. I hesitate for a moment and
then take up the hunk of meat between my fingers. "Isn't
it good just to abandon manners?" she asks as the schmaltz

drips down my chin and hands. Isn't it a pleasure to let our instincts rule again? The contrast between her words and her genteel behavior unnerves me. There is certainly a game being played here, though I have no interest, at this point, in determining the rules. She offers me more of everything. I eat until I am stuffed. The bouquet of branches and berries forms a centerpiece or a screen between us.

01.09.2010

Spent the morning splitting wood, afternoon at the Remington working on Herschel Prager. I can close my eyes and see him walking the streets of Berlin - the grimy alleys in the Scheunenviertel, the leafy streets in Grunewald and Zehlendorf. I resolve to bring down the letters from the attic that I retrieved from Dr. Hoffman. I know it is the only path forward for my work. Yet it is precisely the path I want to avoid. What paths are there other than those we want to avoid?

01.10.2010

I come home from a long afternoon walk and discover Leah's picnic basket on my kitchen table. Leah is nowhere in sight. I haven't seen her since we ate the goose together. Though I am not one to fervently guard my privacy, the notion that Leah has come into the house without me being there is unsettling. It occurs to me that the intrusion might not have stopped at the kitchen. There is a chance she went further and higher - perhaps all the way into the attic. It isn't likely. It would take a certain type of courage to pull down that ladder and ascend into those regions. Leah doesn't possess such courage, I conclude, though I have reason to doubt my judgment here.

Opening the basket, I discover a pot wrapped in a towel. I remove the pot from the basket and take off the lid. A soup sits inside. The basket also contains an envelope and I open it up. "Dear Abel," a note reads, "here is a borscht for you. I know you liked it so much as a child. If it is cool by the time you come to it, reheat it and add some sour cream to your bowl. Clip some of the fresh parsley I have left for you."

The soup is delicious, reminiscent of the borscht my mother made. I wonder if I mentioned this to Juliet and she said something to Leah, for it is impossible that I would have told Leah directly. The thought doesn't linger long. After I finish two large bowls of soup, I empty the rest into a smaller vessel and wash the pot. I take the pot and basket down the road to the Klein house, though, finding that Leah is not home, I leave both in front of the door.

01.11.2010

A warm winter day. Night. In one of the pines not far from the house I hear the hoot of a barred owl. This is the fifth or sixth straight night the owl's voice keeps me company. It is a peculiar feeling to have this fierce predator living close to me. If I were to consider the totemic value of this beast, I would postulate that either I needed to become fiercer or that some acute danger lurked nearby. It strikes me that if I am a mouse, Leah is an owl.

01.12.2010

I write a harsh letter to Juliet and mail it in the afternoon from the General Store. I tell her to return immediately to Casco. Winter has gone on for far too long
already. Last night, late at night, I heard the owl unfurl
her wings and slash through the branches. It flies through
the darkness, hunting.

01.13.2010

Little sleep last night. I blame the owl. The night stretched
on forever - and sleep came only with the break of dawn.
I woke up in the early afternoon and had the strong sense
that someone had been in the house. There was nothing to
conclusively prove this - but I sensed it, I know it.

01.14.2010

I walk across the frozen lake to the girls camp. The camp,
of course, is idle and empty now. I realize that although
I have observed the camp from across the lake for years,
I have never been to the grounds. It's true that I have
ventured with my canoe near the camp's edge, close enough
to see the girls in the field dressed in their white and
blue uniforms, and many times I have crossed paths with the
girls' vessels in all regions of the lake. Blue and white
with yellow details - these were the camp's colors, a far
cry from our forest green and brown.

When I set foot on the snowy ground I immediately feel
like an intruder, like one of those characters in the camp-

fire stories that the counselors there undoubtedly tell
each summer. I am the crazy loner from the other side of
the lake: the other side - a truly horrifying thought. And
why? Why are we frightened by spots which can be filled
only by the imagination? Why is our imagination as dark,
as thorny as it is? The lone, bearded man from the other
side of the lake. I am he. We had a story of such a man -
a man, as the story went, whose youngest son accidentally
drowned in the lake many years before. He, the man, sits
on his dock and gazes across the lake at our camp, imagin-
ing that one of the young boys he sees there is his young
boy, his dead boy, still among the living. After some time,
the man becomes so convinced that his boy is there that he
decides to ride over to the camp in his small motorboat to
bring him back, though, as we all understood, he is simply
intent on kidnapping a camper. His plot is foiled and he is
sent to a mental asylum in nearby Augusta, where for many
years the doctors try to rid him of his delusions. Finally,
he is placed on medication and released. He returns to the
lake, back to his dock - staring across the lake again at
the camp, thinking again about his son. We trembled at the
thought of him - as the girls trembled at the sight of me,
the lone canoeist.

There is a large field and there are rows of bunks. Everything is well maintained, every structure boarded up
and padlocked for the winter. A boathouse near the lake, a
large structure I assume to be the dining hall, the assembly
hall, an infirmary. I walk around a bend in the path. There
is a basketball court, half a dozen tennis courts, a baseball diamond, and a soccer field in the distance. In short,
it is a camp like hundreds of others, but also, I am sure,

singular, singular to the girls, to each girl who wears the blue and white.

Beside the assembly hall sits a cluster of tall pines situated close enough together for their branches to have interwoven. The sun, now directly behind them, casts its light through the tangled mesh of needles and snow. This produces a strange visual effect. A figure appears to emerge from the thicket, emanating from the boughs like a puff of smoke or steam coming off the surface of the water. It is my Fata Morgana. There she is, struggling to free herself from that tangle of arms and fingers. She is ready to ascend into the sky, into the airy ocean. Or perhaps this being of light is the camp's angel and she is now flying away to warn the others that the bearded man from the opposite bank has finally come ashore. There is no way to know. It could be that the angel is headed to the Fieldston place to tell Betty Fieldston - Elizabeth - that an interloper has come from the future. I take one step to the side and the light angel, my Fata Morgana, disappears.

The docks have been disassembled and taken in. The boats are quietly hibernating in the boathouse. It is a camp in winter, a lake in winter, a life in winter. I pause and consider that Leah Klein is such a life. It's true that I met her once in the summertime, on a summer evening, but she has since transformed into a winter being. Winter is her molting time, a time to slowly grow new feathers. I, too, perhaps, have been molting for these years - unable to lift myself and fly. At once, I realize that my wings are now strong and ready. I can burst into the air and follow that angel of light into the hidden realms beyond the blue, into the ultra-violet.

Spots formed, vanished, and reformed in my field of vision. It was the familiar notice: too much reading, tired eyes—a condition known to all historians. I set the stack of papers down on the window seat and rocked back and forth a few times before standing up. Slowly, I walked to the bathroom. The image of Abel watching me at my desk bent over the Hebrew Bible came to me—but I didn't know what to make of my friend's observation. I never really knew what Abel made of my plunge into medieval Jewish history, partly or primarily because I wasn't sure what to make of it myself. When I was a boy, I always imagined my future work would somehow connect me with Major League Baseball—a scout, perhaps, or an analyst, or, as Paul Freeman said, a statistician.

The house was starting to grow dark again. The light was draining out quickly, as it did each late afternoon. I went downstairs and lit a few candles on the coffee table. "A life in winter," I murmured. "A life in Casco."

The painting on the wall caught my eye. I gazed at it now, for the first time really studying it in detail. It was a lake, a lake in winter. The view was from a clearing—and the frozen lake stretched out from the shore in three directions. I moved closer to it. There, on the right side, was a spot that must have been Abel's El Dorado. The spot of white could be, I thought, the little, windowless shed or boathouse. As I stepped back, the scene came into increased focus and I was sure of it. The sand. The shed. That was the spot. Across the lake from the painter, on the only stretch of shoreline cleared of trees, was the girls camp. Tiny dots seemed to designate the rows of bunks. Larger splotches indicated the dining hall, assembly hall, and boathouse. There was no mistaking it— this was Pleasant Lake painted from the perspective of the end of Abel's forest path.

For the sake of some ordinary curiosity, or perhaps out of a vague intuition, I went over and removed the painting from the wall. The first thing I noticed was that the blue paint on the wall behind the painting was a different shade than what surrounded it, clearly indicating that the painting had been hung long ago. After moving a couple of the candles out of the way, I set it down on the coffee table. An inscription on the back said, "Pleasant Lake in Winter," and below it, "Lillian Blumenthal, 1965."

I stood up. She had been here—not only on this lake but on this property and in this house, this room. Lillian Blumenthal, Lillian Prager, Abel's mother.

Thoughts swirled in my mind. None of them made any sense to me, and I was gripped by a feeling that all the progress I thought I had made over the last days had been deceptive and futile. I stood in the living room, amid the candlelight, as coherence crumbled around me. The thought occurred to me that I should abandon the fort now, flee into the wild to graze and live among the beasts, like Nebuchadnezzar. Indeed, I was a beast like the Babylonian king, afraid of knowing, afraid of understanding. I was a historian afraid of the sources and terrified of the reality of the past. Lillian Prager, née Blumenthal. How old was she in 1965? Twenty, maybe. Twenty-five? It was six years before Abel was born. Pleasant Lake in winter, an austere scene—a view of the boarded-up camp across the way. I looked again at the back of the painting, scanning the words slowly and deliberately. Then I noticed a small slip of paper folded up and stuck into the upper left-hand corner. I carefully removed and unfolded it. The brittle paper immediately broke into four pieces. I positioned them together and saw, written in a sweeping, elegant script, "Thank you, my dear Betty. I owe you life itself. Love, Lilliana."

I ran my hands through my hair. It occurred to me that the house might not be properly ventilated and that a creeping rise in carbon monoxide from the Franklin stove could be causing some sort of delusional state of mind and, accordingly, that all that was happening might not really be happening at all, might not be real. For a moment this hypothesis seemed the most likely, especially because it occurred to me as the house grew increasingly dusky and the candles emerged from the background into the foreground of my perception.

All eight of us had helped build the set for Abel's one-camper show during that final August. It was nothing more than a wooden cube, 10′×10′×10′. We had framed it with the help of Uncle Sandy, the director of woodworking, and covered it with pressed board. On the back wall we installed a door, painted gray (the rest of the interior was whitewashed), with the words "Assistant Principal" stenciled in large black letters. Inside the cube stood a row of four chairs and nothing else, besides a large clock hanging in the upper right-hand corner of the back wall. The clock's tick was so loud it could be heard, when all else was silent, in the very back of the assembly hall.

The curtain opened and the lights came up. There was Abel, alone on stage, sitting in one of the four chairs with his elbows propped up on his knees and his chin resting in his hands. He had a blank look on his face; he gazed out into the nothingness. For a minute or two—as that clock ticked—he sat there without saying anything. Finally, he spoke. "Josh Hamburger," he began. "I've known Josh Hamburger for nearly ten years. Every year we've ended up in the same class, chained together, as day is chained to night." Where did he come up with this stuff?

A certain Manichean nature, it seemed to me, carried over from Abel's youth to his adulthood. Always pairs. Josh Hamburger and . . . and . . . I struggled to remember. And . . . Yes, Benjamin Gilman was one. Juliet and Leah Klein formed another. Perhaps Ezra Stern and Leo Schulz a third. Or Abel Prager and Ezra Stern. Could it be? I wondered. Abraham Prager and Lillian Blumenthal. In the end, though, Abel was too clever to stop there, for the ultimate character of darkness, whether it be Hamburger or Leo Schulz, was always, in some way, more heroic than the hero, whose determination to smite the evil, to claim victory over the other, allowed that very same darkness to creep into his heart. Hamburger and Schulz, on the other hand, wound up discovering some deeper humanity, some glimmer of vulnerability—something flawed and alloyed but human and true. A message crystallized before me: only through darkness do we find light, only through sin are we redeemed.

"No!" I said aloud. These were ready-made answers, I thought, as my mind trailed back to my first lecture of the semester, on Augustine. Yes, this was it: Abel and Augustine were linked by the death of a mother. The scene of Monica's death came to me as if I were back in the lecture hall. I leaned back, beyond the immediate reach of the candlelight. There she lay, her sickness ready to claim her, her son, Augustine, bent over her bed in grief—a storm of sorrow in every heart. When her eyes finally closed, when she was gone, this storm erupted in her son, one of grief and sorrow that would propel him further into the realm of the Lord, for it was the divine healing of that deepest of wounds that brought him near to God.

An idiotic analogy, I reproached myself. Foolish, pedantic nonsense. Nonsense! I thought again. There had certainly been no closing of Abel's wound. It could be that he came here to close it or, conversely, that he came here to pry it open again and feel fresh the pain. The lights cut out after the final scene, leaving Abel stranded there in the darkness in the middle of the $10'\times10'\times10'$ cube. Only the noise of the assistant principal's door opening could be heard. The play was over. The lights came up. All the campers hesitated for a few moments, not knowing what to do, and then broke into applause. Punishment awaited him, but it was a meaningless, external punishment. The great struggle of guilt and innocence had already taken place in the waiting room, in the mind of the lonely student.

The wind picked up outside. I had let the fire burn down low and worked to get it back up. When this was done, I hung the painting back on the wall, repositioning it three times before I was satisfied that it was level. A knock on the door, I thought as I sat back down, a boot print in the snow, squirrels scampering on the roof above the attic, an owl in the pines, a loon in the shallows—the images and sounds of solitude and madness.

I leaned back on the sofa and listened, hearing nothing besides the sound of the crackling wood in the stove. What a contrast to home, I thought, where Sam and Sybil seemed to try to outdo each other in clamor. Endless noise, until the latch caught on the office door, then muffled sound, the city version of silence. With half-closed eyes, I watched the flames of the candles dance in the drafty room, the Fieldston house.

A whiskey and a sandwich, those were just the things I needed. My family was probably just now sitting down to dinner—Sam picking at his food with maddening slowness and willful opposition, Sybil shoveling in the comestibles as quickly as possible in order to get back to her play. A wave of alienation from my family passed through me. I missed them. I needed to go home.

In the kitchen, I examined the remaining provisions. The cheese was gone, as were the apples and bananas. I still had a chunk of salami, a quarter of the milk, three quarters of a jar of peanut butter, the maple syrup (unopened), about half of the whiskey, and eight slices of bread. In addition, there remained a few pieces of moose jerky. I took a piece and munched on it as I prepared a peanut butter sandwich, reducing the available bread to six slices, or three more sandwiches. I poured a glass of milk and took both it and the sandwich back to the living room. I closed up the Franklin and sat down on the sofa. Slowly, I ate, churning the food over and over in my mouth. I wished I had brought the medicine my doctor had prescribed for me after particularly difficult months when even the over-the-counter stuff had failed to do the job. I certainly wasn't getting enough fiber here and was likely dehydrated, having failed to regulate my intake of eight cups of water each day, as recommended by Dr. Bennett. In general, Bennett told me that I needed more exercise, less stress, to eat more fruits and vegetables, and to be more systematic with the timing of my attempts to move my bowels so that the body would become acclimated to performing at regular intervals. Irregularity, inconsistency, Dr. Bennett said, only encouraged the rectal diffidence.

I drank the milk and went back to the kitchen for the whiskey. On my way back to the living room I had the idea of sleeping in Abel's bed, instead of spending another night on the sofa. While a few days ago I had rejected the thought as somehow unsavory, now it seemed appropriate or even necessary.

With whiskey in hand, I sat down in the armchair next to the Franklin and looked at the coffee table. A Fieldston piece, I thought, and wondered precisely where Leah had "slammed down" her glass. Thanksgiving was coming. My mother would make the central components of the meal—turkey and stuffing. Sophia would prepare vegetables—potatoes, both mashed and sweet, green beans, Brussels sprouts. Sophia's parents would bring pies. My father and I, like last year, would take the kids on a short trip somewhere to keep them out of the way. Judith had been there last year. In truth, I wished she were coming again. After I got in touch with the Reynolds boys and got the car running and the phone charged, I might call her, I thought, to see if she would come.

Not now, I reproached myself. None of this now. It seemed to me that I wasn't thinking with a clear mind. No decision seemed conclusive or better than the next. Everything would have to be reconsidered when I was back in my office in Whitefield Hall. Everything would have to be run by Sophia. Luckily, I had found a woman who knew right from wrong, good from bad. By contrast, ambiguity and ambivalence seemed always to cloud my mind.

Slowly, I made my way upstairs and into Abel's bedroom. It was dark there and I had to feel with my hands for the edge of the bed. There it was. I took off my clothes and slipped under the blankets. Abel, I thought, Abel Prager. "Abel Prager," I said to myself in a whisper, "does not exist. I am Abel Prager." Louder, I repeated, "Abel Prager does not exist. I am Abel Prager." I fell into a deep, winter type of sleep.

Day Six

I awoke with a massive urge to urinate and rushed into the upstairs bathroom to relieve myself. Tired, bleary-eyed, I ran my hands over my face and through my hair as the urine fell into the toilet bowl. After I finished, I contemplated going back to bed—the sleep in Abel's bed had been far more comfortable than what I had experienced on the previous nights—but then dismissed the idea. I had to finish up; I had to leave this house.

Wood. Fire. Coffee. I ran through the morning ritual like a priest. A line from Abel's transcription of the Thoreau journals came to me: "If I am not quite right here, I am less wrong than before." As I sat in the chair by the Franklin stove and sipped the coffee, I wondered whether the same was true for my friend.

The story of Cain and Abel returned to me, the first murder, the first unnatural death, a slaying of brother by brother. Both make a sacrifice to God. Abel, a herder, gives the choicest newborn from his flock, while Cain, a farmer, brings fruits of his harvest. God prefers Abel's offering to Cain's. Cain is sullen. God speaks to him and says, "Sin crouches at the door; its urge is toward you, yet you can be its master." Cain says something to Abel. They go out into the field. There, Cain kills his brother. "Where is your brother?" God asks. Cain responds, "Am I my brother's keeper?" There was much to think about in all this, and I considered the idea of taking a break from the Karaite manuscript to look into the story of Cain and Abel in a deeper way, maybe in a theological or moral way. "Am I my brother's keeper?" Yes or no? The story of Adam and Eve teaches personal, individual responsibility before God—a moral universe in which every actor (Adam, Eve, Serpent) takes responsibility for his or her own actions and faces the just consequences of them. Adam is not the keeper of Eve. Eve is not the keeper of Adam. Are we, then, meant to infer from the tale of Cain and Abel that we are not only responsible for ourselves but for the well-being of others? Or is our only obligation not to harm them? If Cain had let Abel starve to death, would God also have punished him? Thoughts tumbled through my head as I sipped my coffee. *Its urge is toward you*, I said softly to myself, *yet you can be its master*.

"Abel," I said, "Abel Prager. Cain and Abel." Where, I wondered, should I go from here? Upstairs—yes, I would have to go upstairs again. There, I would skip ahead to the last months, or even weeks, of my friend's life to gain the closure I needed. After that, I would walk to the General Store, get hold of the Reynolds boys, and go home. That was it; it was that simple. The rest of it—whatever "it" was—could wait. It could wait for springtime. Sophia, it occurred to me, must be beside herself with worry by now. I wondered why no scout—some local policeman or county trooper—had been dispatched to check up on me. It could be that Sophia knew me well enough to know what was going on, to know what sort of quest I had undertaken. I found this idea both comforting and horrible. If she knew me so well, how could it be that I knew my friend so poorly? I went upstairs and into the office. I discovered that the wood basket there was empty and went down again to fetch some logs from the pile. Back I trudged with the logs. After a few minutes the fire was blazing.

There were four large stacks on the desk with somewhere around two thousand pages in each. This represented an incredible amount of labor. Eight thousand pages of material typed on the Remington—and all just an expression of what I assumed to be a much larger archive in the attic. I removed the stacks one by one and placed them on the window seat. After this was done, I took the first of them and sat down with it in the rocking chair, feeling its ponderous weight on my lap. I started to flip through the pages. It contained a mix of journal entries and a combination of notes and narrative about Herschel Prager, the latter of which made up more than half the stack. The journals were some of the first Abel wrote in Casco, beginning in June 2005, Abel's first month there. Perhaps, I thought, the beginning was a better place to start than the end, for the beginning of something often does a better job forecasting the fate of that thing than the period leading directly to ultimate demise. I paused and considered this, finally rejecting it, not on the basis of its merits, but because I had made a decision and wanted to stick to it, to see it play out. Hagerson was right, I thought, when he said that men can't help playing out losing hands.

I placed the whole pile on the floor beside me and took up the second stack. More Herschel Prager, more Casco atmospherics, poems, journal entries, transcriptions of quotes from Simone Weil, Kierkegaard, Defoe, at least a dozen long pieces on Jeremiah the ice fisherman and mantic, lists of mushrooms discovered on Abel's acreage with short descriptions of the specimens, the localities in which they were discovered, and the dates of the finds. Again, I deposited the pile on the floor and took up the next, the third one. Here I encountered more journals, a long treatise on Thoreau, miscellaneous pieces—observations, aphorisms, short vignettes. About three-quarters of the way down the third stack I saw the year 2011 emerge. January, no February, no March, April, May, June, July, no August, September, October, November 1, the final day of the journal, at least of the journal that had been transformed from pen and paper into the Remington's black ink—if, in fact, a pen-and-paper version existed. Curious, strange, peculiar that he would have taken it up so close to the day of death. What to do about this? Taken together, the 2011 journal was huge—much more than I would be able to process if I were still to leave for home later in the day. I needed a method.

After some minutes of considering options, I concluded that the best tactic would be to follow the mind of my friend through those final weeks, to really focus all my attention and energy on that segment of time leading inexorably to the end. October 1, 2011 seemed like a good place to start. October 1 through November 1. It was an orderly decision. As for the rest, the behemoth totality of the journal from June 2005 until November 1, 2011—this would have to wait until I was back at my desk in Whitefield Hall.

10.01.2011

He writes of his mother, Elena Ivanovna, "All she picked were species belonging to the edible section of the genus Boletus." He could have been talking about Lillian Blumenthal. Love of the Boletus links them - as much as the leaving behind of a son at death; one son (Vladimir Nabokov) an adult, the other (Abel Prager) a child. We fall back on memory. Here is his:

"With great clarity, I can see her sitting at the table and serenely considering the laid-out cards of a game of solitaire. She leans on her elbow and presses to her cheek the free thumb of her left hand, in which, close to her mouth, she holds a cigarette, while her right hand stretches toward the next card. The double gleam on her fourth finger is two marriage rings - her own and my father's, which, being too large for her, is fastened to hers by a bit of black thread.

"Whenever in my dreams I see the dead, they always appear silent, bothered, strangely depressed, quite unlike their dear bright selves. I am aware of them, without any astonishment, in surroundings they never visited during their earthly existence, in the house of some friend of mine they never knew. They sit apart, frowning at the floor, as if death were a dark taint, a shameful family secret. It is certainly not then - not in dreams - but when one is wide awake, at moments of robust joy and achievement, on the highest terrace of consciousness, that mortality has a chance to peer beyond its own limits, from the mast, from the past and its castle tower. And although nothing much can be seen through the mist, there is somehow the blissful feeling that one is looking in the right direction."

My dead appear to me the opposite - full of life, radiant, sauntering through my dreamscape with airy legs and rosy, cherubic faces, their eyes gleaming from some inner luminescence.

I doubt very much that there is a "terrace" that provides such a view as this, at least not one accessible to my consciousness, however robust and whatever the "achievement" - if such things as "achievements" really exist. I peer into the mist, in any case, but whether it is the right direction or the wrong one, I do not know and do not care.

10.02.2011

I enter her room at the end of the hall after she has vacated it to take a rest, following a morning and possibly a night of painting. Her aura and scents still linger there and mix with the smells of wet paint and cleaning agents, the combination of which both titillates and stings my nose. I see on the easel that against a deep black background she has painted a scene of a small village carnival. A sidelong view has a glowing and spinning carousel in the foreground, with its white, brown, and gray horses bobbing up and down. Its movement creates a horizontal whirl of color. Behind it, and above it and all else (food vendors, carnival games, crowds of human-like forms), stands the Ferris wheel, which seems to be as ephemeral as an exploded firework. Indeed parts of the structure have already vanished into the night sky. Even at a young age, I cannot help but feel a sense of enchantment and also nostalgia - even sadness - as I stand there and gaze at what she has just created. An evening, a night, she has drawn out from her memory - a summer night. I find it magnificent to behold - to grasp onto such a scene conjured from her spirit. I long to inhabit this space, to plunge my whole being inside this alternate universe of color and light. A morning of solitude, a yearning for her attention and embrace - while she was here, viewing a village carnival from the perspective of the music tent. Such a morning culminates with this emptiness. She is gone to another world while I remain in this one, this reality, which she constructed and then abandoned in search of sleep.

10.03.2011

Gathered apples from the trees in the field. They are tarter than last year. HDT comes to me: "So there is one thought for the field, another for the house. I would have my thoughts, like wild apples, to be food for walkers and will not warrant them to be palatable, if tasted in the house." A letter arrives from her. It says she is coming in a few days to spend some time in Casco. A rare autumn migration.

10.04.2011

Walking through my woods, I find four young porcinis. I think of V.N. again: "In classical simplicity of form, boletes differ considerably from the 'true mushroom,' with its preposterous gills and effete stipal ring. It is, however, to the latter, to the lowly and ugly agarics, that nations with timorous taste buds limit their knowledge and appetite, so that to the Anglo-American lay mind the aristocratic boletes are, at best, reformed toadstools." I carry my four noblemen home and fry them for lunch. I sit in the office for hours, doing little but listening to the sound of the autumn wind in the trees. In the distance, the loon calls out, marking the passage from evening to night. That red, demonic eye is out there blazing in the darkness. Wail, my friend, for she is coming in autumn. I contemplate the idea of abandoning my rural outpost and finally, once and for all, setting out in pursuit of the wilderness.

10.05.2011

There is no greater moment for a reader than discovering, with Crusoe, that footprint in the sand, after decades of isolation and solitude. True horror grips us. It is perfect campfire horror. I come home from a long afternoon walk and find the following poem typed on a piece of paper and shoved under my door:

> Where had I heard this wind before
> Change like this to a deeper roar?
> What would it take my standing there for,
> Holding open a restive door,

Looking downhill to a frothy shore?
Summer was past and day was past
Somber clouds in the west were massed.
Out on the porch's sagging floor
Leaves got up in a coil and hissed,
Blindly struck at my knee and missed.
Something sinister in their tone
Told me my secret must be known:
Word I was in the house alone
Somehow must have gotten abroad,
Word I was in my life alone
Word I had no one left but God.

I had read this poem aloud to them on that last night of that last summer. He told me afterwards he was deeply moved by it, though he wasn't entirely sure what it meant. He was, and is, by nature, melodramatic, but at the same time is aware of this and works hard to compensate for it. The result is often tense and bothersome, but in any case it seems that I have drawn him in. He lurks beyond the house, barely visible, as a crow wheeling around a tree against a charcoal sky. Crusoe's footprint meant cannibals were on the island.

10.06.2011

Very little sleep last night. She will soon arrive. I sense that he has arrived already, though I do not know what has drawn him here after many years. "Word I was in the house alone, somehow must have gotten abroad." I look at the page on my desk. It is as sinister as those hissing leaves. He is roaming in the dark woods, I suspect, and an impulse grasps me to throw on my jacket and boots and head out there in pursuit of him. He has turned into what my grandfather would call ein Alp, a demonic elf of the night. The footprint Crusoe discovered was much larger than his own. By contrast, the print of the elf will be the size of a crow's foot. "We have two ideas," Borges writes, "the belief that dreams are part of waking, and the other, the splendid one, the belief of the poets that all of waking is a dream." After days of insomnia, my mind struggles to keep any system of categorization.

10.07.2011

It's nighttime and so dark that I can barely see a few paces in front of me. I know he is out here; I am on my way to find him. The logic is inescapable. He is here, and because he is here, I must find him. I do not think about anything - but feel the pulling sensation of being drawn (by the forces of fate) into the woods beyond the field. I start down the forest path. I stop to listen, and listening, I hear nothing but forest sounds. Branches, pine cones, and pine needles crunch under my tread as I plunge into the woods, leaving the path behind me. A noise resounds somewhere around me. I turn around and see nothing. Darkness. I pause. I feel him watching me, tracing my way, tracking me. My heart begins to beat wildly. I know that he is coming to murder me - and that, it's true, he has always carried with him this desire. Another noise. I turn and start running in no particular direction, but after only a few strides my foot catches on a root and I fall to the ground. I am lost now, a mouse for the owl. I lurch from bed in terror and glance quickly at the clock. Only half an hour has passed. Reluctantly, I rise from bed and sit again, as I had all day, at the Remington. Letters - black and inky - bang into place. Words form. Sentences. Pages fill. The night mare - the horse of night - gallops toward the horizon of my consciousness.

10.08.2011

She arrives in the early afternoon and enters the house without knocking. I am in the office, fully absorbed, and don't hear her until her footsteps clack on the wooden stairs. I know her at once by the rhythm of her progress - three quick steps, one slow, two quick, another slow, three quick, one slow, two quick, and the last two slow. I wonder if she climbs all stairs in such a manner or only these Fieldston stairs.

A soft knock on the office door announces her. I rise from my chair and the suddenness of the movement causes dizziness and blurriness of vision. For a moment she appears nothing more than a mass of color, a smudge. I brace myself on the back of the chair and wait for my vision to right itself.

10.09.2011

I reach into the drawer of my bedside table and pull out a slip of paper. I read: "Come to my house without delay." I wonder who wrote this note. I rise from bed with a feeling of dread inside me. Without changing, I go downstairs, put on my gray sneakers, and head outside. From the quality of the light I know it is just past dawn. Intuition pulls me down the road and onto the long path toward the Klein house. She arrived only yesterday and already my cosmos has been reordered. Somehow I know she is waiting for me. When I get to the house, I hesitate and then knock. No answer. The door is unlocked and I enter. Her bedroom door is wide open and I turn the corner expecting to see her there. The bed is unmade and she is not there. All of the other rooms are open and I check them one by one - all empty. Down at the end of the hall I see that the only closed door leads into the small room on the left. Dread courses through me. A sudden image flashes to mind of my hands around her throat, squeezing tighter and tighter. I have murdered her and have stashed the body in the closet in the little room on the left to conceal the crime. Despite this, I sense that I will soon be found out. They are coming and will surely do a thorough check of the house to find the missing woman. The only option remaining is to fetch the body and burn it in the fire pit. The idea disgusts me. It must be done. Accordingly, I rush into the room and open the closet. The body is gone. Somebody has been here. Someone has moved it. I turn in a panic and there is Ezra Stern. Convulsions wrench my body from sleep. Ten minutes have passed, ten minutes is all!

10.10.2011

The thought comes to me that it is possible she never left and what I took to be her return to Casco was nothing more than a return from a short outing to the General Store. Certain things supported this view, like the small glass bottle of orange juice she left on the kitchen table. In

her hand she held a bunch of red seedless grapes, half of
which she broke off and gave to me. Her demeanor was not
of a new arrival. She seemed wholly at ease. Her clothes (T-
shirt, moth-eaten sweater, jeans) were of a Casco type. When
she came into the office she sat down on the rocking chair
by the stove. I had lit it some time ago, and though I hadn't
attended to it, the room remained a pleasant temperature.
She peeled off her sweater and underneath was wearing the
blue and white of the girls camp across the way. I gazed
at her for a while and then asked where she had gotten
the shirt. She told me she had found it in one of the
old trunks in the attic. She was puzzled by my bemusement,
she said, because she had already worn the shirt a dozen
times without me taking any notice. I realized that beneath
my flannel shirt I was also wearing old camp attire - my
usual forest green. Two adults, dressed as children, summer
children, while outside the leaves changed colors and fell
to the forest floor. Camp had passed. Summer was far away by
now. I turned to the window and slowly ate my grapes. They
were sweet and crisp. In the reflection in the window I saw
her eating grapes while slowly rocking back and forth.

10.11.2011

An autumn feeling has taken hold of me. "Now the time of
year," Thoreau writes, "duly begins to be ripe - ripened by
the frost, like a persimmon."

"Like the fruits," he says, "when cooler weather and
frosts arrived, we shifted from the shady to the sunny side
of the house and sat there in an extra coat for warmth -
we too were braced and ripened. Our green, leafy, and pulpy

thoughts acquired color and flavor, and perchance a sweet nuttiness at last, worth your cracking."

Who is doing the cracking here? Surely not the squirrel. Did she come back to taste my autumnal "nuttiness" - back from either the south or the General Store? I hear her move from the bedroom into the bathroom. Moments later I hear the toilet flush. She goes back across the hall and flicks off the light.

10.12.2011

"Summer was past and day was past." The line lingers in my mind, filling me with emotion. The page sits here on my desk. The poem's title, "Bereft," has been left off, clearly the messenger's decision. I can find no meaning in this. He has molted his breeding feathers and is now ashore - the Loon Man.

10.13.2011

A dazzling autumn morning greets me as I wake. With four hours of sleep, I feel refreshed, for it is far more than I have managed in the previous days. The sun is up, the dew has settled - and any thought of frost seems like a distant memory. A warm air - somewhat humid and heavy - lingers in the field behind the house. The untended grass sparkles in the morning light. I stretch my body out and issue a bear-like roar.

Four eggs, two pieces of toast, a tall glass of orange juice constitute my breakfast. It is a great deal more than I usually consume. I sense that such a day as this should be embraced fully, for it carries with it warnings of winter. One thought stands above all others: to the canoe!

Passing through the field, I see dozens of fallen apples rotting on the ground. It is a pleasing sight to all who love the apple and an apple orchard in a semi-state of wilderness. The Fieldston Field - where Betty Fieldston tended her garden, a garden known throughout Casco and perhaps beyond. Often during my first years in the house, I pondered how she managed to guard her fecund plot against the squirrels and rabbits without so much as an inch of wire or fencing. This was one of many mysteries. She, my mother, once spoke of the garden as "Eden" in her wistful, abstracted voice. Though I now own the land, I have not yet found this Eden, and suspect that one must be a skilled archaeologist to discover it - and not, as I am, an amateur hunter of arrowheads. I gave up the garden long ago. Henceforth, God said, man must toil for sustenance from the ground. Here we have the beginning of work, of labor, linked at its origin with punishment. It could be that this coupling of work and punishment was why HDT rejected the domain of labor almost entirely, in favor of another world where work is not a product of punishment but a calling of love. In such a world, the pure Walden water is "mingled with the sacred water of the Ganges."

Beside the path down to the lake I find a cluster of Galerina autumnalis busy breaking down a fallen pine. I touch the log with the toe of my sneaker, watch as pieces flake off, and carry on. The lake is calm when I arrive, not even the slightest breeze disturbs it. A paddling of ducks seems content to drift along on a barely perceptible current. I go down to the lake and dip my arm in to test the water temperature; it is much colder than it was the last time I was down here, some weeks ago.

Flipping over the canoe, I find three spiders taking refuge in the cavity and sweep them out with my hand. From a closet-sized structure at the edge of the clearing, which I constructed my first fall here, I remove a life jacket and the Morehouse paddle. I marvel again at the latter's grace and beauty - sorry that the Morehouse brand is long since deceased. While dragging my canoe to the edge of the lake, I think about where to go, and though creating a goal seems both arbitrary and pointless, I decide I will ride over to the small public beach below the village and walk up to the General Store to do the shopping I had planned for the afternoon. With a few heavy strokes, I set off. The ducks look on, undisturbed.

The problem with fixing a goal like the General Store is that by fixing it, the journey is instantly transformed from an end in itself to a mere means. Accordingly, I spend nearly the whole trip mentally composing my shopping list (chicken, milk, coffee, bread, potatoes, carrots, lettuce, garlic, onions, yogurt, butter, eggs, lemons) and missing out on the lake's splendor. Perhaps I am tired of the lake's splendor.

Coming to shore, I see Jim Bussy and Phil Crawford as they leave the General Store and get into Jim's red Ford pickup. I hang back to avoid them, knowing they are likely to engage me in discussion about certain happenings I am wary of discussing. For years, I have tried not to participate in any of it, and the longer I am away from it, the more I fear it: the domain of people drawn together in pursuit of overlapping self-interest. I fear this type of community.

To think that at one point I was sitting at negotiating tables in Central Asia and Africa hashing out treaties over the life-giving substance of water, and now I am afraid of talking about lake issues with Bussy and Crawford. The truck idles in the parking lot until the store's door opens and out runs a German shepherd. It bounds down the stairs and hops into the pickup, squeezing its way between the two men on the front seat. Bussy pulls out and heads down the road in the direction of Raymond.

Upon entering the store, I order my chicken from Warren, who dispatches Carl to the back to fetch it. It has been a long time since Warren has tried to converse with me and now he simply leaves me to my shopping and continues to work over some sort of puzzle in the back of the daily paper. Now and then I see him eyeing me as I slowly move up and down the store's narrow aisles. There is something menacing about these glances. The thought comes to me that while I did not talk about anything of significance with Warren or Carl, others might have - and probably did. There was no telling what he knew about me, about my current situation, about the happenings (or lack thereof) on that short stretch of Mayberry Hill Road. The sight of Bussy and Crawford, together with Warren's looks and Carl's slowness with the chicken, gives rise to a creeping anxiety that later culminates in my locking the front door of the house for the first time since arriving in 2005. I also lock myself inside the office.

I paddle home against a strong current. By the time I make it back to the end of my forest path I am exhausted and barely have enough energy to walk the short distance to the house with the two bags of groceries. Once home, I crave a roasted chicken but do not feel like roasting it. I long for her to come and put it in the oven, for her to baste it, slice it, and serve it to me. She has not returned.

From the desk of the locked office I gaze out over the field. Something feels not quite right with the world. The day before, I saw Bussy's pickup turn into the McKenneys' driveway as I was on my way to the Klein house. From the sounds of it, Bussy was trimming or cutting down trees with a chainsaw. He worked from mid-morning until the early afternoon. The McKenneys on one side, the Lasalles on the other, Bussy and Crawford down the road toward Otisfield, the Kleins, the young Aiken family who bought out the Wilkinsons five years ago - it could be that a Westphalian system had emerged to guarantee the peace on Pleasant Lake, a peace that could be threatened by the rise of an ambitious actor. Was I seen as such an actor? And was this the reason for the unlikely alliance between the Lasalles and the McKenneys, who had been bitter enemies for many years? I consider this and other possibilities until late into the night.

10.14.2011

A rainy afternoon. We draw down the canvas flaps over the large screen windows and listen to the rain batter the roof of our bunk. Ethan is there, as are Ezra and Walt. Only Paul Freeman is missing. We are playing a game of bridge on two beds we have pushed together. As always, I am paired with Ezra, Ethan with Walt. We play for a while - maybe one or two rounds - and then I start to become increasingly concerned with Paul's whereabouts. Nobody else seems to notice he is gone. The next time I am dummy, I decide, I will head outside and search for him. In all likelihood, he was in another bunk or over playing table tennis in the activities shed. Nothing to worry about, in other words - no reason for concern. The cards are dealt, the bids made, and game after game I am either in control or playing defense. Half an hour passes, still no Paul. Increasingly, I find it difficult to focus on the cards and start losing tricks that should have been easily won. Ezra glowers at me from across the bed.

At some point it becomes clear to me: something has happened to Paul, something horrible. I tell myself to calm down, that I could be dreaming up the whole thing. But no, I conclude, it isn't a dream, it isn't delusion. Paul Freeman is out there in the rainy afternoon and something has gone terribly wrong. Without saying anything, I throw my cards on the bed and dart from the bunk.

I rush down toward the lake, which is being churned by the combination of the stiff winds and the cold rain. "Paul," I shout. "Paul, where are you?" From the dock I see a figure standing on the high-dive platform out on the raft. Without my glasses, I can't tell who it is, though the form looks too slender to belong to Paul. I dive into the lake and swim out there. I haul myself out of the water and find myself face-to-face with Leo Schulz. I look down and see blood on his hands and arms.

"I did it for you," he whispers, "I did it for you."

10.15.2011

"Word I had no one left but God." Isn't being alone with God enough? Alone and forsaken by God would be far worse, as Robinson Crusoe came to learn one feverish night. Worse still, among men and forsaken by God - one would become a being without spirit, without soul. What will become of Casco if the Westphalian balance of power is disrupted? What will become of me if the alliance holds between the McKenneys and the Lasalles? Bussy and Crawford will fall in line. Crowley, Samuelsson, and Winthrop will array on the opposite side. I have little chance, even if I remain neutral, of surviving such a conflict. The casus belli might have been the breach of sovereignty of the Klein domain.

10.16.2011

A sickness of the spirit has kept her bedridden in my bed for three days. She rises only to use the bathroom and eats and drinks very little. I have tried to increase her appetite by preparing dishes I know to be to her taste, but she rejects them, even the chicken I roasted some days ago. "Let me live where I will," Thoreau writes, "on this side is the city, on that the wilderness, and ever I am leaving the city more and more and withdrawing into the wilderness." A Lethean stream, he calls the Atlantic. What would the opposite be, a body of water that when drunk causes everything to be not forgotten but remembered? Such a body of water is Pleasant Lake.

HDT: "In Wilderness is the preservation of the World. Every tree sends its fibres forth in search of the Wild. The cities import it at any price. Men plough and sail for it. From the forest and wilderness come the tonics and barks which brace mankind. Our ancestors were savages. The story of Romulus and Remus being suckled by a wolf is not a meaningless fable. The founders of every state which has risen to eminence have drawn their nourishment and vigor from a similar wild source. It was because the children of the Empire were not suckled by the wolf that they were conquered by the children of the northern forests who were."

Yes! I say with HDT, our hearts yearn for barbarism, but of what type? We strive for Wildness, but where do we find it? "Hope and the future for me are not in lawns and cultivated fields, not in towns and cities, but in the impervious and quaking swamps."

As I sit here at night at the desk with her sleeping in the room across the way, I feel the wolf roaming in the woods beyond the field. I think of Robinson Crusoe and his encounter with a pack of 300 wolves while crossing the Pyrenees on his way home from Portugal to England, after finally escaping the island. The wolves attack the small pack of travelers. They lust for human flesh and horsemeat, but are unable to breach the wall of fire. Packs of wolves, an army of wolves, or Demons, as Crusoe calls them. I fear but one wolf out there beyond the field, a lone wolf lusting to devour only me. Crusoe, of course, was, on the one hand, a great civilizer and, on the other, a man who became wilder and more savage with the passing years. Proof of the latter was his own lust to kill, both wolves and men - and oh how he slaughtered those men on the island with calm detachment and military precision! The wolf is after me and I am after him. We are locked and each determined to kill the other. When Crusoe's party reached the nearest town they found it in a state of high alert, for the night before it had been attacked and plundered by bears and wolves. They must have known what Crusoe knew - man must become a savage to kill a savage, a wolf to kill a wolf. Such is our yearning for the wild.

10.18.2011

She wakes me from a deep sleep by stroking my cheek with her smooth, cool fingers. As I open my eyes and struggle against the blurriness of vision, I feel as though I have been asleep for a long time. When I ask her how long I've been sleeping she claims I have been asleep for eighteen hours. Immediately, I glance to the window and realize it is already nighttime. I have missed the entire day. Beneath the tightly fitted sleeve of her shirt I notice a bulge. When I ask what it is she rolls up the sleeve and shows me a large bandage. I can see from the state of the bandage that the wound is quite fresh. "What happened?" I ask her. She remains silent and looks away.

"Don't think about it now," she whispers and slips under the blankets. As she presses her body against me I close my eyes and try to remember some scenes from my dreams. Alas, I have lost it all. The week of near-total insomnia has driven my dream world too deep into my slumbering consciousness. Not a single grain of oneiric material could be dug out from

it. Quietly, I reorient toward the throb of our bodies pressing together. My own body seems to have shrunken during the
long sleep and her body seems to wrap completely around it,
enveloping me in a fleshy pocket. Under the blankets I feel
her work off her pants and underwear. Her nakedness presses
against me and causes me to become engorged. Slow movements
bring the arousal to a heightened state, and though I feel
like I want to prevent climax I know I am powerless against
it. I focus on holding it inside for as long as I can, but
when she reaches down and grabs hold of me, there is nothing I can do. The orgasm lashes out and soaks the sheets. I
shift my body to escape the wetness but it is everywhere.
The whole bed is full of it. I roll over and she is gone.

10.19.2011

The field is a sea of yellow and brown. The woods beyond
it rage with color. Amid the withering grasses no wildflow-
ers have survived the violent October frost. Besides the
apples, the only other fruits are those for the squirrels
and chipmunks, who busily cache them away for winter in
their forest redoubts. Though I sense that winter will come
earlier this year than last, I don't dread it. I am ready to
settle into a long winter without fear of being buried by
the snow.

I think of my father and his clockwork schedule, his
unbothered fastidiousness, the way he controlled the feeling of a room by some sort of gravitational force that, by
dint of his internal density, determined the paths of all
orbiters. I think now of his silence. What a grandiose silence surrounded him - or emanated from him, the way noise

or speech comes from others. It could be that by nature he
was a mute, a mute who happened to find himself within a
body capable of speech. It could be that his brain felt no
impulse to translate thought into sound. Most meals passed
without him uttering a word. Long drives were dominated
by his silence - an oceanic silence, I once said to Ezra. I
recall that during the entirety of one nine-inning Yankee
game, my father never said a word. Was he really sitting
right there next to me? Often I try to remember what it was
like before her death and whether or not he spoke more when
she was alive, but my memory is too fuzzy to find answers.
Increasingly, I am forgetting that world.

My father's silence wasn't caused by a lack of interest.
Those long and detailed letters he wrote to me at camp after
she died testify to how deeply he thought and felt about
my life. Each day we ate breakfast and dinner together, all
the way up to the breakfast on the day he died. When I was
sick as a boy, he would stay home from the bank and sit
with me, flipping through stacks of papers he had brought
home from the office the day before. Each day he wore a dark
suit of charcoal, black, or navy blue. Every day he wore a
perfectly clean and plain white shirt with a striped tie.
He never exercised, though never gained weight. His form,
even as he grew older, remained basically the same. He was
tall and thick without being fat, like the trunk of a tree.
He had become a banker. A banker. Why? Why was he like he
was? Why wasn't he what he was not? I could not understand
him and felt that I loved him passionately without knowing
him. I lived with him for all my life without inhabiting
the same space. He died without giving me that chance - a

son's birthright - to sit by his bedside. Perhaps he mistook
his Jacob for an Esau.

10.20.2011

It is a warm evening, the last Saturday in July. Juliet and
Hagerson have gone to the carnival already, in the late
afternoon, to see the parade and listen to the performance
of the high school band. It's tradition, they told me. Not
being a dedicated adherent even to my own ancestral tra-
ditions, I was disinclined to add new ones and told them
I'd meet up with them later in the evening, around nine,
near the big tent. By eight, the Remington starts to lose
its ink. Over the past days, I have noticed that it's become
increasingly gummed up inside, such that I will be forced
to take the machine into Portland for its annual tune-up.
I break off from my work to get ready for Casco Days.

A strange delight grips me as I move down the hall and
draw a hot bath. I strip off my clothes and climb into the
tub, where I steep myself with my eyes closed and my head
tilted back, trying not to think of much, certainly not
Juliet's pending departure. After the bath, I shave for the
first time in weeks (or is it months?) and then select a pair
of pants and a shirt unworn since leaving the city behind.
Wearing brown leather shoes instead of sneakers, I head off
into the night.

The night air is cool and pleasant - convincing me that
I should walk the two miles to the village center instead
of taking the car. I walk quickly, with a childish sense
of giddiness and excitement coursing through me, covering
the distance in less than half an hour. As I approach the

village square, upon which the carnival has been erected, I fill my lungs to their full measure and expel a hearty laugh, perhaps a guffaw. A guffaw, indeed, for the sight of the carousel, with its black stallions and regal white mares covered with oriental finery, together with the majestic Ferris wheel and the brassy sounds emanating from the tent, which conjures in me memories of Coney Island as a child and thoughts of my grandfather's stories of the Prater in Vienna, where, alone as a young man, he searched for and discovered all sorts of wonderment. The grand old Habsburg Empire had become a riverside carnival in much the same way as the carnival in Casco has transformed this ordinary village green into an imperial palace unmatched by the splendor of Versailles or Schoenbrunn. I gaze at the scene as I climb the hill from the lake. Peering back, I see the carnival lights reflected on the surface of the dark water.

At the carnival's edge, I run into George Aiken holding a large stuffed brown bear with an enormous pink bow around its neck.

"A successful hunt," he says to me with a boozy smile as he proudly holds up his prize.

"It seems so," I say, peering over his shoulder in search of Juliet and Hagerson.

"Haven't seen you around much, Abel," Aiken says as he touches me on the shoulder with his free hand. "We've been up here since mid-June. It's been the best summer here since we bought the place. I'm working from here. The kids are both in camp, the weather's fantastic. I'm finally convinced that Jane was right about the place. Can't say I ever thought of myself as a lake guy. Not to mention the house itself.

We had to dump another hundred and fifty grand into it to make it habitable."

"I imagine Rose will be pleased with the bear," I respond, ignoring the rest.

"Actually, it's for Jane. She's got a stuffed animal thing. The bigger, the better, if you know what I mean."

"Where is Jane?"

"She's over by the carousel with Mindy and Sally."

Under the glow of the neon lights, with the whirl of carnival games and amusement park rides swelling in the background, George Aiken's drunken face seems half-clownish and half-sinister, as if he were a traveling impresario or an itinerant peddler of nostrums, some cure-all stuff in small glass vials last seen during times of plague.

Without a farewell, Aiken stumbles off in the direction of his wife. I look around and spot Juliet and the wrestler on the far side of the big tent. When I come to them, I see they are drinking bottles of beer. Hagerson, like Aiken, shows signs of inebriation. Odd, I think, because I had seen him drink amply before with little effect on his behavior. The wrestler, under normal circumstances, could handle his booze, and it is surprising to see him now unsure on his feet and to hear him slurring and searching for words. Their drinks being almost empty, I offer to go get the next round. When I return I get the first focused look at Juliet in her short blue skirt and white blouse. Her hair has been cut shorter, exposing the bottom part of her neck. Her makeup, nail polish, lipstick all seem more generously or luxuriously applied than usual.

After a few minutes Hagerson breaks away to chat up a woman in a pink dress with whom he has been exchanging looks. She is with a friend, who is busy tossing dimes and quarters onto a large board in hopes of matching George Aiken's success. I watch as Hagerson approaches without the slightest drunkenness in his gait. He has apparently stead- ied himself for the task at hand. He moves with confidence now, the confidence of a skilled social practitioner, a mas- ter of the art of seduction. He tells her something, putting his mouth quite close to her ear. She laughs and touches his arm just above the elbow. Hagerson pretends not to notice it and again leans in and says something. She seems surprised by it. He reassures her. She touches his arm again.

Juliet takes me by the hand and tells me she wants to ride the Ferris wheel. As she pulls me along I feel a rising anxiety, for as a child, sometime before my mother's death, I developed a deep and lasting fear of Ferris wheels and had not ridden on one since I was in Paris in the mid-1990s hunting down letters my grandfather wrote long ago. I consider telling Juliet that I can't do it, I can't ride it, but I don't - possibly because the sight of Hagerson picking up that woman seemed to call my own manhood into question.

We wait for a bucket to empty out and then get in. The carnival worker pulls down a heavy metal bar across our laps and we slowly start to rise along the wheel's perfect curve. "Summer was past and day was past," I think to myself. The wrestler was set to leave the following day, Juliet two or three weeks later.

We climb into the starry night. The carnival noises fade away. Below us the lake stretches out in a sheet of silky blackness. We reach the top of the wheel and the whole structure comes to a halt, causing our bucket to sway back and forth in the night sky. I clutch the metal bar that runs across my lap. Juliet places her hand on my arm. We look straight into each other's eyes for the first time that evening.

"What now, Abel?" she asks.

"Stay here," I say to her, "stay here in Casco."

The wheel turns. The starlight turns back to neon. Smells of popcorn and corn dogs waft through the candy-scented air. She looks down at the carnival grounds.

"Looks like Rick has vanished," she says.

"And the woman in pink?"

"Nowhere in sight."

We reach the bottom and get off. I feel agitated that Juliet has not answered me. When we get to the edge of the carnival I say, "How about it?"

"I don't know," she says.

Through the night I run as fast as I can as the sweat pours down my face and erupts over my entire body. Behind me, the Ferris wheel spins faster and faster, transformed by its speed into a multifarious ribbon of light. Up and down swoops the road, like the twisting and turning of a rollercoaster. From the distance I hear the faint howl of the McKenneys' dog. The lake rises from its bed and becomes a sidereal mist and the Fieldston house, some fifty yards from the road, sits there shrouded in darkness like a molted shell a snail has sloughed off in hopes of gaining its freedom.

When a man is alone, said Emerson, let him look at the stars.

10.21.2011

"Somber clouds in the west were massed." She left these words on my desk. He left them under my door. "Summer was past and day was past." Winter was coming.

The question of why the wolf would stray so far from its den is a perplexing one. I can only conclude one of two reasons - either it has lost its way or it has been driven out. In either case it is desperate and on the hunt. "The whole of nature is a metaphor of the human mind," Emerson wrote. If only our minds could possibly be so grandiose! Poor Emerson, the truth is we comprehend but a tiny speck of nature - a snowflake is too complex for us to understand. Most of the time I feel myself akin to the Ferris wheel - turning eternally and slowly in the same direction, now and then coming to an abrupt halt.

10.22.2011

On the lake in mid-July. Two girls from the camp across the way have capsized their small sailboat, and though they've managed to right the boat, they are struggling to hoist the sail, which has become submerged in the water. I paddle close and hitch my canoe to their vessel. Once aboard the sailboat, I pull the sail up and hand the rope to the girl with dark, braided hair. They thank me nervously and wait for me to get back into my canoe and unhitch my vessel from theirs. I paddle off with a few quick strokes.

10.23.2011

I need to face the fact that there is no wilderness or wildness here. It is pastoral land, at best, becoming, especially in summer, nothing more than a reflection of the wealthy suburbs of the great eastern cities. If wildness means continuous, unending renewal, what does this place mean? I follow in a long line of refugees who have looked for meaning here, here in the New World, this Eden reinvented. Most died believing in the myth of the wild, the regenerative power of Nature.

I wonder what she came here for - that young, beautiful woman. As a child, she had attended the girls camp across the lake. Now she was fleeing something - fleeing, most likely, an immediate threat. She came here for refuge and found something, some sort of something, and then returned to live back in the world again without it. She could have come for love or tenderness - or to escape one or the other. Perhaps she came here for friendship, a friendship that would nourish her and rekindle her animating spark. Or none of this, or nothing. I can imagine it in hundreds or even thousands of ways. The Lake of Memory, Pleasant Lake, is full of invented memory produced by a heart deep underground and far away and then filtered through miles of earth until it comes to us, purified and sanitized and empty of all its grit. The memory it contains is as fictional as the lake itself, as her death was fictional, as mine will be.

10.24.2011

She stayed the night last night. I am unsure how many nights she has stayed now. I tossed and turned in bed and then gave up. I worked in the office until nearly dawn and then finally fell asleep for a couple of hours on the sofa. I woke up as she came down the stairs, bleary-eyed, in search of coffee, which I prepared. She wore the blue-and-white T-shirt from the Fieldston trunk and a pair of gray underwear. The kitchen was cold and gooseflesh rose on her bare arms and legs, prompting me to fetch her a blanket. She draped it over her legs as she sat at the kitchen table looking out into the field.

She is not well. Though she denies it, it is undeniable.

10.25.2011

She is out for most of the day. I don't like being here alone anymore - knowing she is there, or somewhere, and not here. For hours I debate with myself about whether she left for the south or just for the General Store. The question is solved, at least in part, by her return in the evening. When I ask what she was doing, she gives vague and unsatisfying replies. I am overcome with fear and jealousy with an intensity I know only from my short bursts of dreaming, which, these days, jar me awake in the most violent manner. She tells me I need to get more sleep. Somehow, she says, I need to give my mind a rest. Constant motion, she says, has worn it out.

10.26.2011

After days of minimal sleep my days have turned to night,
nights to day, or, more accurately, both have transformed
into an endless dusk, half-lit and somber, as if sprin-
kled with ash. There is something indeterminate and indeterminable about this colorless day. Perhaps the ink has
leaked from the Remington and stained the world.

10.27.2011

The light has not returned. Dawn slumbers beneath an inky
haze. "The descent to the underworld is easy. Night and day
the gates of shadowy death stand open wide, but to retrace
your steps, to climb back to the upper air - there the
struggle, there the labor lies." I give myself over to such
a "mad ordeal."

10.28.2011

Nothing accomplished today - a waste of a day. Sleep evades
me. The "mad ordeal" draws nearer. I sit in front of the
Remington and try to type a letter to Ezra. Nothing comes
out as planned. I burn the letter with the mid-day fire. No
chickens left at the General Store.

10.29.2011

A truck pulls up to the house and Jim Bussy gets out and
knocks on my door. He tells me the McKenneys want to clean
up the old stone wall that forms the dividing line between

our sections of forest and field. They've hired him, he tells me, to take care of it before next summer. He wants to begin soon. The issue, he tells me, is that there are a number of trees that have grown such that their roots have stretched out and compromised the integrity of the wall, breaking apart areas of its foundation. He wants to remove some of them, five in total, he tells me - two oaks, a maple, and two birches - which exist on my side of the line. I ask him what "clean up" means and he tells me he intends to rebuild sections and reinforce others. For what purpose? I ask him. He doesn't know, but assumes it's to maintain an orderly border. The border, I suggest, has been perfectly orderly since anyone can remember, with those trees occupying their current places.

"Should I tell the McKenneys," Bussy asks, "that you refuse on account of five trees?"

I consider this way of putting it. I don't feel anything sentimental for these particular trees. What concerns me, I realize, is the integrity of my realm.

"Tell them," I say, "that they need to first survey the line."

10.30.2011

From the end of my forest path I wade into the frigid water for my last swim of the year. The coldness takes my breath away and I gasp to regain it. When I am about thirty yards away from the shore, I stop and look around in all directions. Everything seems to exist here in perfect harmony, on this quiet autumn morning. The craggy bank on this side of the lake peers across at the smooth, gentle, almost imperceptible curve of the opposite shore.

By the time I get out I am shivering violently and must work to steady my hands and build a fire. I look on eagerly as the flames leap to life and devour the kindling at the bottom of the structure. Soon the logs are ablaze and the heat starts to sting my cheeks. I lie back and fall asleep.

10.31.2011

No sleep last night, followed by a nap that stretches from late morning until nearly dusk. I call for her but she is not at home. I consider going to look for her outside but am overcome by fear.

11.01.2011

A terrible fever has come over me. I must have picked it up from Carl at the General Store when I mailed the packages. Still no chickens there, and at a time when I am in dire need of a chicken soup. In my feverish state, I see the Ferris wheel detach from its axle and roll down the hill and into the lake. The water extinguishes its lights like the smothering of torches. A windy night, a cold night. She upbraids me for sitting at my desk in such a state as this. I am not able to let it go. Every time I close my eyes, I see, floating over the dark lake, the red eye of the loon.

I placed the pages down on the window seat and looked on as hard, driving rain shot down like rifle fire into the snowy field. An unspecified craving came to me, and when I focused on it I realized it was for the moose jerky from the General Store. Yes, I thought, I craved that spicy, salty, tangy flavor of cured and dried moose. Slowly, I rose from the chair and made my way to the kitchen, pausing only to add a large log to the Franklin stove. Almost mindlessly, I pulled a long stick of jerky from the bag and began to chew on the end while gazing out at the expanse of field and forest. For a while, I stood there watching the rain, listening to the rainwater batter the roof and stream through the gutters. If only, I thought, the rain would wash all this away—all this, the house, the papers, myself. The rainwater, flowing together, could, I imagined, form the river Lethe.

Far away seemed my office in Whitefield Hall, as far away, or further, than the medieval world, the Karaite challenge. How, I wondered, would I move beyond this point to that, from this A to that B, as Abel had moved from A to B, from November 1 to his death, days later? I surveyed the possibilities. The first was in accordance with the lawyer: Abel killed himself by eating a handful of the mushroom *Galerina autumnalis*. The second was that *he*, the lone wolf from the woods, emerged one night and murdered Abel, or killed him in the woods in self-defense. But the implication of the journal, at least in places, was that I, Ezra Stern, was the lone wolf and, I concluded rather absurdly, I was sure I hadn't murdered anybody. There was the chance the lone wolf was Leo Schulz—a demon who emerged from the depths of Abel's dreams. It could be that Abel and Schulz shared a secret, one which dated back to camp, and that Schulz had acted to protect this secret from being divulged. Had Abel, I wondered, written recently to Schulz? Did Schulz come to Casco to seduce Leah Klein? On the other hand, it might be that one of the sisters was involved in the death. Or both. "That young woman" had found Abel in the woods, according to Warren at the General Store (or was it Carl?). *She* was living in the house—at least part of the time, according to the journal, the accuracy and logic of which were dubious. It would never hold up as a source—as history or legal evidence, the journal was worthless. Which one was it, I wondered, Leah or Juliet? Parts indicated one, parts the other. Parts seemed to combine them into one. The Ferris wheel ride, its aftermath—did Abel drive to the carnival or walk? My mind twisted and turned, somersaulting from one notion to the next, posing question after question with no attempt to answer. Maybe it was Jim Bussy, after all, I thought, who killed Abel, in order to reinforce that crumbling wall.

The stick of jerky was gone and I prepared a peanut butter sandwich, which I ate while standing at the window and mulling over the options again: Ezra Stern, Leo Schulz, Leah Klein, Juliet Klein, Jim Bussy, Rick Hagerson, the McKenneys—and what about Paul Freeman or Ethan Weiss or Hannah or Warren or Carl? No! The lawyer had said it clearly, Abel had killed himself. He knew what he was eating and knew it to be deadly. Though seemingly true, the lawyer's words made the least sense. Suicide was the least satisfying explanation. At that moment, I wished I could deny something completely, like Sybil often did, in order to believe, beyond all reason, in the veracity of something else.

Outside, the rain was falling. There was no point in hiking the two miles to the General Store. Plus, I thought, the Reynolds boys were unlikely to venture out in such conditions for someone they didn't know. I wondered what time it was; the gray sky was little help. I wondered when the General Store closed for the day—five or six or nine or ten? "No," I said aloud, in hopes of reorienting and focusing my mind, "there is nothing else to do but climb to the attic. No other option remains." The idea unsettled, even repulsed me—but there was no way around it, no way to avoid it or postpone it any longer. I had to face whatever I found there.

As I passed through the living room, I paused to take a look at the fire burning in the Franklin stove. I took a deep breath. It could be, I considered, that this precise moment was the one I had been avoiding for all these years—the possibility of gaining clarity, of confronting truth. I had found comfort in memory, in the consistent albeit hazy and derivative existence of my friend. Was this also true of life at home? I paused to think about it. No, I thought, that was taking it too far, for surely there was reality, new, unfolding reality in my life with Sophia, Sam and Sybil; maybe there was even some in Whitefield Hall. True enough, a student in my spring course on Medieval Spain had called me a "fraud" in an extended screed on his final course evaluation form. Though anonymous, I knew the student to be Jay Gold—a nasty thorn in my side all semester. I hated to admit it, but Gold unnerved and even intimidated me—especially when he threatened to take his grievances to the administration and beyond, to the eager rightwing attack machine that guarded the official orthodox, Zionist line. Gold's threats were partly authentic and party extortion, for he never missed a chance to come to my office hours to demand a higher grade. The usual strategy of bumping up the grade by half a letter misfired with Gold, for he took my flexibility as a sign of weakness, which encouraged him to press harder for me to yield more ground. With every victory, Gold became more determined in his resistance, a resistance that culminated in the long and scurrilous evaluation, "a copy of which," Gold wrote at the bottom, "has also been sent to the dean of faculty affairs."

I retrieved the stepladder from the bathroom closet and placed it below the entrance to the attic. "Night and day," I mused, mulling over the line from the journal, "the gates of shadowy death stand open wide." I peered up at the rectangular cutout in the ceiling and wondered whether I should carry the metaphor further. But was I entering hell or leaving it? The divisions in this house in Casco, it seemed, were, unfortunately, not as clear as those at Apollo's temple at Cumae. If this was the exit, the point of access back into the land of the living, was this rectangular door made of ivory or of horn? Ridiculous notion, I abused myself. Absurd nonsense. "The simple truth," I said aloud, "is that my friend, my best friend, killed himself, and I did nothing to stop it, nothing to help. I didn't come here for him. I didn't intervene in any way." There had been signs—Paul Freeman and the peculiar letter had only been the last clue of many. Abel had drowned in the stormy sea of his mind, in a hurricane of mental life. In this way, I thought, Abel was indeed like Ahab. Like the mad captain, Abel pursued a simple, clear, and yet delusional and unattainable goal. For Abel, this goal was solitude. No, for Abel, it was pure self-sufficiency. No, for Abel, it was the simple life. No, for Abel, it was experiencing the wilderness. No, for Abel, like Thoreau, it was discovering a kernel of the wild. The Wild. The Spirit of the Wild, the Wild within a man. And this Wild overtook him, killed him, as the lust for revenge, the pursuit of evil, overtook and killed the captain.

Come now! This is sophomoric stuff with the logic and intellectual sophistication of high school journaling, nothing more. This was not how to get from specific events to big questions and big answers, the grand narratives that swirled around Abel Prager. Ahabian Abel, Ismailian Ezra. Who was the noble savage, the harpoonist Queequeg? Neither. He remained myth; he remained impossible. I tried to regain focus. None of this, despite my desires, changed the basic trajectory I was on; I was headed up into the attic.

With a quick yank, the rectangular door slid open. I unfolded the ladder as dust glittered through the air. When it was set up and stationed securely on the floor, I gazed up into the dark, geometric void.

Darkness. I hadn't considered the darkness and ran back downstairs to retrieve as many candles as I could carry. With the candles and candleholders under one arm, I climbed up the ladder and into the cold, dark, dusty space. I placed the candles on the floor. Above, I heard the rain on the roof.

The space had a central aisle about four feet wide and seven feet high from which the ceiling sloped away. To my right, dozens of boxes sat on deep wooden shelves, and on closer inspection I saw that each box was labeled with a name. All the expected characters were represented: each Klein sister had her own box, Ethan Weiss, Paul Freeman, Lillian Prager, Abraham Prager, Herschel Prager, Henry David Thoreau, Rick Hagerson, Jeremiah the Ice Scratcher, Leo Schulz. And there, practically in the middle of the shelf, was the box labeled "Ezra Stern – Allstar." I reached out and ran my finger over these words.

Turning around, I was surprised to see a desk at the far end of the attic space. With a candle in hand, I walked over to it and saw that it was a beautiful antique piece with a single thin drawer on either side. I slid open the drawers and found them empty. On the desk, Abel had left a thick cloth-bound notebook. I opened it.

Stuck inside the front cover was a piece of paper containing a short note typed on the Remington. I read:

Dear Allstar:

I had always planned on typing out the contents of this novel on the Remington, but somehow I haven't managed it. I want you to read it. That was the primary purpose I had in mind. I want someone other than myself to read it. Families can become entombed units. I needn't tell you this. We will discuss it in the summer when you are in Casco. I imagine you'll be passing by on your way back from bringing Sam

```
for his first summer at camp. It is as good a reason as any
to stop for a swim in Pleasant Lake.
```

```
Your Friend,
```

```
Abel
```

I flipped to the next page and was surprised to discover a title, *Thin Rising Vapors*, written in an elegant hand. Underneath it: *Lillian Blumenthal*. On the first page was this epigraph:

> *My instinct tells me that my head is an organ for burrowing, as some creatures use their snout and fore paws, and with it I would mine and burrow my way through these hills. I think that the richest vein is somewhere hereabouts; so by the divining-rod and thin rising vapors I judge; and here I will begin to mine. – Henry David Thoreau*

I leafed through the rest—hundreds of closely handwritten pages. Carefully, I placed the note back inside the book and set it down by the ladder. I would have to examine it closely, I thought, when back at Whitefield Hall.

I went back and sat at the desk, which was positioned directly against the outer wall. Did Abel work here? If so, why? If not, what purpose did this desk serve? Was it, as it seemed at first glance, a shrine of some sort, a preserved setting for a scene from the life of Lillian Blumenthal circa 1965? Perhaps, I mused, she had come to live here and had experienced something that inspired her to write a novel called *Thin Rising Vapors*, which, years after her death, her son, Abel Prager, would discover in a box or trunk after his father passed away. And perhaps this discovery had caused him to abruptly change everything and to abandon New York for this place, the Fieldston place—a fictional and at the same time real space, a fictional and at the same time real *Thin Rising Vapors*. Then what? The Klein sisters arrived. City life infiltrated and Abel realized that whatever it was he came looking for didn't exist. No, I continued, Abel realized he had duped himself into believing in the impossible, that he could find his way back into her life, that he could be a little boy again. Of course, it could have been otherwise. All this could be nonsense. Abel could have found the book here, for example, and that would then invalidate all the subsequent conclusions, bringing me back to the original question, the initial problem: what had happened to my friend?

I sat at the desk and allowed these thoughts to fade away until no thoughts, but rather a hazy emptiness, remained, together with a slight pulsing throb behind my temples. The wooden desk had a pleasant texture, and I ran my hand over the top, enjoying the feeling of the grain. In all likelihood, I concluded, for no particular reason, the desk had belonged, at one point, to Betty Fieldston. It was a Fieldston desk, a Fieldston piece. The thought and all connected to it faded into the candlelight, into the arrhythmical pattering of raindrops and the whoosh of the wind passing through the wet boughs of the surrounding evergreens.

Tiredness seized me, but just as I put my head down on the desk and closed my eyes a fit of sneezing overtook me. Sense or nonsense? I thought. Sense or nonsense? Did one really exclude the other? Perhaps both existed side by side here—here in Casco, in this life—and met only in death, in the underworld. It could be that this was the essence of what Abel had meant by his "mad ordeal."

Thoreau, I thought, was no reliable guide to life. Abel should have been well beyond Thoreau by now, well beyond these pond-side musings. I closed my eyes and saw Abel's short, thin body, his curly black hair, that pale face, those round wire-framed glasses, those hairy arms and legs. That was Abel, my Abel. There were no words here, no meaningless words—it was flesh and blood, a person, a man, a friend.

I found my way to my feet and carried the candle back to the other side of the attic. On my left, under the sloping roof, were three large trunks, similar to the type that had sat at the foot of our beds at camp. In front of me were the labeled boxes. Had I come here as Job's friends had come, to scorn, judge, and ridicule? They were friends—friends as adversaries, friends as prosecutors.

Slowly, I moved closer to the boxes. I put a finger on my name again and then withdrew it, taking down the box labeled "Juliet Klein" instead. I set it on the floor and positioned candles on either side. I opened it up. The box, about the size of a normal shoebox, was half full of papers, most of which were typed on the Remington. In addition, there were a few handwritten pages, some in Abel's hand, some, though no more than a dozen, in another. The light was too poor for reading, and so I closed the lid and pushed the box aside. I would have to bring down the materials for investigation. After placing "Juliet Klein" over by the ladder next to the notebook containing *Thin Rising Vapors*, I pulled "Leah Klein" from the shelf. Inside, to my surprise, were no more than twenty or thirty pages—and all were typed on the Remington. This puzzled me, for I'd expected to see those letters, those original copies that Abel mentioned in the journal. It could be that they were somewhere else, or that someone had taken them to conceal something, or that Abel had destroyed them for an unknown purpose.

There was no more avoiding it, I would have to look into the "Ezra Stern – Allstar" box. My chest heaved and my heart began to beat so vigorously that I thought I might lose balance. I grasped the wooden shelf for support. Feeling more stable, I pulled out the box and set it between the two candles. Upon opening, I discovered it was completely full. The sight of this amount of material startled me. I felt a sudden and unexpected wave of feeling pass over me. My eyes erupted in tears. I was crying—not because of the dust but for some other, more vague, less material reason, or simply for no reason at all. How little I had known myself, how little I knew myself even then!

I put the lid back on the box and moved it over by the ladder. Then I proceeded to do the same with the rest of the boxes, emptying the shelves and putting them by the hole in the floor. Once they were all there, I carried them downstairs and placed them in stacks in the office. I worked slowly, partly out of fear of tumbling from the ladder, partly because I had undefined moral scruples about the act, and partly because my head felt hazy, my body exhausted. Finally, when I was done, I went back into the attic and looked at the empty shelf. As I started to gather up the candles, my glance fell on the three trunks.

I moved a few candles over to the side of the attic where the trunks sat and unclasped the first one. Inside, I found stacks of old bedding and a few thick woolen blankets, one of which was light blue in color—presumably, I thought, an artifact from the camp across the way. I rummaged around but didn't discover anything of particular interest at the bottom. First trunk closed, second one opened. The second trunk contained mostly clothing—old clothing, a girl's clothing. I lifted out a small blue camp T-shirt and held it up in front of me. It seemed tiny—far too small for a grown woman like either Juliet or Leah Klein. Shirts, sweatshirts, pants, two old pairs of shoes. Again, I fished around but came up empty-handed. I submerged my hand again, this time all the way to the bottom, and there touched something. Carefully, I drew it to the top. It was a group photograph taken against the backdrop of Pleasant Lake. There were some twenty girls in all, teenagers. Mostly, they were smiling and had their arms wrapped around one other's waists or dangling over their neighbors' shoulders. They stood in a long row. Beneath the photograph was a list of names. Third from the left was Betty Fieldston. To her right, from my perspective, was Lillian Blumenthal. I placed my finger on the girls, as if this would establish the reality of their being. Betty Fieldston was the bigger of the two. She had dirty blonde hair, thick hips, muscular arms, muscular and athletic legs, and a wide and somewhat squishy face. Her smile radiated from the image, a joyous, even splendiferous look of pleasure, the pleasure of communing. It was more—it was pleasure in the aggregated history of communing, and she basked in it, as did the other girls, their faces alive and glowing. Blumenthal was darker than Fieldston, and thinner. She had a narrow face and dark, wavy hair. Though she wasn't as beautiful as she would be later in life and possessed here a certain amount of teenage awkwardness, I could see in her that tremendous inner beauty that years later would become fully externalized. It seemed to me suddenly that I had made a fundamental mistake. Abel had taken much more from his mother than I had ever realized. And this mistake, it seemed to me, changed everything. It voided my understanding completely. The whole being, the whole essence of my friend, had not been as I thought it was. He was as much Blumenthal as Prager— and perhaps a whole lot more.

My gaze moved along the string of girls. Nancy Fishl, Jean Klemput, Augusta Messer, Samantha Brown, Liz Wright. It was a group like all others. I looked at it for a few moments longer and then placed it back in the trunk. I moved on to the third trunk. The contents of the first two had somehow stirred me, and now I felt sure that the third would reveal what I was searching for, the secret, the key to the mad ordeal. My hand trembled as I unclasped the top of the trunk and slowly lifted the lid. For a brief moment, perhaps due to the play of candlelight and shadow, I glimpsed a human face staring up at me with washed-out, murky eyes. It seemed to be lifting, moving toward me out of the dark, misty depths, and then, suddenly, it vanished. Everything vanished. The severed limbs, the mortifying flesh, the soupy pool of blood and guts. The trunk was empty now. I probed it with my hand, knowing that trunks like this one often had false bottoms, which concealed an inner space. Indeed, this particular trunk had such a bottom, and I removed the cardboard shelf. The area beneath the shelf was also empty. The question came to me: why would Abel have kept this empty trunk? Two full and one empty—it didn't make sense. No, the more likely scenario was that at one time the third trunk had also been full and then had been emptied, deliberately emptied. And why? A pale, gossamer image of a face remained there. The remnants of her body remained. Her—Betty Fieldston or Leah Klein or Juliet Klein, a body that had been hacked to pieces and then locked up in this trunk for days or weeks or even months and years. And then the trunk was emptied. And then the trunk was cleaned. *Thin Rising Vapors*: a novel by Lillian Blumenthal. The answers were in there, in that notebook. I noticed then that my hand was still trembling. My legs started to wobble. The whole attic space jerked suddenly to the left. I fell.

With a thump I hit the floor and came back to consciousness. In that brief moment when my knees buckled and my body crumbled I felt as though I might be dying—death by falling down a gyrating vortex of darkness, similar to a recurring falling dream I had experienced as a child. With a sharp pain in my left hip and the taste of blood in my mouth, I carefully rose from the floor. Sweat was issuing from my sticky skin. I sensed an aching, flu-like feeling spreading out from my core. It was all I could do to blow out the candles, gather the Blumenthal notebook and climb back down the ladder. I crawled, helplessly, pathetically, into Abel's bed.

I lay there with my eyes closed, opening them now and then to peer blankly at the ceiling. I missed my friend—that boy—that boy sitting in that whitewashed cube assailing the likes of Josh Hamburger while awaiting his dismal fate. I missed that boy—Ezra Stern—sitting breathlessly in the audience, praying for the performance to be a success. He died alone, my friend, Abel Prager. I rubbed my throbbing temples. Abel was calling me out—me, Ezra Stern. "At the sight of misfortune," Abel would say, as Job once said, "you take fright."

The clear picture of Abel that had come to me while gazing down at the picture of the teenage Lillian Blumenthal receded. The thick, tangy taste of blood filled my mouth and I pressed my tongue time and again against the gash in the inside of my cheek while forcing down a gulp of blood mixed with saliva. Outside, the rain started to fall harder. Evening had arrived. Occasional cars sped down Mayberry Hill Road. I rose from bed and made my way downstairs. It was warmer there, and I started to feel my body calming, my mind slowing, my feverish sickness dissipating. I drank three cups of water.

I poured a glass of whiskey and took it over by the Franklin stove. I added a few logs and gazed at the play of embers and flame. Flame and coal, I thought, a kabbalistic metaphor. When I returned home, I thought, I would need to search for something like that, something beyond the ordinary that I could share with Sophia and the kids. That was the lesson here. Or maybe not. There was no way of telling. Faith, yes, but in what? In whom? I felt positively barred from the medieval world. It was smoke and mirrors. My work, and by extension my life, was a fraud. Jay Gold had been right—I was living life dressed in a costume, whirling around an endless, tiresome masquerade ball.

Stripped of the most external of layers, I was still a boy—a boy who loved nothing more than the Boston Red Sox.

Too simple. There was more to that boy. I sipped the whiskey and slumped deeper into the chair, again running my tongue along the cut inside my mouth. Sophia was wrong. She should have called the sheriff. A rescue party was needed here.

I went into the kitchen and fetched the bottle. When I returned, I poured another glass of whiskey and drank it in one tilt. The first glass had already improved my general state of being and the second added to the creeping sensation of blissful haze or foggy apathy. After a third glass, this apathy was suddenly all-consuming, and I could do nothing but give over to it and stretch out my legs toward the Franklin to warm my toes. After the fourth glass, weariness took hold.

With great effort, I climbed back upstairs, folded the ladder back up into the attic, and fell into Abel's bed. The face from the trunk appeared to me again—but then quickly vanished. In its place was Lillian Prager, Abel's mother, caressing her nine-year-old son as they sat on his bed during rest hour on that late-July afternoon. Her long, thin fingers ran through his hair and stroked his cheek. Abel wasn't smiling. Rather, he was feeling each touch, each movement, with the full capacity of his being. To be touched like that, I thought now, to be stroked in such a manner, would be the most pleasurable thing in the world. My mind wandered. Sleep came.

Day Seven

I woke up three times during the night, sweaty and in a feverish delirium—convinced that I had fallen very ill. When morning came, however, the fever was gone. My body felt sore and fatigued but otherwise healthy and fundamentally strong. I rose from Abel's bed and went to the window. The rain had passed with the night and had taken the snow with it. The landscape appeared soft and muddy, full of greens and browns. The sun was shining—creating a scene at once barren and fertile. There was nothing to distinguish this day from its equivalent in early springtime, after the last snowmelt of the year.

When I went downstairs, I saw that the Franklin had gone out. I poked in the ash to find some live embers, but none remained. That was it. It was time to go. I would return in the spring or summer after taking Sam to camp—or not at all, or never again. Abel, who had crept closer to me over these last days, had quickly withdrawn, and I felt the house empty of his spirit. I felt no urge to chase my friend into the underworld.

For the first time in days, I opened the front door and stepped outside. I drew a deep, greedy breath and slowly exhaled it, then another and another. To my surprise, the air was pleasantly temperate. The temperature must have climbed up to around fifty degrees or more. The house belonged to me. "What an inexplicable thing," I muttered. Everything happened without purpose—without clear purpose, I corrected myself, or perhaps without my knowledge of the higher purpose, if such a thing exists. Still, even if there were no purpose, I needed to pay attention, in a broader sense, to what was going on around me. In baseball, they say to keep one's eye on the ball, but in life, I thought, this didn't seem to work very well. There were the primary variables—the bat, the ball—and then secondary ones and tertiary ones. Everything related to everything else. The ball floated through relative space, subjective time. I had been swatting at it, I realized, with a chopstick.

What thoughts! What silly notions! Abel would have taken them and molded them into something interesting, something profound. Abel could see the deeper connections—the position of the fielders, the contours of the stadium, the force of the countervailing winds, the play of light and shadow on the outfield grass—and he would have swung with all of this in mind, hitting right at the sweetest spot of the bat and sending the ball into deep, uninhabited terrain.

Parked awkwardly in front of the house and washed clean by the melting snow and rain, my gray Honda gleamed in the sunlight. For some reason, perhaps out of faith in the alignment of my car's internal workings with more complex cosmic forces, it occurred to me to attempt to start it. I rushed back inside and found the keys on the kitchen counter. I returned to the car and slid the key into the ignition. I turned it. The car jumped to life—its engine sputtering and groaning before settling down into its familiar purr. Just to be safe, I let it run for ten minutes and then turned it off.

Back in the house, I went upstairs into the office and glanced around. I would take it all—the papers, the boxes, the cloth-covered journal containing Lillian Blumenthal's handwritten novel. As quickly as possible, I carried the materials downstairs and packed them into the trunk and backseat of the car. When this was done, I found a brown shopping bag in the pantry and loaded in the remains of my provisions—including the final two sticks of moose jerky. Still in the kitchen, I looked out over the field to the woods in the background. On such a clear day as this I could see the gap in the far corner where the road leading to the lake began. I considered whether or not to walk down there to see the extent of the property, as I had intended to do on that first day here, but was anxious to go and decided that I would look everything over in a thorough manner another time.

I returned to the front of the house and closed and locked the door behind me. The car, full of Abel's posthumous papers, felt warm and comfortable and inspired a feeling of homesickness that connected me back to youth and road trips with my parents and Judith.

"Enough memory," I said aloud, "enough nostalgia." I put the car into reverse, backed it up, pushed it into drive, and turned toward Mayberry Hill Road. A few minutes later I was at the General Store. I went inside and poured a large cup of coffee. The man behind the counter was not the same as the one before. I felt no impulse to engage him in conversation. I paid for the coffee, a bottle of orange juice, and an English muffin sandwich, which contained egg, orange American cheese, and two slices of bacon. I ate the sandwich while idling in the car. After the sandwich was gone and I had taken a few sips of coffee, I placed the cup into the cup-holder next to the orange juice and pulled back onto the road.

Seth Rogoff, author of *First, the Raven: A Preface*, was born in Portland, Maine in 1976. He has translated several works by Franz Kafka, including *The Castle* (2007). He is currently working on a collection of fictional lectures and a non-fiction book on the politics of dream interpretation. He has been a creative writing Fulbright Fellow in Berlin, where he lived for ten years. Since 2015, he has lived with his wife Jana and their two children in Prague.